THE FALL OF DARKNESS

by
R. A. McClanahan

Strategic Book Group

Copyright © 2011

All rights reserved—R. A. McClanahan

No part of this book may be reproduced or transmitted in any form or by any means, graphic, electronic, or mechanical, including photocopying, recording, taping, or by any information storage retrieval system, without the permission, in writing, of the publisher.

Strategic Book Group
P.O. Box 333
Durham CT 06422
www.StrategicBookClub.com

Design: Dedicated Business Solutions, Inc. (www.netdbs.com)

THREAD ID: 1-7Y77E7

ISBN: 978-1-61204-310-4

Dedications

*This book is dedicated to my
children Anne, Sami, Jesse,
and to all of my 'adopted' kids.
Your lives have made my life complete.
And to my father, the true farmer
Don of New London,
'You have been my moral support
through all of my crazy endeavors,
And for that, I will love you forever.'*

Acknowledgements

As Mama always says, "Give credit where credit is due."
The first person I would like to thank is Joe Mann for telling me the story of Lilith, and for picking a fight with me and getting me over a severe case of writers block. If it weren't for you Joe, I would still be stuck on chapter 20. Thank you.

To my father, I owe you the biggest thanks of all for suffering through several edits in the process of writing this book and offering excellent suggestions for improvements, my deepest thanks and eternal love.

I would like to thank my children for giving me ideas to add to their characters. Annie suggested her character should be a pyromaniac, Sami insisted that her character should be a wolf, and Jesse wanted to have a cool power. Sorry buddy, you'll have to wait until the second book.

To my beloved leprechaun of a grandfather and his magical rocking chair; thank you for teaching me the importance of imagination. We traveled the world and had great adventures all from the comfort of that old chair. You were my inspiration as a child, you will always be missed.

To my friend Brandi Fredericks for being my first reader and for also helping name this book; reading a dictionary just wasn't accomplishing much. I greatly appreciate your friendship and encouragement. And also to my friend Nancy Houston for reading my story and quickly becoming my biggest fan. I promise to have the second story done soon so you can be the first to read it.

Last but not least, I have to acknowledge all of my musical muses that inspired me throughout the book. Music has always been a huge part of my life.

    Evanescence / Lincoln Park—'Wake Me Up Inside' (My theme song)
    Plain White T's—'Rhythm of Love'
    Alabama—'The Devil Went Down to Georgia'

Gavin Rossdale—'Love Remains the Same'
Kevin Rudolf—'Let it Rock'
John Meyer—'Waiting on the World to Change'
Peter Gabriel—'In Your Eyes'
Skillet—'The Last Night'
Owl City—'Fireflies'
Kris Allen—'Live Like You Were Dying'
Ludwig van Beethoven—'Ode to Joy'

Table of Contents

Preface ix
1. Graduation 1
2. The Party 12
3. Vacation 18
4. Chichen Itza 25
5. Bad News 36
6. Alone 47
7. The Funeral 54
8. Birthday 65
9. Answers 74
10. Lilith 89
11. Deals 99
12. Leaving 109
13. Dreams 119
14. Oasis 128
15. Profound Effects 139
16. Fighting 148
17. Goodbyes 158
18. Friday October 13th 174
19. Losses 185
20. Scheming 191
21. Strategy 201
22. Offensive 211
23. Darkness 219
24. Déjà Vu 225
25. Confirmation 235
26. Home 250
Epilogue 253

*Darkness is not defined
By the absence of light,
But by the absence of
Faith, Hope, and Love.*
—*Kai*

Preface

Myths, Legends, Superstitions

We have been called many things, but we are real, and we have been a part of history since the beginning of time. We have witnessed mankind's meager beginnings. We have watched you grow and create great civilizations. We have witnessed your ability to learn. We have seen you destroy one another. Mankind is on the brink of a new era and it is no longer up to you to decide your own fate. It is our turn. It is our job. It is our time. This is one legend that you will believe in.

Chapter 1

GRADUATION

I knew he was behind me. I didn't have to turn around to look. I could feel his presence just like the beating of my own heart. I held perfectly still waiting for the conformation that he was there. I felt his hands gently caress my shoulders and I sighed in relief, like medication eliminating pain. Slowly he moved his hands down my arms to my hands hanging at my sides. He intertwined our fingers and then pressed up behind me.

I shivered as his breath tickled the back of my neck, and then he whispered, "Annie." His voice was so soft and melodic. He wrapped his arms around my waist tightly, but it wasn't tight enough for me. My breath was becoming ragged as he gently kissed my neck. I wanted to turn and face him, look into his icy pale blue eyes that were set into his beautiful bronze face, but he held me firmly.

He was trembling with desire but resisted. "Forbidden fruit to torment me and test my will," he murmured softly. My heart was pounding out of my chest; it was becoming unbearable to even breathe. I wanted him more than anything. I could feel the tears welling up in my eyes....

"Annie." That wasn't his voice. "Annie? Are you getting up?" I was only vaguely aware of my mother coming into my room. Not wanting to let go of the dream, I mumbled something unintelligible and put the pillow I had been hugging over my face.

"Annie, we have a lot to do today. You don't have time to lay in bed all day dreaming about *him*." Mama always referred to my dream as 'him' because I had never been able to put a name to his perfect face. I have only been dreaming of him since early childhood. When I was little, he was a comfortable companion and a mentor. It wasn't until recently that he began taking on a more seductive nature.

Mama pulled the pillow off of my head in an attempt to drag me unwillingly into reality. "You know, if you would just allow yourself to have a real relationship, you probably wouldn't have such vivid dreams," she prodded me mockingly. "If he is as gorgeous as your sketches make him out to be, then I can understand your fascination."

She stopped talking for a moment, I slowly opened my eyes and she was right there, leaning over me. "Come on, get out of bed. You need to be at the salon by nine o'clock. Graduation is at one o'clock, which reminds me, did you polish your cornet for the ceremony?" She paused to wait for an answer. I remained silent, still trying to recapture the dream.

She continued with the schedule. "Your party starts at five o'clock, the caterer will be here by four-thirty. You should take your speech with you and practice while at the salon." She was sweeping through my room as she rattled off the agenda, picking up all the clutter as she went. The energy she exuded reminded me of a tornado. She snapped open the purple velvet curtains on the two windows in my room and the sunlight glowed off of the electric lime green walls with waves of neon blue and the purple carpeting that matched the color of the curtains. I love the colors of my room, but it is a hard adjustment on the eyes when waking up.

"Mama! Enough already!" She knew if she kept up long enough I would eventually give up on the dream and accept reality grudgingly.

"I think you are more nervous about graduation than I am. Actually I'm certain you are, because I'm not worried about it in the least." I teased her. "I polished my cornet last night, my speech is memorized, everything is set up for the party, what more do I need to do?" That was a loaded question and I regretted it before I finished asking.

Did you pack for your trip yet?" She knew she had me before I could even answer. My graduation present was a two week trip to San Miguel, Mexico with six of my friends.

It's not that I wasn't thrilled to go, but the idea of leaving my mother all alone for so long made me anxious. Two months out of every summer, my mom and I would go to San Miguel. It is the closest city to the ancient Mayan ruins of Chichen Itza. My mother and I are drawn to the ancient city like a heroin addict for the next fix.

"I'll get the packing done when I get back from the salon. By the way, why do you think it's necessary for me to get my hair done when it's going to be tucked under that stupid cap anyways?"

The look in her eyes told me I had pushed it too far. She was about to get all mushy on me. I interjected before she could start.

"Besides, with the speech I have to give, everyone will be asleep in seconds," her smile reached her eyes as she laughed softly at my cajoling.

"By the way, I did have a boyfriend once," I corrected her.

"The five second rule only applies to food dropped on the floor, not boyfriends," she chided.

It wasn't a story I was fond of, one of those moments in life that you are supposed to learn a lesson from. I was a freshman, and Brad was a junior, a jock. He grabbed me in a big bear hug, planted a kiss right on my lips, and said that I was his girlfriend. When he let me go, I punched him in the face and knocked him to the floor. I stood over him and told him I was breaking up with him. I was so mad at him I wouldn't accept his apologies. Two days later, he drove his car off of a cliff. Whether it was an accident or suicide, no one knows. Lesson learned; don't hold a grudge, life is too short and precious.

I dragged myself out of bed and headed for the shower.

* * *

I've been told that you should take stock of your life when you reach the precipice of a monumental occasion; so as I stepped into the shower, that is exactly what I did.

Anyanka Paylea Cain, that's me, though the only person to ever use that name is my mother and only when I'm in serious trouble. Most people just call me Annie Cain. I am five foot six inches and one hundred twenty pounds with light brown hair and green eyes. I live outside the small town of New London, Ohio with my mother, Lillian Cain, in a large log cabin style home completely surrounded by woods. I think of myself as a well-rounded human being. I enjoy horseback riding, reading, martial arts, nature, sports, art, and music. I also love history, but not the well-documented type, ancient history with all the mystery of the unknown.

All of this is influenced by my mother whom I call 'Mama' as a more affectionate term of endearment. Mama is quite the adrenaline junky. If any type of extreme sport can be done, the chances are, she has tried it and drug me along too, sometimes unwillingly. We've been skydiving, parasailing, bungee jumping, cliff diving, rock climbing, and surfing. That is just a few of the extremes she has done in order to experience an adrenaline rush. I honestly can't even guess at my mother's age. She acts like a teenager and looks like she's twenty. Of all the things I love about my mother, it's her philosophy on life that I truly appreciate the most: "If you spend your life worrying about dying, you will never have learned to live." It's obvious that she truly believes that.

I have friends, six of which are more like family than friends:

Jesse Burton, my deer hunting buddy who from October to December every year is faithfully at my side bow hunting until we both harvest our limits. (Venison is preferred over beef in my house for the nutritional value). Jesse would fit right in between line backers on a football field if football didn't interrupt hunting season. He is well built, tall with light brown hair and big brown cow eyes. He would be intimidating if it weren't for his teddy bear personality.

Mike Stover, also a big muscular kind of teddy bear, has short dark brown wavy hair and the most beautiful hazel eyes. I always think of him as a protector, my own personal body guard, though in the sleepy village of New London, I don't really need to be protected. Oddly, Mike's favorite hobby is cooking, the yin to my yang because I hate cooking.

Ryan White, who is tall and wiry in stature, is the most deceptive of my friends. He has long red hair that he keeps pulled back in a ponytail, and glasses that are always falling off of his nose, he looks like he would be a permanent fixture in a library. What is so deceptive about his appearance is that no one would ever guess that he is a second degree black belt in tae kwon do. We tested for first degree black belt together, but I was too busy to continue with him for second degree. I often think that Ryan was a brigadier general in a previous life. During our paintball wars, he is usually the last man standing, like he has a sixth sense for military combat.

Katie Brown, the athletic one. I spend the least amount of time with her because if a sport is in season, Katie would be at a practice or a game, whether it's volleyball, softball, track, basketball or soccer. Her competitive nature keeps her busy most of the time. We are built the same, height and weight anyways, but she has short, spiky light brown hair and muddy brown eyes in contrast to my long brown hair and green eyes.

Jenny Chapman is a very unique individual. Blond hair, blue eyes, but not what you would call beautiful. She is just downright adorable. She is a mechanical genius, she can fix anything with a motor, and she has a knack for problem solving.

And last but not least, Sami McKenzie, petite with straight long sandy blond hair and bluish green eyes, is the most energetic, bouncy, outgoing person I know, almost to the point of unbearable, but I adore her anyways. She has a unique way of seeing the world as if she could see through to the souls of people. In spite of the fact that she can't hold a thought for more than a few minutes, she is the most interesting person to talk to.

The water from the shower started to run cold, it was time to get started on the day. I reflected that taking stock of one's life is very similar to counting your blessings.

* * *

The weather was absolutely perfect as I drove the five miles into town . It was already eighty-five degrees and it wasn't even nine o'clock yet. The weather forecast predicted ninety-six for the high. For the rest of my class, this was horrible news because the graduation ceremony was to be held on the football field instead of in the gym. The school was having the floor refinished for the next basketball season. I love the heat, so ninety- six degrees was a welcoming treat for me. I had the windows rolled down and the music turned up as I drove my metallic midnight blue '65 mustang into town. Mama had bought me the car for my sixteenth birthday. Not that either one of us is a car fanatic, but according to Mama, the Mustang is more than a car, its art at its' finest.

When I arrived at the salon, the door was standing open and the fans were on. As I walked in, the two stylists started to sing 'It's Miss Valedictorian' to the tune of 'It's Miss America.' I put my hands over my face and shook my head. I had considered forgoing all my homework assignments for the last quarter just to avoid moments like this. The only thing that kept me on course was the scholarship I earned to Ohio State University. I was planning on majoring in archeology with a minor in anthropology.

"So what kind of torture do you two have in store for me today?" my voice dripping with sarcasm. Sue and Judy knew me well enough to know I didn't consider my hair an important issue. Most days I didn't care to even brush it, let alone spend hours styling it like they obviously did. Only on windy days did I bother to even pull it back in a ponytail to keep it from whipping my face.

"I think a shorter style will be good for you, easier to take care of. Maybe just off the shoulders," Sue smiled wickedly and it made my stomach lurch. What did my mother get me into?

I submitted to Sue and Judy as my mother knew I would. After all, the two of them were practically adopted mothers to me anyways. Katie and Jenny are their daughters and for the last six years I practically lived at their houses or they at mine. I sat in the salon chair and closed my eyes. I figured it would be best if I didn't see what they were doing.

For an entire hour they gabbed between themselves, every now and then asking me a question about the trip to San Miguel. Katie and Jenny were going with me and Sue and Judy wanted to make sure they had all the necessities packed.

When they were finished, they spun the chair around to face the mirror. "What do you think?"

As well as they know me I would have thought they would avoid that particular question. Before I looked in the mirror, I glanced at the floor. It looked like cousin It from 'The Addams Family' was curled up around the chair. I had to muster up my courage before I could look in the mirror. To my surprise, I loved it. It was a strange wild kind of style that fit me perfectly. Spiky, but not so short that I looked like a guy, and not so long that it would take more than twenty seconds to deal with in the morning.

"You two are absolutely amazing! Thank you. You know, it kind of looks like Katie's style, just slightly different." They were beaming at the compliment, knowing it meant so much more coming from me.

"Are you guys coming to the party tonight? We're having a bonfire after dark. I bet Mama pulls the guitars out again." I had to laugh at the memories of the last bonfire when Judy tried to sing like Patsy Cline, tried and failed miserably.

"Of course we'll be there. Did anyone think to buy the marshmallows?" Judy asked.

"Mama bought five bags this time so we won't run out. Hey, I better get going, lots to do today. I really love the hair though, thanks."

Just as I was about to step out the door, I had an afterthought. "Would you guys mind doing me a favor?" I paused to see their reaction. They were looking at me intently so I continued. "Would you mind keeping my mom occupied while I'm gone? She doesn't let on, but I think she's dreading this trip, and I'm worried about her being alone."

Sue gave me a wink, "Already made plans to take care of it," she smiled mischievously. It probably should have made me worry even more, but it was Sue and Judy, Mama would be alright. I sighed, smiled, and left.

* * *

The graduation ceremony was as boring as could be expected. We marched onto the football field between the rows of folded chairs filled with family members to the band playing 'Pomp and Circumstance.' Then the senior band members, all ten of us, played 'Ode to Joy,' my favorite song. When we were seated again with our class mates, Father Jack from the Catholic Church led us in the invocation. After the "Amen" (some of my classmates saying it a little more enthusiastically so it sounded like an exclamation that the prayer was over), the superintendent walked to the podium.

"With great honor, I would like to introduce the class of 2012's valedictorian, Anne Cain." As I stood up and walked to the podium, the superintendent continued. "While Anne is making her way to the podium, I would like to say that in all my years in education, this is the first time that I have had the privilege to present this award for perfect attendance from kindergarten through 12th grade. Anne." As he handed me the plaque I began to feel like a blinking neon sign was hanging over my head saying "GEEK! GEEK!"

"Thank you, sir," I mumbled as I shook his hand. I felt the blood rush to my cheeks.

I had to take a few moments to compose myself before I could begin my speech. "My fellow classmates, we began our journey thirteen years ago. The first step of our journey we learned the alphabet, counting, colors, how to share and play. The next step we took. . . ."

Why is everyone staring at me like that? Maybe it's the neon sign still blinking over my head. Didn't I ever miss a day of school? Did I ever get sick? I don't remember ever being sick. Come to think about it, I don't remember ever having a broken bone or stitches or ever needing a doctor. Wow, gotta give Mama credit for that.

"In sixth grade we went to camp. We learned how to canoe, identify trees and plants, hunt, and wilderness survival skills. We sang songs by the campfire and had epic marshmallow wars...."

They're still staring. Is my speech that boring? I knew I should have stuck to the original speech, much more interesting. Why did I listen to mother and rewrite this thing?

"High school was like starting all over again...."

Wow, what is that look on their faces? Are they scared or concerned? Oh, it must be the new hair style. I knew I should have avoided the salon this morning. Even Sue and Judy are staring at me, though. Maybe that's not it then. Did father Jack just cross himself? Is he praying? Is something wrong with me?

"Graduation is a great crossroad in our journey. It is a time when we have to choose the road best for each of us. Our Journey is far from over, but the memories and friendships that we have gained will always be cherished as we travel down these new roads."

Is my mother starting to hyperventilate? What is going on? Did I say something wrong? Finish the speech and blend back into the crowd.

"So my parting words of wisdom to you is 'carpe diem,' cease the day! Don't wait for life to happen, go out and make it happen. Live each day as if tomorrow may never come. My friends, good luck to you and congratulations!"

It was silent for an unbearable five seconds. My mom started to clap and then everyone joined in.

I hurried back to my seat and slouched down so that the row in front of me was hiding my head from the crowd. The superintendent returned to the podium and started calling our names to come up and receive our diplomas. As he called my name I stood up and realized that everyone seemed to flinch as they caught sight of me again. I kept my head down as I walked to the podium to shake the superintendent's hand. As I looked up at his face, he appeared to be in pain. He didn't say 'congratulations' like he did to the rest of my classmates.

"Thank you," I mumbled as I hurried to join the rest of the class now huddled to the side of the spectators, ready to throw their caps in the air. All of my classmates were edging away from me as if I had the plague. Except my friend Sami, who I could always count on no matter what, even if I had just committed the worst social faux pas at the podium.

"Are you alright, Annie?" She didn't quite bridge the gap between us but she was closer than the rest of the class.

"I'm fine. A little embarrassed. How bad was it?" I whispered at her, not wanting to hear the answer, and yet mortified by not knowing what I had done wrong.

She was about to answer when the superintended spoke into the microphone. "Congratulations class of 2012!" There was a roar of cheers as caps went flying into the air. I pulled my cap off my head so I wouldn't be so obvious. Sami just stared at me not bothering with her cap.

"What's wrong?" I croaked. Before Sami could answer, parents were swarming in. I turned to leave quickly, suddenly needing the safety of my car. I called over my shoulder, "I'll see you in a couple of hours."

I got in my car and waited for my mom to catch up. She had seen me running off of the football field and didn't make me wait too long. I started the car as soon as she put her seatbelt on. I didn't realize I was crying until she reached over and wiped a tear from my cheek. I looked at her and all I saw was concern.

"Annie, are you alright?" I couldn't answer immediately so I just nodded.

"How bad was it Mama? Don't sugarcoat it either, I need to know." I was sobbing and practically yelling at her.

"Annie, the speech was fine, but, you know how on a hot summer day you can see heat waves coming off the road?" I looked at her, completely confused. She continued on her analysis. "When you were standing at the podium, there were heat waves coming off of you. The grass at your feet actually looked like it was wilting." She stared at me with wide eyes. "So, how are you feeling? Be straight with me, no sugarcoating."

"I feel just fine Mama, just a little embarrassed. Everyone was staring at me like I was speaking in a different language." I started to feel a little more relaxed. I knew my mother would give me the truth no matter what. 'Painfully honest' is what we called it between ourselves. The idea that I didn't just publicly humiliate myself with a horrible speech was a relief.

No sooner than we got home, the phone was ringing off the hook. I let my mother handle the brunt of the attacks. After about the tenth call, she had her speech memorized. "Annie is fine . . . Yes, I know she looked like she was about to burst into flames, but really, she is fine. Must have been an optical allusion the way the sun was glimmering off of the cap and gown. . . . The party is still on. We'll see you in a little while then." I gave my mother the look of pure appreciation. She understood and smiled at me. Life was always good when I had her to look after me.

Chapter 2

THE PARTY

Mama had turned the air conditioning on in the house. She probably thought I needed to cool down from being out in the sun all afternoon. It was too cold for me though, so I went outside to wait for the caterers to arrive. Sami was just pulling in the driveway as I walked out.

"Are you alright?" She asked as she was getting out of her car. Unlike at the ceremony, this time she was demanding an answer immediately.

"I'm fine, just glad it's over." Sami was giving me a stern look, and I knew I needed to placate her. "Don't worry; I'm not going to internally combust. I'm alright, promise."

"Well, one thing can be said about it. *You are so HOT!*" She gave me a wink and I knew the conversation about my health was abruptly over, sarcastic comments and all.

Sami gave me an impish smile. "I brought my luggage over for the trip. Your mom thought it would be easier if we all spent the night since we have to leave so early in the morning. Where do you want it?"

"The music room, no one will be in there tonight during the party." The music room was my favorite room in the house. It was a large room on the first floor that we had dedicated solely for our musical instruments. The room was done in thick black carpet with extra padding, the walls done in white cork that had sheet music painted on them, and on the one end of the room there was a raised platform with a blood red baby grand piano on one side and a twelve piece drum set on the other. On the opposite wall from the platform was a huge bay window that looked out over the pond in the back yard, draped in red velvet curtains. And just under the bay window was an oversized black velvet couch with big red pillows. The acoustics in the room were perfect for when my friends and I got together to play. We weren't a band per se, but we all enjoyed playing our different instruments. The extra padding of the carpet made the music room the best for sleepovers.

"Jesse and Mike are on their way over, and Katie and Jenny will be over around six. I don't think Ryan will be here until after nine. At least he won't miss the bonfire," there was a gleam in her eyes that made me dread what was coming next, "or the epic marshmallow war." We both started laughing at the memory of sixth grade camp and the huge marshmallow fight that broke out, guys against girls. It was the night that started the friendship that the seven of us shared. We had been almost inseparable ever since. When my mother decided to send me to San Miguel for a graduation present, she knew it wouldn't be complete unless the other six went with me. She made all the arrangements without my knowledge and completely surprised all of us on the last day of school.

* * *

The graduation party was in full swing by five o'clock. My mom and I saddled up two of our four horses to allow the guests to ride through the woods. Volleyball and corn hole were set up near the pond in the backyard and the pile of wood for the bonfire was set up at the far end of the pond. We had a stereo playing on the back porch, the music was of every genre my mother and I could put together. Our friends were having a great time. It seemed that most of my classmates were here as well as the rest of their families, over two hundred people in all, but the back yard, as big as it was, never seemed overly crowded. The caterers had done an excellent job with the food, most of which had already been eaten before I had the chance to get a plate for myself. As the sun began to set and guests began to dwindle, we all made our way out to the bonfire pile to begin the after dark festivities.

Mike, Jesse, and Ryan (who had just arrived from another party he was obligated to go to) walked out to the fire together, all with their hands behind their backs and devilish grins on their faces. As they came within ten feet of the rest of the group they pulled out what looked like pvc pipes shaped into guns. Before the rest of us even knew what was going on, the war had begun. The guys were shooting mini marshmallows at us. Sami and Katie grabbed a bag of marshmallows sitting on a chair and started throwing them at the boys while Jenny and I hid behind Mama as she held up a chair as a shield. Sami started licking the marshmallows before throwing them and actually got a few of them to stick on the boys. Sue and Judy were there too, as well as several of our other classmates, all of which quickly became victims of the battle that ensued. The only reason the war ended was because we all ran out of ammo. It took a good half hour before the laughing and screaming finally quieted down. Fortunately, our closest neighbors were over a mile away, or the police probably would have been called for disturbing the peace.

I sat down on the ground close to the fire and Mike came and sat down next to me. I leaned into him and he wrapped his arm around me. To anyone who didn't know us, this would have seemed intimate, but Mike was like a brother to me. That went for Jesse and Ryan as well. Sami, Katie, and Jenny were more my sisters than friends, we all felt the same about each other. None of us had ever dated each other; it just would have been awkward.

Mike murmured softly to me. "Can I ask you a question?"

"You already met your quota, one question and you already asked it?" Sarcasm is one of my finer personality traits. I looked up into his big hazel eyes with an impish grin, and he laughed.

"I'm trying to be serious, believe it or not. I apologize if this offends you, but I was wondering. . . . . ." he paused, not sure of how to word the question, truly not wanting to offend me.

"I promise I won't get upset, you can ask me anything." This gave him the courage he needed.

"Well," he began, "I knew everyone at the party, and I know you don't have any relatives in this town. I was wondering if you have any other family, you know, like grandparents, aunts, uncles, cousins. . . ." He hesitated and then added. "You don't have to answer if you don't want to."

"It's okay, I don't mind. It's just me and Mama. You know I don't know my father. Mama was an only child and her parents died in a car accident before I was born or something like that. "

"That doesn't bother you?" He asked in earnest.

"No. Mama raised me to believe that family has nothing to do with the blood that runs in your veins. It's how you feel about another person that makes them family. That's probably why I think of you as a big brother, not just a friend. You guys *are* my family. Mama feels the same way about you too, you know. She thinks of you as her children rather than just her daughter's crazy friends that show up to raid the fridge." We both laughed at the imagery.

Mike continued, "You are a unique individual. The most emotionally stable person I ever met, even considering your family, or lack thereof. Nothing bothers you, you don't get mad, you don't get upset or anxious, nothing. You are always happy, the one true constant in the universe."

I settled my head back into Mike's broad shoulder, just as Sami came bouncing over to us. I mumbled under my breath, "T I double Gerrr." Mike and I were doubled over laughing at the inside joke. Sami has always had such a bouncy personality (I actually compared her energy level to a class five hurricane) that we had nicknamed her Tigger back in the sixth grade, but the nickname annoyed her so we refrained from using it in front of her. Behind her back was another story. She cocked her head to the side with a quizzical look, realizing she just missed a good joke.

Sami sat down on the other side of Mike and leaned into his shoulder the same as I was, and he wrapped his arm around her as well. He leaned over and kissed both of our foreheads, sighed and whispered "Family" and gave us both a squeeze. That was exactly what it was for all of us.

Mama, Jesse and Katie, who I hadn't even realized were gone, came walking up just then. Mama was carrying a guitar, Jesse had a wooden box that was used as a type of drum, and Katie had the violin. The jam session was about to begin. It had become a contest amongst our friends to try to come up with a song that my mom or I didn't know. Only once had we ever been stumped. Sue knew a song from a local band that we had never heard of.

Sami and I got up from sitting with Mike. I took the guitar that Mama had handed me and sat down in a chair. Sami took the drum box from Jesse and sat down on it next to me and Mama took the violin from Katie.

"Let's get this jam session started," Mama announced. "How about 'The Devil Went Down to Georgia'?"

We all knew the words so everyone sang as we played. "The devil went down to Georgia; he was looking for a soul to steal. He was in a bind, because he was way behind and he was willing to make a deal. . . ."

When the song ended, Katie was the quickest with a request for 'Let it rock,' and so the night progressed. By two in the morning the party dwindled down to the last ten people. Sue and Judy were the last to say their goodbyes.

We all were just getting up from our chairs when a burning log rolled off the fire right towards Jenny! I didn't think about what I was doing, I just reacted. I jumped towards Jenny pushing her out of the way before she could get burned and grabbed the log with my bare hands and threw it back into the fire. Everyone was staring at me; it felt like the graduation ceremony all over again. No one was even breathing. The only thing I could hear was the crackle of the fire and the bull frogs singing in the pond.

Instead of placating everyone by telling them I was fine, which just didn't seem to be the right thing to do, I tucked my hands into my arm pits. "Ow! That wasn't the smartest thing I've ever done."

I looked at Jenny who was still on the ground from me pushing her over, "I'm sorry Jenny, are you okay?"

I could hear everyone start breathing again. Jenny shook her head and rolled her eyes. "I think the appropriate question is, are you okay?" Another knee jerk reaction, I reached my hand down to help her up. Instead of grabbing my hand, she grabbed my wrist and inspected my hand. "It doesn't even look burned," she said it more as an accusation than a statement.

Mama, as always, jumped in to save me for the second time today. "Let's get you in the house and put ice on those before they start blistering." She grabbed me by the shoulders as Jenny let go of my wrist, and marched me up to the house.

Chapter 3

VACATION

Mama had taken me straight to the bathroom to inspect my hands. As I suspected and to her amazement, there was nothing wrong with them. I asked her to wrap them up to avoid all the accusing questions that my friends were sure to bombard me with.

Mama had finally gone off to bed; she would be up before us to fix breakfast. We were leaving for the airport at nine in the morning; she would be up by seven. The rest of us set up our sleeping bags in the music room in a big circle, pillows facing in so we could talk until we fell asleep.

"That was the longest day I have ever had," Jesse mumbled with exhaustion. "Wow, we finally graduated! Honestly, Annie, if it weren't for you, I probably never would have made it."

I blushed, not that anyone could see it in the dark. "Jesse, you would have done just fine with or without me." I felt the need to change the subject before the conversation got mushy. "Hey, where did you guys get the marshmallow guns?"

Ryan started to answer but he was laughing too much to get the words out. Jesse interceded, "Ryan found the blue prints on the internet about two months ago. You know how hard it is to keep a secret from you girls for that long?"

"I think I got a bruise from a rogue marshmallow," Jenny feigned injury. "What did you do, petrify them before shooting us?"

Katie was done with the subject. "Just think, guys, by tonight we will be sitting on a beach sipping on pina coladas. I am so hyped up; I don't think I can sleep tonight."

The conversation then turned to all the activities that we wanted to cover while in San Miguel. Snorkeling, sunbathing, swimming, deep sea fishing, a two day trip to Chichen Itza, and a lot of drinking were the main plans for the trip. Although the last part only applied to the other six who were already 18 and were of legal age to drink in Mexico, I was only 17 and would not be 18 until after we got back to Ohio. Of course, the others assured me that it wouldn't be a problem, since none of them had an aversion to contributing to the delinquency of a minor.

It seemed that we had all just drifted off to sleep when Mama came in to wake us up. Not likely for her to do it in any normal fashion, oh no, she walked over to the drum set in the corner and woke us up with a very loud rendition of "Wipe Out". I love my mother, but sometimes. . . . . . .!

"Anyone want coffee with their breakfast?" She asked as she was heading out of the room.

Sami's head perked up so fast to say yes, but before she could, the rest of us screamed "NO!!" out of terror of having to sit on a plane next to a caffeinated class five hurricane of a Sami. The image my head conjured was the plane crashing from an electrical short circuit. Sami's natural energy tended to have a bad effect on electrical devices, mostly that they just quit working if she got too close. Her parents wouldn't let her use a computer or a cell phone anymore because they had spent a small fortune replacing them on a regular basis. They even bought her several disposable cameras for the trip just to protect their digital camera from her wrath.

We all managed to get showers and eat breakfast in record time. The minivan that Ryan borrowed from his mom and the SUV that Jesse borrowed from his dad were loaded up. Mama went through the checklist to make sure we had everything: passports, plane tickets, bikinis, swim trunks, toothbrushes, sunglasses. . . . . Her list was thorough and complete from years of experience. Before we left the house, everyone took turns giving Mama a hug and thanked her for the trip. When it was my turn, (she saved me for last) I was crying. "I love you, Mama. I'm already missing you."

She gave me a big bear hug and then wiped the tear from my cheek. "Tell Choc Mool I expect him to continue his duties as a guardian and tell him I miss him. Have fun, and be careful."

She gave me a kiss on the cheek and then pushed me out the door. "Now go, find the man of your dreams."

Sami, Mike and I were riding with Ryan, and Jenny and Katie were with Jesse. We had an hour long ride to the Cleveland airport and I knew we wouldn't be five minutes into the drive before someone would ask the question. To my surprise it was Ryan, the quietest one of the group. "So, who's Choc Mool, a friend of yours or something?"

I laughed at the thought of Choc Mool being considered a friend, "Not exactly. Choc Mool is a stone sculpture that was used as a sacrificial altar in Chichen Itza. He and I have a history together." I paused for a dramatic effect. "My oldest memory was from when I was three years old. Mama was doing rubbings of the glyphs on the Temple of Warriors; I got bored and wandered off. Mama found me a half hour later curled up on Choc Mool, sleeping. It wasn't until I was older that I understood the look Mama had on her face. It was a combination of relief and horror. She was relieved to have found me, but terrified that I looked like the sacrificial lamb ready for the slaughter. Definitely a look that is hard to forget."

"Why did your mom want you to say hello to *that?*" Sami asked.

"After the incident, she thought of Choc Mool as my guardian rather than a sacrificial alter, so it's kind of her way of telling me to be safe and she will miss me while I'm gone." They all gave me a look that they had no idea what I was talking about. I guess you just had to be there to understand.

The airport would have been uneventful if it weren't for Sami setting off the metal detector as we went through security. The security guards took her aside to use the wand to scan her, but that didn't seem to work right either. Once they determined that she wasn't a security risk, we all headed to the gate to wait for the boarding call. All of us seemed to be absorbing Sami's energy, eager to start our vacation. Jesse and Katie were discussing the benefits of having tranquilizers to calm Sami down, but didn't think that any amount less than what would be used to bring down a full grown elephant would have any effect on her.

The flight to San Miguel felt shorter than the six and half hours that it really was thanks to Jenny sitting next to me. We kept up a conversation the whole way so I couldn't let my fear of flying get the best of me. Mike and Jesse sat with Sami, trying to keep her contained. It was ironic how two big muscle bound boys could have such a hard time with someone as petite as Sami. Ryan and Katie sat across the aisle from Jenny and me, but they fell asleep twenty minutes into the flight, so they weren't much into the conversations.

Jenny was hesitant to ask me a question, but I could see it in her eyes. "What is it, Jenny?" I tried to encourage her.

"Um. . . . . I was just wondering. . . . . . about your hands. I see you didn't bother to put bandages on them this morning." She was still hesitating, not really wanting to ask a question. "They look alright. Do they hurt?" Finally, she asked a question.

"I think Mama got to them quick enough to keep the damage to a minimum. There's no pain, but they feel hot, which is strange for me, because I never think anything is warm enough. I always feel cold unless the sun is beating down and the temperature is above ninety degrees." I put my hands on her arm. "See what I mean?"

Jenny flinched when I touched her. "Ow, that is so weird. It's like your hands are still on fire." As I removed my hands I saw that her arm was bright red where I had just touched her, a perfect imprint of my hands.

"Sorry." I murmured, feeling ashamed and embarrassed. It was time to change the subject again before she realized I was becoming a freak of nature. "So, did you have fun at the party?"

Talking to Jenny was as easy as buttering toast. She started to rattle off a play by play of the entire party, filling me in on some of the things I missed while I had to play hostess.

When we landed at the small airport outside of San Miguel, we all breathed a sigh of relief that Sami didn't crash the plane. The moment we stepped off of the plane, my friends all looked as if they were wilting in the heat. For me, however, one-oh-two with heavy humidity, I felt like I was finally home. Everyone was in agreement; the first thing after we got to our rooms was to hit the swimming pool to cool off until the sun went down.

We spent the next five days in and around San Miguel. We did some sightseeing, (it was nothing new to me, having been there so many times), snorkeling on the reefs, and we spent lots of time at the pool. We had a flight scheduled to take us to Chichen Itza for a two day tour on Friday and Saturday, so Thursday night we decided to go to a local dance club three blocks down from the hotel.

Just as we were walking through the door to the club, I realized I had left my wallet at the hotel room.

"I'll walk back with you. It's probably not safe for tourist to be out after dark all alone," Mike said. I think he was trying to scare me, but I was confident that I could take care of myself.

"No, Mike, I'll be fine. You go and have fun. I'll be back in twenty minutes." I assured him.

I was two blocks away from the club when I heard footsteps behind me. I figured it was Mike just being overly protective. I turned to face him, and realized my mistake. Barreling towards me was a large man. He had a scowl on his face and a knife in his hand that showed his intensions, he was trying to kill me! I instinctively went into a fighting stance. Just as he closed the gap to three feet, I threw a side kick into him. I made perfect contact with his chest and he fell backwards onto the ground with the wind knocked out of him.

All of my training told me to run, but I didn't. I wasn't afraid of this man, I was curious. I took the few steps needed so that I could look him in the eyes. He was grabbing his chest with his hands, and gasping to catch his breath. The knife he had held was now lying at his side. I picked it up, it was a dagger in the shape of a dragon, it looked sinister with ruby eyes, but it was much lighter than I thought it should be. I used the dagger to point at my attacker. "Maybe you should pick on someone your own size. Or better yet, get a different line of work. You suck at this one." I left him lying on the street, still gasping for air. I made it to the hotel room with no more incidences. I put the dagger in my travel bag taking note that it looked to be made of ivory. I grabbed my wallet and headed back to the club.

It had only taken me fifteen minutes to make it back to the club. Jesse was by my side as soon as I walked in. A steel drum band was playing on a small stage so he had to yell for me to hear him. "If you hadn't come back in two more minutes, I was sending the Calvary out after you." He paused to look at my face. I'm not sure what he saw, but he was concerned. "What happened to you?"

"Is it that obvious?" I took a deep breath to calm myself. "Una suveza por favor." and gave him a half-hearted smile.

"Are you going to tell me about it now, or am I going to have to get you drunk first?"

"Drunk first, please. Where is everyone?" I was already scanning the crowd and spotted Mike and Katie at a small table, and the rest out on the dance floor. We shimmied between dancing bodies to go sit at the table. Jesse went to the bar to get me a beer.

As I took my first drink, the beer seemed to wash the anxiety away. The rest of the night was spent dancing and laughing as if nothing had happened. The next morning, on the other hand, was a whole other story. I would have sold my soul for a bottle of aspirin and a few more hours of sleep. Lesson learned; don't drink in excess.

We made it to the airport ten minutes before the flight to Chichen Itza was taking off. We all climbed aboard what my mother always referred to as a puddle jumper. There were several other tourists on the flight with us, but the plane was not filled to capacity, so we were able to stretch out and take a nap for the forty five minute flight. By the time we landed, I was feeling much better and ready for my favorite part of the vacation.

Chapter 4

CHICHEN ITZA

"Welcome to Chichen Itza!" I couldn't contain myself as we walked through the entrance gate of the national monument. To me, it felt like coming home. I was in an ecstatic mood, and nothing less than the end of the world was going to change that.

"¿Como estas, Annie?" I heard a familiar voice behind me.

"¿Muy bien, Raul, y tu?" Raul had been a tour guide so long at Chichen Itza that he seemed like as much a permanent fixture here as the stone monuments themselves.

"Follow me; you can put your gear in the observatory. It's closed to the public, so no one will bother it there. It is under reconstruction, another project funded by your mother. I assume that is why your mother was granted special permission for this sleep over tonight?" Mama had donated so much money towards the excavation and reconstruction of the city that she was granted almost any favor she asked for, including an overnight stay and access to the observatory.

As we made our way to the south end of the city, I rattled on about some of the buildings we passed, not wanting to get into too much detail until we had a chance to visit each of the sites. "The south end of the city is known as 'Old Chichen', the architecture here is mostly Puuc and Mayan. Archeologists believe this was built around eight hundred A.D., but there are still debates on that. This part of the city is dedicated mostly to Chak, the Rain God. Since the economy of this area was dependent on agriculture, Chak was a very important deity." Raul rolled his eyes at me, and I understood immediately that he was feeling like the proverbial fifth wheel. It wasn't that we needed a tour guide, but it was required by law because the city was a national monument. Raul knew he was just a babysitter for this tour.

As we entered the observatory, my friends were awestruck by the spiral staircase that led to the observation platform. Raul, needing to feel useful, interjected, "Amazing, isn't it?" The Mayans were the epitome of artisans. This structure is also known as El Caracol or the conch because the design of the staircase was taken from a conch shell." We dropped our extra gear off at the base of the stairway, keeping our backpacks with bottled water and light snacks with us for the day.

"Where to first, Annie?" Raul asked, trying to be a gracious host.

"The pyramid, I want to show them the interior before it gets too hot." Raul nodded in understanding, and led the way to the huge pyramid that towers over the rest of the city.

Raul started up his tour guide speech as we were heading to the north side of the structure. "The Castillo, or the Castle . . ." I couldn't let him finish the sentence.

". . . Is not really a castle! Why do you still use the Spanish names in this place?"

"A rose is a rose, Annie!" He looked smug when he turned to me. "But, Annie does have a point. *The pyramid* is actually a calendar, a very precise one at that. The structure is seventy-five feet tall with ninety-one steps on each of the four sides plus the top platform for the three-hundred-sixty-five days of the year." He rambled on until we made it to the entrance of the interior of the pyramid. "This is the second pyramid built on this spot, right over top of the first pyramid. The larger pyramid is dedicated to Kuklukan. *He* is the plumed Serpent God. The smaller pyramid is dedicated to the Red Jaguar." As we stepped through the entryway, we were greeted by a statue of the Red Jaguar. It's inlaid jade eyes staring blankly at us.

"So you still haven't accepted the fact that Kuklukan is a female deity?" I prodded Raul. We had this argument before, that not all deities represented here were male. It was illogical for me to argue this point with him again, but I wanted my friends to hear the arguments so they could decide for themselves, and I may have been showing off a little as well. "The first pyramid is superimposed in the second pyramid, like an infant in the womb of its mother. Also the symbol for Venus is prominently displayed on the larger pyramid, and in every other religious belief, Venus is definitely female."

Katie, Jenny and Mike seemed to agree with me, but the other three still had their doubts. A millennium of beliefs that women were inferior to men ingrained into their beliefs would take a lot more than a brief argument to convince them otherwise. I wondered if it was because of their hobbies. Katie is the sports nut, which seems kind of masculine. Jenny is the grease monkey, definitely masculine. Mike the chef, could be construed as feminine. Whereas Jesse the hunter, Ryan the military genius, and Sami, though a little crazy, still seemed to remain gender oriented. Interesting thought; I could probably argue my point a little longer to get the other three to at least see my point of view, that females probably played a more important role than history has lead us to believe.

"This smaller pyramid has sixty-one steps on each side plus the platform equals two-hundred-forty-five days which represent the days of Venus cycle around the sun. This leads me to believe that the Red Jaguar was also female." Speculations are not my strong point but I really wanted to get Raul agitated. Not that I cared to argue with him, but he made the funniest faces when he was mad, and I needed a good laugh.

"Annie! That's enough!" And there was the face I so needed to see. I couldn't help myself, I actually snorted from trying to hold the guffaws in. As soon as I let it out, the rest of my friends joined in as well. Poor Raul didn't understand, he just thought that the heat was getting to all of us, so he quickly herded us out of the pyramid.

As we walked out of the pyramid, I had the strangest feeling that we were being watched, or maybe a sensation that something was about to happen. I couldn't quite explain the feeling; it was something I had never felt before. I was pondering the feeling when Sami came up behind me. "What are you staring at, Annie? You look like someone just walked over your grave."

"Don't know. I can't quite put my finger on it. Do you feel like someone is watching us?"

Sami, being the type that could sense anything out of the ordinary, just shrugged. "Nope, all is well in our happy little world. Hey, did Jenny tell you she thinks this place was set up as some kind of superconductor? I'd say I have to believe her, the energy in this place is amazing." Leave it to Sami to change the subject. At moments like this I truly appreciated having her around.

Raul led us up the north face of the pyramid rambling on about the spring and fall equinox, but I couldn't shake the feeling preventing me in paying attention to what he was saying. Mike caught up to me and put his arm around my waist as we ascended the stairs. "Don't worry, Annie, no one will get anywhere near you with us around." He looked down at me waiting for me to meet his gaze. When I looked into his eyes, I found his confidence reassuring.

"Thanks Mike. You guys are a true comfort to me. What would I do without you?"

"Probably starve. I've tried your cooking. I think my dog would turn his nose up to it." We both laughed. I was definitely feeling better. Mike stayed close by my side for a while just to keep me reassured that everything was fine.

Raul was still rambling on in his tour guide duties. "This structure represents three of the most important gods of the Mayan religion. Kuklukan was the most powerful, he controlled the skies and the heavens. The Red Jaguar, we believe, was the God of War. And Chak was the God of Water or God of Rain. Chak is represented in the temple at the top of the pyramid." We spent what seemed like hours on the pyramid, calculating out which steps represented our birthdays, and asking Raul ridiculous questions about leap year and day light savings time which we knew he couldn't answer, because neither concept existed during the Mayan era.

When we were done messing with Raul (and laughing at the expressions on his face) we started to head to the ball court. I knew this would be a real treat for Katie, the sports fanatic. I stopped everyone twenty yards out from the pyramid. "Ryan, give me your loudest yell." Ryan looked at me like I had truly lost my mind, but he yelled anyways. The sound echoed off of the surrounding structures. "This is a 'clap zone', one of many in the ruins. The Mayans were geniuses in their construction. The ball court has a very unique feature to it. It's best to just show you, it's too complicated to explain."

As we walked into the one-hundred-eighty-nine yard by seventy-six yard playing field in the shape of a capital "I", Katie was wide eyed with wonder. "Think of it as a prelude to modern day soccer and basketball. The players moved a hard rubber ball around only using their hips, knees, and elbows in an attempt to score by getting the ball through those stone rings." I pointed at the huge rings engraved with feathered serpents nine feet up the walls. "And the really strange thing is, the captain of the winning team was sacrificed to the Gods."

Katie was bouncing with joy. "Can we play a game? Mike can be captain." She teased.

Raul scowled, "I don't think so."

"Party pooper!" Katie stuck her tongue out at him.

Before she could throw a temper tantrum, I intervened. "Let's split up, I want to show you something. You four go to the Temple of the North, and we'll go to the Temple of the Red Jaguar." We split up, Mike, Sami, Ryan and I went to the south end of the playing field, while the others went to the north. I turned and spoke in a normal voice. "Can you hear me now?"

Raul responded, "Plain as day, as always."

"The acoustics in this place allows you to hear people on the opposite ends of the court as if they were standing next to you. Stay where you are, we're coming over. Race you guys there." The four of us raced back to the other end of the field. Mike and I tied, but Sami and Ryan were right behind us.

"This is one of the strangest temples in this place. It's dedicated to the Bearded Man. Since the Mayan men did not have facial hair, it's a curiosity where this man came from. Also, since he is opposite the Red Jaguar, what was his connection to *her?*" I emphasized the "her" just to see if Raul was paying attention. If he was, he didn't show it. "The engravings on the balustrades here represent the Earth Monster, and of course, Kuklukan is represented on the panel overhead." I gazed up at the faded carving of the bearded man. The face, what could be seen of it, looked strangely familiar. I tilted my head to the side (not that the view was any better) just to get a different perspective. It didn't help.

"Where to next?" Jesse asked, he seemed a little bored with all of the history lessons. I was going to have to come up with something good to keep him interested.

"How about a little death and mayhem to peek your interests? The Platform of Skulls is right this way." I smiled when I saw the spark in his eyes.

"Just as the name says, this wall is covered in carvings of skulls. This is where the Mayans used to put the heads of their enemies on poles and display them like trophies. Isn't that lovely?" My sarcasm was still intact.

Ryan was enjoying this temple as well, but if I knew him well enough, I would say his favorite would be the Temple of Warriors. Unfortunately, that particular temple had been closed to the public to protect the painted artwork that was surprisingly still visible on the walls.

We made it through most of the northern part of the ruins by five in the afternoon. It was quitting time for Raul, so he handed us off to the second shift security guard that had to accompany us while we were here. His name was Miguel, but he wasn't the talkative type. He kept his distance, but he was ever vigilant in his duties to keep us out of trouble. When the last of the visitors left the city, we headed back to the Observatory to collect our gear and make camp. We each brought a sleeping bag and pillow to sleep on the ground and I had brought a mesh tent to keep the insects away. We weren't allowed to make a campfire so we settled on energy bars and water for dinner. Katie thought to bring a Frisbee, so we kept ourselves entertained until it was dark enough to enjoy the observatory. There was a full moon so the ruins were lit up as bright as dawn.

"The Mayans were excellent astronomers. They were able to calculate the length of a year by mapping the location of the sun and the stars. They even calculated the length of a year for the planet Venus. This, if you remember, is represented by the inner pyramid of Kuklukan's temple." As we reached the top of the winding staircase of the observatory, I pointed out the remaining windows of the observation level. "Every night they would plot the stars that could be viewed from each of these windows. When the stars lined up again, a year had passed. They kept extensive documents to keep track of the movements. On a drearier note, the Mayan calendar ends on December twenty-first this year, end of the world or something." With that, six sets of eyes turned to glare at me. "What?"

Ryan spoke up while the others were still trying to figure out what to say. "Do you have to put it like that? Is there a pleasant explanation for this, or is it something we don't want to hear?"

"Just a couple of speculations: Maybe they were predicting their own demise that came much sooner than they expected, or . . . . Oh, you said pleasant explanation. I'll keep that one to myself then." The glaring eyes intensified. "I'm just guessing at this. Mama could probably give you a hundred different scenarios that aren't so . . . . . catastrophic."

"Well, that would suck!" Jesse added. "We just wasted the last twelve years of our lives in school to find out the world is going to end six months later."

"It may not be the end," I tried to be positive, "just a new beginning, the next cycle."

Miguel, who had been silent all night, spoke up. "Annie, you are forgetting an important fact. The Mayans believed that there are only four cycles, and this is the end of the fourth cycle, there is no fifth cycle." I was beginning to not like Miguel, he was such a pessimist.

Jenny yawned, "Guys, it's been a long day. Let's get some sleep. If you're going to have us hiking all over this city tomorrow like you did today, we need to get some rest." Amazingly even Sami agreed with Jenny, but I was feeling restless. The feeling that someone was watching us, came back to me. I shivered as if cold fingers just ran down my spine. I nonchalantly moved closer to Mike as we headed down the spiral staircase and back to our makeshift camp. Being closer to Mike always made me feel safe.

"What's for breakfast, anyways?" Jesse asked. I thought I heard his stomach growl, but it could have been the wildlife out in the jungle.

"We have to be at the airstrip by eight. The pilot is bringing us a continental breakfast." Mama had made the arrangements, she thought of everything. This trip was a great idea, I would have to remember to pick her up a thank you gift for this.

It didn't take long for us all to fall asleep. Trekking around an ancient city really does take a lot out of a person. I began dreaming as soon as my eyes were closed. It was hard to tell where reality ended and the dream began.

He gently caressed my arm to wake me. I wasn't surprised to see him, after all, I was just dreaming, although it seemed almost too real. He took my hand and helped me to my feet. My friends were still sleeping in the mesh tent so we quietly left. He held my hand as we walked, but we didn't speak until we were halfway to the pyramid.

"This place was built for you." He spoke softly so he wouldn't disturb the soft music of the jungle. "I hope you like it. I've always felt drawn to this place myself."

I looked into his eyes and answered him. "This place has always felt like home to me. I love it here, the beauty of the architecture, the mystery of the people, and the energy of this place. I feel like I have always belonged here. What was it like before it was abandoned?"

"*See for yourself.*" I looked away from him unwillingly towards the pyramid. It was breathtaking. Instead of the crumbling, half restored ruin that it had been during the day, it was complete and magnificent, painted in bright greens, reds and yellows and completely lit up with torches on every step leading to the temple at the top. He led me up the stairs on the north side and stood aside for me to enter the temple before him. I gazed in astonishment at the beauty before me. In the center of the temple was a huge gilded bed with a canopy overhead of bright colored silk in hues of purple, blue, pink, and silver. On the floor surrounding the bed were dozens of terra-cotta vases filled with wild flowers and palm fronds. The aroma of the wildflowers permeated the air with their sweet fragrance.

He gently picked me up and cradled me in his arms. I looked into his eyes and my heart began to race. He held my gaze as he carried me to the bed, and laid me softly in the center with my head on his arm for a pillow. His fingertips tracing my cheek bone left my skin tingling. I arched my neck to kiss him, but he put his fingers on my lips to stop me. "We must not, Annie. I do not think I would be able to restrain myself, and I do not want to hurt you. It is hard enough to keep control with you so close, but to allow myself to give in even in the slightest. . . ." He closed his eyes and turned his head as if he was ashamed of some great weakness.

"Why did you bring me here, then?" Frustration was obvious in my voice, but it was softened by sympathy for his anguish.

"I need to be near you, even if we are limited. I have suffered centuries without you. I have no more patience left to wait for you as I should." He pulled me closer and held me tight. I could feel his cool breath permeate through my hair. My blood was boiling and my skin felt like it was on fire. I reached my hand up to caress his face and I realized that my hand was on fire!

I sat up quickly, and jerked myself awake. It was still and quiet in the tent, except for my heavy breathing. My heart felt like it was trying to pound its' way out of my chest. I was surprised that the noise of it didn't awaken anyone else, to me it sounded like a base drum getting thoroughly abused. It was the strangest dream I had ever had. It was so life like, vivid. I even remembered the smell of wildflowers. The good news was I wasn't on fire, the bad news was it was still hours before dawn and there was no way I could get back to sleep after that dream. I lay back down on my sleeping bag and tried to decipher what it had all meant. The only conclusion I could come up with is that I was destined to be alone for the rest of my life. I couldn't even have a normal relationship in my dreams, how could I ever have one in reality. I mentally shrugged, as long as I have my friends I would be fine. Of course, someday *they* may actually have a chance for normal relationships. I would be happy for them, and I definitely wouldn't stand in the way, but the thought of it made me feel even more alone than before. I was startled when Jesse nudged me awake. I wasn't even aware that I had fallen back asleep again. Thankfully it was a dreamless sleep this time.

"Hey, sleeping beauty. We don't want to miss breakfast, so get up!"

"But I don't want to go to school, mommy!" I couldn't help but smirk when I said this. The façade was up, so I got myself moving.

We packed all of our gear, making sure nothing was left behind before we headed to the airstrip. We were to stow our gear in the plane and head back to the south part of the ruins for the day. The plane had arrived before we reached the landing strip, and the pilot had gone off to find a friend. The stewardess helped us stow our luggage and brought us our breakfast. We ate out on the grass in the shadow of the plane. Breakfast consisted of a bowl of fruit, cereal and milk, and blueberry muffins. We chatted casually about the plans for the day. Katie and Jenny wanted to have time for the souvenir shops outside the city before we left; everyone else quickly agreed that it was a good idea.

We were just cleaning up the trash from breakfast when the pilot returned to the plane.

"Katie Brown? Are you Katie Brown?" He asked Jenny. Jenny pointed him in the right direction.

"Katie Brown?"

"Yes." Katie sounded a little leery.

"I have a message for you from the hotel." He handed her the message that was sealed in an envelope with her name on it, and then boarded the plane.

"Thank You?" She called after him a little late.

Chapter 5

BAD NEWS

Katie opened the envelope, "It's from my mom." She started to cry before she even finished reading the message. She handed it to Mike hoping he would be able to explain what was wrong so she wouldn't have to.

It was odd that even Mike was having a hard time finding his tongue. "Annie," His voice cracked. I didn't know what was coming, but I froze in place expecting the worst. I could hear the blood pulsing in my ears. Mike's voice sounded distant. "I have some bad news to tell you." My head was spinning. "Your mother was. . . . ." He swallowed hard, and tried again. "Your mother was killed in a car accident last night. I'm so sorry Annie. I. . . ."

I didn't want to think. I couldn't think. I needed to get away, from my friends, from reality. They were all trying to hug me, I couldn't breathe.

"NO! Get away from me!" I was screaming, the tears were pouring down my face. I pushed them away and started running for the tree line on the south side of the ruins. When I reached the tree line, I just kept running. I was afraid that if I stopped, I would have to face the pain, so I kept running. My legs were burning and my heart was pounding out of my chest. My legs, arms and face were stinging from the foliage whipping at me, but I still couldn't slow down. The physical pain was so much easier to deal with than the emotional pain. My lungs were on fire and I couldn't breathe anymore. Finally, exhaustion got the better of me and I tripped over a tree root and fell to the ground. I laid curled up in the fetal position and let the pain consume me.

I had no concept of time, but it must have been hours later because the sun was directly overhead now. I could just catch glimpses of the light through the thick canopy of leaves overhead. I felt numb physically but the pain in my chest was like someone had ripped my heart out. There was a big gaping hole where it should be. My eyes were dry and sore from the crying and my vision was blurry. The blood still pounded in my ears, but I thought I heard something. I tried to concentrate on the noises in the jungle. I heard the birds cawing, the leaves rustling in the breeze and I heard what sounded like a footstep, but muffled. I pulled myself up into a crouch and held still to listen for the noise again. What I heard sent cold chills down my spine. It was the sound of a large animal on the hunt and I wasn't sure if I was the prey. I stayed in the crouch position and slowly turned in a circle as I listened for the sound again. Just as I turned one hundred eighty degrees I caught sight of a large wolf stalking me thirty yards away. My worst fears were realized, I was being hunted.

I knew I couldn't outrun a wolf, but my sense of reason evaded me as self-preservation became necessary. I turned to run but was abruptly stopped. I thought I ran into a tree at first. I looked up to see the most amazing icy blue eyes looking back at me. They were glowing.

"Sleep Anyanka," His voice was calm and soothing. The strangest sensation swept over me. My mind was no longer in control of my body. My eyes shut and I couldn't open them, I felt like I was being swept up by the wind. I thought I heard voices speaking in a strange, soothing melody. It was like a dream but I couldn't see anything, just the darkness. I heard the words but I couldn't make out the meaning of what was being said.

"You seem in a better mood, brother. How long has it been?" It was the most beautiful female voice that I had ever heard. It was so light and airy that it seemed to be riding on a breeze.

"Can we discuss the situation at hand, please?" The voice was so familiar to me. I knew it was him, the man I had been dreaming about my whole life. So I must have been dreaming.

I felt comforted by his voice so I allowed myself to drift into the dream.

"This is a peculiar turn of events, I must admit." The female sounded confused.

"Did Lilith not tell you about her?"

"No, I have not heard from Lilith in almost two decades. I have not felt her presence either."

"How can this be? It is not as if she could leave."

"I am as baffled as you are, but those are the facts. And this one is just as baffling."

"It is her, I am certain." There was so much jubilation in his voice as he stated this proclamation.

"It is improbable. There can only be four. She is gone, we failed her."

"Then explain her!" The man snapped. "You heard her soul. That is why you called for me. It is not impossible. We have been here long enough to know that nothing is impossible."

"Yes, I can hear her, but her song is not the same. It sounds similar, but still very different. How does she appeal to you?"

"The same, but I am in control, for now at least." He growled.

"We should test her, to make sure she is our Anyanka."

"How do you propose we test her?"

"With fire. Here, use this. It will be a more effective test if she is awake." The female voice suggested.

"And if she proves to be Anyanka, she will be in grave danger."

"She has guardians. They are in her city waiting for her to return."

"Do you think I have any faith in guardians?" The man growled again in uninhibited rage. "Watch over her. You can keep her safe."

"I cannot. You will have to watch over her, for now at least. I will be able to join you in a week's time."

"I do not know if I am ready for that. It has been a long time since I have had any interaction with humans."
"You will be fine, my brother. I have faith in you."
There was a stiff breeze, and then silence.
I'm not sure how much time passed, but it felt like only a few minutes until I heard him speak again. "Awaken, Anyanka."
As I slowly regained consciousness, I became aware of a presence. Someone was carrying me through the jungle; someone that, oddly, smelled like a fresh spring rain. I opened my eyes. My head was nestled into a muscular chest covered with a form fitting white t-shirt.
"The wolf!?" I blurted out as I looked around for signs of the giant predator. I looked up to see the strangest blue eyes staring back at me. The eyes had a reflective quality, like cat eyes reflecting light in the darkness but it was still daylight. I was mesmerized by them. We stared at each other for countless seconds. I took in his face, bronze and smooth, like a sculpture, perfect. High cheek bones, strong angular jaw with a hint of stubble, smooth lips that were set in a scowl, long light brown hair down past his shoulders that glimmered brass when the sun filtered through the canopy overhead, and a strong brow over those beautiful icy blue glowing eyes. He seemed so familiar to me, but it took a moment for my mind to catch up to reality. I gasped as I put the puzzle pieces together. It *was him*, the voice, the face, even his hair. The only thing different about him was his eyes.
He was staring at me, not breaking stride as he continued to carry me through the jungle. I forgot how to breathe.
"The wolf was only curious, he never meant you any harm." He snapped at me. I sensed he was angry with me, but that barely registered. There was something strange about the way he spoke. His lips didn't move to the words as he was speaking. It was like watching an old martial arts film where the actors were obviously speaking in Japanese, but the audio had been dubbed in English. Since that was

completely impossible, I was certain I was still dreaming or going crazy. But I felt very much awake.

"Who are you?" It wasn't the question on the top of the priority list, but it sounded better than, *where have you been all my life?* I couldn't resist the urge to reach up and run my fingers over his face to verify that he was real. He jerked his head back, obviously not wanting me to touch him. I pulled my hand back and continued to stare at him.

"I have many names, but you may call me Kai, Anyanka." He took me by surprise calling me by my name, my real name that only my mother ever called me when I was in serious trouble.

My heart fluttered as a surge of adrenaline ran through my veins. "How do you know my name?" He stopped walking, and glared at me intently. I noted that he was the most beautiful man I had ever seen.

"Lilith would not have changed your name . . . ." He stopped abruptly with an anguished look on his face as if he was remembering something that was best left buried and forgotten. He recovered quickly, and started walking again.

"No one calls me by that name, not even my mother." I still wanted an answer for the question.

"What does your mother call you, then?"

"Annie, Annie Cain."

"Cain? Lilith was pushing her luck with that one. She was never that reckless." The scowl on his face only deepened. He was quite intimidating.

I had to muster the courage to continue questioning him. "Do you have a last name, Kai?"

"The last name you called me was Jora." I noted that his response was strangely worded as if he was insinuated that I already knew him. At least his mood seemed to improve, but only slightly.

"Well, Kai Jora, thank you for rescuing me. It seems I owe you my life."

It finally dawned on me, that my one hundred twenty pounds might be a bit of a strain on him, as he was still carrying me, "Kai? You can put me down now. I think I can walk." I noted, however, he wasn't breathing hard or even sweating in the one-hundred-two degree temperature with ninety-eight percent humidity. His skin felt quite cool to the touch.

He kept his composure stern. "I will not put you down. You are a stupid child for running out into the jungle without your guardians. Are you trying to get yourself killed? Do you have any concern for you own life?" He was yelling at me. I was terrified by him, but also a little put off.

"Where are you taking me?" I tried to sound authoritative, but I heard the panic seeping into my voice. I tried to remain calm, panicking wouldn't help the situation. Though I knew his face well, he was a stranger to me.

"I am taking you back to Chichen Itza. Your guardians are here to protect you. You should not have run off like that; especially now that the transformation has begun. To anyone that would know the signs, you will be all too easy to identify. This is a very dangerous time for you, but apparently that is no concern to you." He wasn't making any sense to me.

"I think you might be mistaking me for someone else. I don't have any guardians." That was the only logical conclusion I could come up with. Although there weren't many people in the world with the name Anyanka, how could he know me?

He stopped walking and set me gently on the ground as he spoke. "I can prove to you that I am not mistaken." He reached into the right pocket of his faded khaki shorts and pulled out a butane lighter. With a movement so quick it looked like his hand was blurred, he grabbed my left wrist. He didn't hurt me, but my heart felt like it was going to pound out of my chest. He saw the look of terror in my eyes and tried to calm me. "Stop fighting me, this will not hurt if you hold still." He threatened.

His assurances did nothing to calm me as he struck the flint and held the lighter closely under my exposed forearm.

"What are you doing?" I shrieked and tried to pull away. The flame on my arm was a strange sensation. It didn't burn me like it should have. It felt like velvet gently brushing across my skin. I stopped struggling to free myself and stared wide eyed at the flame and then at him. "How . . .?" I couldn't form an intelligent question.

"Fire is your gift, or talent, whatever you want to call it. When you have fully transformed you will be able to control it, but for now, you are only able to endure it." He removed the flame from my skin and released his grasp of my wrist to let me inspect my arm. Other than it felt warmer than normal, there was no sign of the fire ever touching me, just as when I caught the burning log at the bonfire. I looked into his eyes trying to find the answers.

He seemed frustrated with me. "Your guardians should have told you when you were younger. It is easier for a young mind to accept the unacceptable. Perhaps they kept you ignorant to help protect your identity." He sounded almost apologetic.

"Who are these guardians you speak of? What were they supposed to tell me? What am I transforming into? Am I a freak of nature? " The flood gates were open and I flung one question after another at him without letting him respond.

"You know nothing of who you are? You are nothing more than a silly child!" He insulted me again. "Your guardians are the ones who raised you and protect you from danger. They are the ones that came here with you." He raised a brow; he obviously didn't understand why I would ask such a question.

"They're not my guardians, they're my friends." I yelled back at him. "I only had one guardian, my mother." The gaping hole in my chest burned again, reminding me why I was here in the first place. "She's . . . .," I sobbed. I couldn't say the words to make him understand. "I have to get back home." The tears were running down my cheeks again.

A piece of information clicked in my head. "How do you know I'm here with anyone? Have you been watching me?" I accused.

"Yes, I am not one to believe in coincidences, but I cannot explain how flawless the timing was. Ariel was here for an annual memorial ceremony, she arrived two days ago. She said she felt your presence and summoned me here. I arrived yesterday morning. I had to see for myself that our Anyanka has been returned to us. You are not supposed to exist and yet Lilith must have found a way." As he said this, the paranoia I had felt in Chichen Itza, the feeling that I was being watched, finally made sense.

"What do you mean I'm not supposed to exist? Am I a freak of nature?"

"A freak of nature? No. Much more than that, you are a violation of God's Law."

"I think I would prefer being a freak, it doesn't sound as bad." I don't think he was even minutely aware of how much he kept insulting me. "What did I do to violate God's Law?" I probably sounded more sarcastic than I intended, but I was feeling a little irked by his constant scowling at me. He may have looked like the man of my dreams but he definitely didn't act like him.

Kai sighed; he acted like I was a five year old asking 'why' too often. "God allowed Lilith to create four of us and only four, you are the fifth. The fourth . . . . is gone." He whispered the last part, his eyes burned with an unfathomable pain. He quickly recovered, "Your life was not sanctioned by God." The scowl quickly returned to his face, but he had to make an effort to accomplish it.

"I'm the fifth what?" I sounded a little more annoyed than curious.

"There is no word in your language that describes us. Immortal is the best I can tell you, but it is like calling an ocean a pond."

"And you expect me to believe this?"

"It does not matter if you believe me or not, it does not change the truth of my words. Believing will only make your transformation a little easier if you know what to expect and why." He stated with a superior attitude.

I couldn't deny that his strange kind of fuzzy logic appealed to me, it made sense when he put it like that. I was still debating with myself whether this was real or just a figment of my imagination. He must have been real, because I would have imagined him with a better personality. The way his lips moved against the words that I heard was just that much more incredible. I couldn't help myself, I just blurted out the next question. "What language are you speaking?"

He leered at me, but answered anyways. "It has been a long time since I have spoken to anyone. I tend to take my gifts for granted. I am speaking in Mayan, but you hear me in your native language."

"How is that possible?"

"That is one of my gifts to mankind, to help them understand one another."

"Oh." What a brilliant response, before I could come up with anything better to say, Kai swooped in, picked me up and began carrying me through the jungle again.

I didn't want him to see how annoyed I was with him, so I continued questioning him. "So, what is this transformation?"

He looked down at me with a little smirk, pleased that I was so easily willing to accept the impossibility of what he was saying. "We are created human so that we learn to empathize with them. You have always had some gifts that you were born with, but not obvious ones. People near you tend to feel the tenor of your emotions and gravitate towards you, especially when you are happy. You inadvertently control their moods. What you are experiencing now is the beginning of the transformation. Your more impressive gifts will surface, such as your gift with fire. You will also have a more profound effect on the people around you as you begin to change."

"What do you mean by profound effects? Am I a danger to my friends?"

"It is different for all of us, or perhaps different because of the people around us. It is a trivial point, no matter. Where is Lilith, Why has she not told you any of this?"

"Who's Lilith?" I wasn't sure I could handle any more, but not knowing would drive me mad. It all seemed so surreal.

"How is it that you do not know her?" He realized that I had no answers, so he continued. "Lilith is a long story, but to sum it up, she is our creator. We were not created the way humans are. We are not born into this world. We are *made* of this world. Do you believe me?"

"Does it matter?" I snapped at him.

"No, not yet anyways," He snapped back. "I am certain you have questions, but we are out of time. For now, I need for you to understand that there are people in this world that fear what you will become, and will try to destroy you before you are complete."

Just then, we broke through the line of trees back into the ancient city. Kai breathed deeply as if he was inhaling my scent and then set me on the ground. "You must go now; it is not safe for you to be seen with me."

I took a step away from him before I turned around. I was about to say goodbye and good riddance, but there was a different look on his face that I could not read. It was possibly a look of sorrow, but more than that. I felt a stabbing pain in my heart for him. I never realized I was such a pushover for a pair of sad glowing blue eyes. "Will I ever see you again? After all, I owe you my life for saving me from that wolf." I tried to keep my voice light, in hope to see him smile at least once.

"You owe me nothing; it is you that has saved me." He reached his hand up to caress my cheek. "You are everything I remember and yet so much more then I imagined." He gave me a halfhearted smile, but he seemed so sad my heart ached for him. He stiffened and I could tell his mood changed. "Be careful, and stay with your guardians!" His face was set in a scowl again. He dropped his hand and turned to leave.

"Kai, wait!" He turned back to me. "You didn't answer my question. Will I ever see you again?"

"Yes; but for now, it will be better for you and your guardians if I stay away."

"How will I find you?"

He laughed softly, "I will find you." He turned and disappeared into the Jungle.

I stood there staring as he disappeared. I had an overwhelming urge to follow him, but I kept still. I heard someone shout my name from somewhere far behind me, and turned to see my friends coming towards me.

Chapter 6

ALONE

I allowed Mike to wrap me in a big bear hug. Everyone else circled around and put a hand on my back or shoulder. Mike growled in my ear. "What were you thinking? You can't run off into the jungle like that, you could have gotten lost or killed!" His voice trembled.

"We don't mean to rush you Annie, but if we want to get back to San Miguel tonight, we need to get back to the plane now." Katie sounded apologetic. I nodded my head, and without another word we all headed to the landing strip at a fast pace.

I sat with Ryan on the plane hoping that he would remain his usual quiet self. Ryan was as comfortable with silence as I was. My hopes were broken before the plane hit cruising altitude. "Are we heading home tonight?"

"No, I am going home tonight; you guys are staying and enjoying the rest of your vacation." I couldn't explain the reasoning behind my decision to Ryan. As much as I needed my friends at the moment, I wanted to keep them away from me in the event that I did have crosshairs trained on my head. My friends were too important to me to allow them to be in danger on my behalf. "I have so much that needs to get done. I will be too busy to spend time with you guys anyways. Besides, I probably won't be the best of company right now either." Ryan nodded his head, not in agreement, but in understanding.

The rest of the flight back to San Miguel, I made a mental list of everything I needed to get done in the next week. On the top of the agenda was scheduling a flight home and making funeral arrangements. Neither of which was going to be easy.

Once we were back at the hotel I was on the phone. It took two hours to get a flight scheduled. Unfortunately I had to have a short layover in Los Angeles before heading back to Cleveland and it was costing a small fortune because of the immediate departure. I had twenty minutes to get my luggage packed and head to the airport. My friends were not thrilled with the idea of me being alone, but they kept their arguments to a minimum.

I took a cab to the airport after saying my goodbyes. On the way, the cab driver had to stop for a crowd of people gathered around a church. A man stood on the top step near the doorway preaching as the crowd grew bigger. On closer inspection, the man looked familiar to me. He looked like the man that had tried to attack me several nights before, only he had a softer, kinder look to him. I convinced myself that it couldn't have been the same person, but Kai's voice echoed inside my head about having profound effects on people. I let it go, still not certain if Kai was just a figment of my imagination or if he truly existed. As I boarded the plane, I heard the cry of a giant cat, it sent a cold chill down my spine. It felt like an omen that I shouldn't be leaving my friends behind.

The flight home was quiet. Most of the passengers were asleep, including the little old lady that sat next to me, and inadvertently used my shoulder for a pillow. I didn't mind, better that she slept soundly than to try to talk to me. I had plenty of time to think. I thought of my mother at first, remembering the words she had spoken several years ago in one of our rare serious discussions.

* * *

"When my time comes, Annie, know that I go willingly. I have never been afraid to live and I am not afraid to die either. I have done everything in this life that I have wanted to accomplish, that makes it a good life. It would be more appropriate if you celebrate my life not mourn my death. I want

you to have me cremated and spread my ashes in Chichen Itza by the pyramid."

"This is a really morbid conversation Mama, is there something you're not telling me? Are you alright?"

"I'm fine, Annie. I had my will written today. It just had me thinking. Sorry, I didn't mean to scare you."

"Why would you do that?"

"It's the responsible thing to do. Most people have their will written when they have children. Think of it as a contingency plan."

"Nothing is wrong then? You're the epitome of good health?"

"I'm not going to live forever, but for now, all is good." She gave me her best mischievous smile. "Come on, I have us scheduled for sky diving this afternoon."

* * *

As the plane descended into the Los Angeles airport, I felt a blanket of peace come over me. Mama was right; it would be silly to mourn over her. I would miss her, certainly, but a life such as hers should be celebrated and cherished and that was what I planned to do.

The plane arrived late in Los Angeles, so my short layover became a mad dash to another terminal on the other side of the enormous airport. I made my plane with no time to spare. I would probably have to pick my luggage up in Cleveland in a few days; it wasn't going to make it to the plane on time. It was still dark in Los Angeles as the plane leveled off at thirty thousand feet. There was a storm rolling in off of the mountains and the captain announced that the passengers should remain in their seatbelts after the seatbelt sign was turned off. Most of the passengers drifted off to sleep, but I had too much on my mind to even close my eyes. The stewardess offered me a pillow. I refused, but asked for a cola instead. I was already deep in thought when the stewardess returned with my drink. I thanked her and returned to my thoughts as I stared out the little window into the darkness.

As I watched the storm clouds roll beneath the plane I thought of Kai. I first had to decide if I believed he was real or just a dream. I felt the heat coming off of my left forearm where he had held the lighter and I couldn't deny that he was absolutely real. So how is it I knew his face when I was a child? I dreamt of him so often I felt like I knew him already, but I knew nothing about him. How old is he? Where is he from? Why do his eyes glow? Why is there a wolf in the Central American jungle? So many questions that I wanted to ask him as he carried me through the jungle that I couldn't find the coherency to ask, came to me now. And then all that he had said to me came flooding back, filling my head with even more questions. Who are the other two of the four? What purpose am I supposed to serve? What happened to the fourth? And then the question that made me shiver, who would try to kill me? Why would they want to? I couldn't answer any of these questions and by the time the plane landed in Cleveland, I was so frustrated and annoyed with Kai, I never wanted to see him again. I was so wrapped up in my resolve that I didn't even notice Sue standing at the gate to pick me up.

"Annie?" I had walked right past her without as much as a sideways glance.

"Sue! I'm sorry, I didn't know anyone was coming to pick me up." I had to double back a few steps to her.

She gave me a big hug. "Katie called to let me know when your flight was landing. She didn't think you had made any arrangements to get home."

"She was right; I didn't think anything of it. I guess I have too much on my mind right now. We don't have to wait for luggage, mine is probably halfway to Florida by now. I just have my carryon with me."

Sue led the way to the parking garage in silence. She seemed to sense that I wasn't in a talkative mood. When we reached the car, my morbid curiosity peeked. "What happened to Mama, Sue? All I know is that it was a car accident."

She waited to speak until we were past the toll booth from the parking garage. "Lillian was supposed to pick me and Judy up at my house; we were going to the movies. She called me right before she was leaving, but she didn't show up. After a half hour, I tried to call her cell phone, but she didn't answer. Judy offered to drive to your house to see if she was alright." Sue paused and looked at me with tears in her eyes. "Are you sure you want to hear this?"

"I need to know." There was no emotion in my voice.

"She ran the car into a tree at the end of your road. She must not have hit the brakes for the stop sign. The damage that was done to the car suggested she was still driving about forty-five. She hit her head on the steering wheel and broke her neck. The coroner said she would not have suffered with that injury."

"How could she have hit her head on the steering wheel? Her car had airbags, didn't they work?"

"Annie, she wasn't driving her car, she was driving your Mustang." It felt like someone had just kicked me in the stomach. My eyes were wide with fear. What if someone was out to get me? Would they tamper with the brakes on my car? Try to make it look like an accident? If so, then my mother died because of me. I took a deep breath to clear my head. I wasn't even sure anyone was after me. I needed to remain calm until I had all the facts, but guilt on top of grief was consuming me.

"Annie, I think you should stay with me and Katie for a while. I don't think it would be good for you to be in that house all alone." I knew Sue was right, but I was even more afraid to have anyone near me, knowing my mother had died in my car.

"Thanks for the offer Sue, but I think I will be more comfortable in my own home." I stared out the windshield at the morning light. It felt like I had lost a whole night from traveling east, and I was starting to feel groggy. The sun was obscured behind dark ominous clouds; it looked like a storm was rolling in from the south. I was hoping that it stayed cloudy for a little while, it would be easier to get some sleep if it wasn't so bright.

Sue dropped me off at my house. Before I could take a step from the car, she rolled the window down. "If you need anything at all, just call me Annie."

I nodded my head, and walked to the front door. I punched in the code, 3336, for the lock and opened the door. I always thought Mama had overdone it on home security, but at the moment I was grateful. She had said that regular locks could be picked or keys duplicated and with the two of us living out in the middle of nowhere, it was better to be safe than sorry. If I could call any place safe at the moment, this was it.

As I walked into the house, I was flooded with a profound depression. All of the photos of Mama and me on the walls were just too much of a reminder that I didn't want. I went straight to the basement and found an empty box and a stack of old newspapers. I returned to the living room and proceeded in wrapping and storing all of the photos, I vowed to myself not to mope, so as I took each picture down from the walls or off of the shelves I took a moment to remember the occasions when the pictures were taken. They were all happy memories of riding horses, or playing on the pyramid in Chichen Itza, band concerts, and group photos with my friends. As I put each picture in the box, I tucked the memory away in my head to save it for when I was stronger and the pain wasn't so overwhelming. I came to a picture in the dining room that I had no memory of. It was when I was an infant and Mama was holding me in her arms. She looked like she was glowing as she gazed down at me. I put this picture aside to use at the funeral; it wasn't as painful to look at. I swept through the whole house except for Mama's bedroom and her craft room. I had rarely ever stepped foot into either one of those rooms in almost eighteen years. I didn't have the courage to do it now. I touched each of the doors with my hand, bowed my head and said a little prayer and then moved on. When I had finished putting the pictures in the box, I took them down to the storage room in the basement, out of sight, out of mind. The house felt less like a home now and more like an empty shell. I was exhausted, having been up for over thirty-two hours. I climbed the stairs to my room, closed my curtains and fell asleep quickly.

Chapter 7

THE FUNERAL

It was late evening on Sunday, when I finally woke up. I had a lot to do, but it wasn't going to get done tonight. I went to the music room and sat on the bench at the baby grand piano. The house was too quiet and I needed to cheer myself up. I sat there for what seemed like hours just staring at the black and white keys hoping they would speak to me somehow. I put my hands on the keys finally and began to play, not a song that I knew, just what I felt in my heart. It was an uplifting and complicated tune, my fingers found the right keys at the right time. The music just poured out of me like water. In my head, I could hear an orchestra accompanying me. Outside, a thunderstorm rumbled on as my percussionist. The song continued in my head long after I was done playing it. It kept the loneliness from creeping in on me, like a candle light keeping the darkness at bay.

I hummed the tune as I went to the kitchen to make dinner; a bowl of cereal, I hated cooking, and fixing a meal seemed pointless. As I ate, I wrote down a list of things I needed to accomplish. Make arrangements for the funeral, have Mama's remains cremated as she requested, get the coroner's report, death certificate, and police report, and have my car towed home. In the back of my head I wondered if Jenny would be able to fix it, and even if she could, would I ever be able to drive it again. Perhaps I would just cover it in a tarp until I could make a rational decision, until then, I would drive Mama's car. With my plan for the next day set, I took the Bible off of the shelf in the living room and went back to my room. I would look for passages to use at the funeral until I felt tired enough to sleep again. I wasn't the type of person that could quote the Bible verbatim, but I remembered several passages that were uplifting that I thought Mama would appreciate. I fell asleep with the lamp on and the Bible lying across my lap turned over to hold the page I wanted.

Monday morning I woke to a thunderstorm. The flashes of lightning shooting across the sky were absolutely magnificent. I stood on the back porch drinking tea and staring into the sky enjoying the light show. The smell of the rain in the air reminded me of Kai. I closed my eyes and inhaled deeply trying to recapture his essence. I was having a hard time separating the dream from reality so my resolve to never see him again was wavering quickly. I imagined his face and those strange beautiful eyes. I could see the depths of his pain and wondered what could have caused it. I had too much to get done so I didn't linger too long. I walked back into the house and got dressed for the day.

I found Mama's car keys hanging by the front door. A wave of fear swept over me. What if her car had been tampered with as well? I laughed at myself "Coward!" That didn't help me find my courage though. I stood behind the steel front door and hit the button on the keyless remote. The car didn't blow up, that was a good sign, "I'm becoming a paranoid schizophrenic." I murmured to myself, annoyed. I walked to the car, got in and put the key in the ignition. Still nothing happened. Just to be on the safe side, I put the car in gear and tested the brakes several times heading down the driveway, I figured if they didn't work I could throw the car in park or jump out and let it crash if need be. The brakes worked just fine. "Get a grip on yourself. No one is trying to kill you." I felt mildly better, but I couldn't fight the urge to scan my surroundings as I drove to town.

The first stop I made was to the funeral home to make arrangements for the cremation.

"How long will it take before I get her ashes?"

John, the funeral director, looked apologetic. "It could take up to two weeks. Do you want to wait until after the funeral to have your mother sent out?"

"Two weeks, really?" I laughed. I couldn't help myself.

John thought I had lost my mind. "Are you alright, ma'am?"

"I'm fine. I just think it would be funny if Mama were to skip out on her own funeral. I guess she would get the last laugh." I continued to chuckle about it, until John interrupted me. He didn't find the joke all that funny. I guess that dealing with death on a daily basis can destroy ones sense of humor. I wondered how I managed to find mine given the circumstances.

"Would you like to pick out an urn for the ashes?" John asked politely.

I nodded, still trying to stifle my laughter. He led the way to a display room. "Would you like a moment alone to choose?"

"Yes, thank you." I smiled at him as he left. It only took a moment to decide. I found a very graceful looking copper urn with handles on each side that looked a little like a trophy cup with a lid. It was unique and beautiful. I wandered back out to the main floor to find John.

"Can you do engravings on this?" I wanted it to be special for my mother, though her ashes wouldn't be in the urn for long, it would be a nice keepsake of her.

"Yes, what would you like on it? Just her name, or would you like a Bible verse, or a quote?"

"Can you engrave hieroglyphs?"

John thought about it for a moment, "Perhaps, if they are not too complicated."

I took a piece of paper and pen and drew the Mayan hieroglyphs for fire, water, earth, and wind, the four elements as the Mayans called them. As an afterthought I added her name and the glyph for mother as well. "Could you put these four glyphs around the base here, and her name on the body, and then this last glyph on the lid?"

"That shouldn't be too difficult, when do you want it?"

"Saturday morning if at all possible."

"I will call you Friday to let you know if I will have it done by then. The engraving doesn't take that long, but graphing out these designs might be time consuming."

I left him my phone number and thanked him for his help. My next stop, I knew wouldn't be this easy. I headed to the Catholic Church to arrange the funeral.

When I got to the church, to my surprise I found it locked. Especially in a small town like New London, the churches are never locked; they remain open for anyone in need. I walked the short distance to the rectory next door and found a note taped to the inside of the door.

> I will be on vacation from
> June 10 to July 4.
> For all your ministry needs
> Please contact Father Robert
> At the Norwalk St. Paul's church
> At 419-555-2355
> God Bless, Father Jack

I called the number; it rang twice before a gentle male voice answered the phone.

"This is Father Robert, may I help you?"

"Hi, my name is Anne Cain from New London. I need to schedule a funeral for my mother." It was odd how business like I was able to keep my voice. I was feeling numb from all of the recent emotional outbursts I had been having.

There was a long pause, I wasn't sure if he was on the phone anymore. "Hello?"

"Yes, when would you like to have it?" He sounded nervous.

"Saturday evening if you are available. Would seven o'clock be good for you?"

"Yes, seven would be fine, and what kind of arrangements would you like?"

"Nothing traditional, I would like to start at the park to dedicate a tree in my mother's honor, and then lead the procession to the church for the funeral service. I would prefer it to be outside, if that's alright."

"And what of the deceased? It wouldn't be prudent to have the body out in public."

"I'm having her cremated. This will just be a memorial service." I chuckled slightly again at the morbid humor.

"And have you thought of any verses that you would like read at the service?"

I listed off several Bible verses for Father Robert. He seemed confused by my choices.

"I will see you on Saturday at seven then." He hung up the phone without a "God bless you" or anything. I thought it was customary for priests to say that. Guess not.

I drove to the local newspaper to have the funeral announcement put in. I added a special request that everyone should dress casually. One more stop to the local tree farm to talk to "Farmer Don" as he was known in New London, to make arrangements for the tree dedication. Farmer Don even offered to talk to the park board for me to pick the spot for the tree. I made it home by four o'clock. I wasn't tired, just drained.

As I walked through the front door, I sighed with relief. No one had tried to kill me today. That's a good thing, I thought to myself. The house was too quiet, so I went to the living room and turned the stereo on and put a CD in to dispel the emptiness. I sat in the plush recliner and kicked my feet up with an art pad and charcoal pencils and started sketching. The image that came to mind was Kai. I had several dozen sketches of him in my room, but I was never satisfied with the way they looked. I could never capture the true essence of him. It was the eyes, how could I ever sketch those beautiful eyes, the way they glow, the sadness in them. I realized I was missing him more than I should. I hardly knew him, but I was obsessed with him. It wasn't normal. I couldn't even explain it to myself. He wasn't very nice to me, and yet it felt like I left half of me in Mexico. I longed to be with him again. I had to remind myself that he was not the man I dreamt of. He may look like him but he definitely had a different personality than what I had dreamt. Still, a part of me wondered if there wasn't something else behind his attitude.

It was a long week. I missed my friends, I missed Kai, the dream version, and above all, I missed my mother. I did my best to keep my spirits up by calling Sue and Judy every day, but it didn't make me feel any less lonely. The phone rang off the hook all week, with friends calling to send me their condolences, and one strange message on the voice mail from a captain of a bagpipe brigade wanting to lead the procession from the park to the church. He mentioned something about being the least he could do for all that Lillian had done for him. Since the procession was turning into more of a parade, I decided to take the horses to ride as well.

I tried to keep myself busy by getting things done. I made arrangements to have the Mustang towed home, Mama's death certificate mailed to me, and asked to get a copy of the accident report, although the police chief wasn't willing to give it to me on account of emotional distress, I reminded him that I needed a copy for insurance purposes. The chief wasn't buying my excuse but relinquished the report to me anyways. I promised myself to wait until after the funeral to read it.

I also remembered to stop by the bank to make sure I had enough money to pay for the funeral. Money was not a topic my mother and I discussed openly. We had money, but I never knew how much. Mama never worked, she volunteered at the school or the library, but never brought home a paycheck. She said we had "old money" and left it at that. So when I went to the bank to check on finances, I was quite surprised to find that I would be comfortable for a long, *long* time. One less thing to worry about if it weren't for the fact that I had no idea how Mama acquired it.

It dawned on me then, how little I knew about my mother's past. I knew her, her moods, her hair, her eyes, her favorite color, and music, everything except her past. Where did she grow up? What school did she go to? What was her childhood like? What were her parents like? Where did she get so much money? So many questions would now go unanswered because I never thought to ask while she was here. I began to feel like she was a stranger that I happened to see often, but never got to know. I felt a greater, more profound loss than the moment that Mike had told me she was dead. Was I truly so self-absorbed that I couldn't see the lives other people lived when I wasn't with them? I vowed to rectify that character flaw by getting to know the people around me more. Lesson learned: don't take the people you care about for granted.

Saturday morning finally arrived. My friends would be getting back from Mexico around eleven o'clock. I wondered if I could get them to pick up my luggage that had finally arrived in Cleveland on Friday. I left a message on Katie's voice mail.

I spent the morning washing the horses and cleaning their tack for the funeral. I had to head to town and pick up the urn at the funeral home. John said he managed to get the hieroglyphs done in time, but my mother's ashes were not ready yet. I had to laugh. Mama wasn't going to show up to her own funeral after all. I wondered if anyone else would find humor in that.

By noon, I was done with all of the last minute details and called Jesse to see if they were back in town yet. They were just coming into town having taken them longer at the airport than expected because they had picked up my wayward luggage. Jesse let me know that Jenny would drop it off within the hour. I was grateful that they had saved me the two hour round trip to Cleveland to pick it up.

I was in my room picking out clothes to wear when Jenny arrived. I didn't hear her car pull in the driveway so I was surprised when the doorbell rang. I ran downstairs to the front door, elated to have my friends home. I opened the door with eagerness and threw my arms around Jenny in a big hug before she could even say hello. She hugged me back

"Um . . . . Hi, I missed you too." She sounded flabbergasted by my outward show of emotion. "I see you had the Mustang brought home. Do you want me to try to fix it?" Her eyebrow rose as if my answer to her question would determine whether I was crazy or not.

"I haven't decided on that just yet." That should keep her guessing on my sanity. "I was hoping you could check it out to see if there was a mechanical malfunction though. Mama's accident just doesn't make sense." No need to explain to her why I was thinking it was a mechanical malfunction. I didn't want to worry her.

Jenny gave me a sheepish look. "I already checked it out, hope you don't mind, I was curious myself. The brakes felt spongy, but the lines were clean, looks like you had a recent brake job done on it?"

"No, the brakes haven't been touched in almost two years. Mama had them done before she gave the car to me for my sixteenth birthday. Why do you ask?"

"The lines still have paint on them. Normally the paint wears off after a couple of months of driving. The brake lines on your car are brand new, I'm certain of it."

"Maybe Mama had it done while we were gone." I wasn't very convincing, and Jenny wasn't buying it either.

Jenny stared at me questioningly. I was tempted to tell her what I was thinking, but I held my tongue. I didn't want to get my friends involved in my clandestine life if I could help it. "You're knowledge of cars is amazing. Where did you learn all this stuff?"

Jenny sensed that I was changing the subject, but she let it go. "I'm the son my father never had. He had me out in the garage since I was old enough to walk. It drove my mom absolutely insane." We both had to laugh at the thought of Judy the beautician with a grease monkey for a daughter.

* * *

Jesse and I made it to the park in plenty of time to get the horses saddled up. He offered to drive the truck and horse trailer for me because he knew I wasn't comfortable with such a big rig. Jesse, Mike and Katie would be riding the other three horses with me during the procession. I was amazed at how many people were showing up for the tree dedication, it seemed like the entire town was at the park for the event. I was overwhelmed by how many people whose lives had been touched by my mother.

Judy and Sue passed out small candles to everyone as we all gathered around farmer Don's tractor that was holding a blue spruce in a tree spade. Father Robert said a prayer and blessed the tree. Everyone seemed to be having a good time visiting with each other. The atmosphere didn't feel like a funeral at all, it was more like my graduation party. Everyone was laughing about their little anecdotes of my mother. This was exactly what I wanted for her, to celebrate her life, not morn her death.

The bagpipe brigade with the accompaniment of drums lined up on the street to lead the procession to the church. We rode the horses behind them while I carried the empty urn, and the rest of the town gathered behind us carrying their candles. The bagpipes began with 'Amazing Grace' as we made our way down the street. Mike, Jesse and Katie were laughing and joking with me as we rode. Even the horses seemed to be happy, as they pranced, not walked, to the beat of the music. What few people left in town that were not a part of the procession, came out to watch as we made our way to the church.

It was a short walk. It only took ten minutes before the procession arrived at the huge yard by the church. Father Robert had set up a podium with a microphone to perform the service. After everyone had filed into the yard, Father Robert started the service with an opening prayer. The mood was anything but typical for a funeral. Everyone was smiling and seemed to be enjoying the warm June evening. The atmosphere was more like a festival than a funeral. Sue handed me a candle and took the urn from me to place by the podium, she made a slight gesture about the weight of the urn. I shrugged in reply.

Father Robert droned on about new beginnings. I stared at my candle. The flame on the wick danced. I tried to make it burn higher, but I didn't have any idea how to accomplish it. Some gift, what was I ever going to need it for anyways? As the service continued, people, some of which I had never met, filed to the podium to share their experiences with my mother. The stories were all the same, someone needed help and my mother came to their aide. She really was an amazing woman. It's no wonder why our house was filled with eccentric gifts from "old friends".

After the last of guests said their peace, the crowd broke into song, 'Oh Danny Boy'. The bagpipes joined in as the crowd began to file out of the yard. I tried to put my candle out with my mind, but gave up after a few tries and just blew it out like everyone else.

Jesse, Mike, Katie and I had to ride the horses back to the park to load them in the trailer. We chatted with the people who were walking home. By the time we reached the park entrance, we were alone. I was tired and not paying much attention to the other three when a loud noise, or several loud noises all at once, spooked the horses.

Time seemed to move in slow motion. My horse reared up and I felt a sharp pain in my shoulder. I almost fell off of the horse. I heard Jesse yell, "Get her out of here!" as Mike was grabbing me around the waist and pulling me onto his saddle.

"We'll meet back at the house," Mike yelled back as he wheeled the horse around to head through a wooded section of the park running at full speed with me draped over his lap like a potato sack. I wasn't worried about getting lost, or even about falling off of the horse, I was worried because I had no idea why my friends reacted the way they did. Did they know what was going on? Did they know that someone might be trying to kill me? Did they have a prearranged plan that I didn't know about?

"Mike, STOP!" He ignored my plea, so I screamed louder. "STOP, MIKE!" I could feel him pull back on the reins and the horse slowed to a fast walk. "Please stop Mike. This is not very comfortable." He pulled back on the reins more until the horse stopped. Mike remained quiet while I jumped off and mounted the horse behind the saddle in an upright position.

"Would you mind telling me what is going on."

"At the moment, I think it's best if we keep quiet." He whispered urgently at me.

"Where are Jesse and Katie?" I badgered on.

"Please Annie, keep quiet."

"What is going on Mike?" I whispered.

Mike knew that I would not stop pestering him until he explained himself to me. He finally gave in after a few more minutes. "Before we left Mexico, a woman approached Jesse. She told him you were in danger and it was our duty to protect you. He said she was pissed off when she found out you came home without us and she was sending her brother here to protect you until we returned." Mike paused, listening to the surroundings. "Are you hurt? Your breathing sounds erratic."

"My shoulder hurts and I'm feeling a little lightheaded." I answered weakly.

Mike stopped the horse and half turned in the saddle to look at me in the darkness. "You're bleeding, I can smell it." Mike took his t-shirt off and held it tight against my shoulder. I resisted the urge to scream out in pain.

"Let's get you home quickly. Ryan should be able to patch you up. Can you hold on till we get there?" He didn't give me a chance to answer. He turned back in the saddle and waited for me to wrap my arms around his bare torso before asking the horse to run the five miles home.

Chapter 8

BIRTHDAY

I spent several hours that night trying to explain to my friends what was going on. The more I explained, the more they all refused to leave me for their own safety. It was official that someone was trying to kill me. The bullet that had grazed my left shoulder was proof of it. Ryan did his best to patch me up. He said I would live, but if it got infected he would drag me to the hospital kicking and screaming if necessary.

"How long were you going to wait before you told us all of this?" Mike glared at me accusingly. The rest of my friends were finally asleep in the music room, but neither Mike nor I could sleep and he took advantage of that fact by cornering me in the kitchen to give me the third degree.

"I didn't want to tell you at all, I figured you might think I was going crazy or something. Stressed out by Mama's death and have me committed to a funny farm. I am so sorry I put you in danger. I really think you should all leave and save yourselves."

"Not a chance, I can't speak for the rest of the crew, but I'm not leaving until I know you're safe. By the way, happy birthday Annie," He smiled and leaned down to kiss me on the forehead.

He caught me off guard. I hadn't been paying attention to the date. "Is it June twenty-first already?" My birthday was my favorite day of the year. Not because I would get gifts and cake, but because it was the day the sun hung in the sky the longest, the first day of summer. I was officially eighteen, a legal adult. A mile stone to most people, but all I could wish for is that I would make it to nineteen. "Don't say anything to the rest of them, it doesn't feel appropriate to celebrate right now, besides, there are more pressing matters that need to be dealt with."

Mike nodded his head in understanding and gave me a big hug. "I will do whatever it takes to keep you safe. My solemn vow to God, I will protect you."

I inhaled sharply when he said this, the words that Kai had said rang in my ears again that my friends were my guardians and were here to protect me. I leaned back and looked him in the eyes. "He was right," I mused, "you are my guardians." A feeling of dread overwhelmed me.

"'He' meaning Kai Jora? " I nodded in confirmation. "The same 'He' you have been dreaming about for as long as you can remember?" I nodded again. "And 'He' told you that we are your guardians?"

"Yes, I told him that you guys were just my friends but he kept calling you my guardians. How could he know?"

"I don't know, but he sounds like a very smart man." Mike yawned and I realized he probably hadn't slept in the last two days.

"You look exhausted, why don't you try to get some sleep." I tried to herd him to the music room but he wouldn't budge.

"I wanted to talk to you about something first."

He paused, it seemed he was uncomfortable with what he was about to say, so I had to motivate him. "You can tell me anything Mike, you know that."

He looked at me with guilty eyes, "I . . . . . . I kissed Katie," he blurted out as quickly as possible.

"When? Where?" I was a little shocked by this.

"In San Miguel, after you left."

"So what's the problem? Did she kiss you back?

"Oh, she kissed back alright. The problem is, as soon as we got back, she won't even talk to me. I don't understand why she's being so . . . . distant."

"And you want me to talk to her, and find out why." It was a statement not a question.

Mike looked up at me under his lashes with a pleading grimace. "You're not mad at me?"

"Why on Earth do you think I would be mad at you? I want you to be happy. I want all of you to be happy. Does Katie make you happy?"

"Yes, she does." He sighed. "I can't explain it. After you left, I accidentally ran into her, but before I could apologize, it was like I was hypnotized by her stare. It felt like she was gripping my heart. Not in a painful way, it was euphoric. I couldn't help myself; it felt like if I didn't kiss her I would explode. When I looked at Katie, I saw everything I ever wanted in a woman, but more. I don't understand any of it. I thought she felt the same way, but I can't be certain now. She's avoiding me." He looked as if he was about to start crying.

I reached up and caressed his face. "I will talk to her today, I promise. You need to get some sleep. You look like you're about to collapse."

"It has been a long day. What about you? You look like you haven't slept in the last week." He accused.

"You're right, as always. I haven't been sleeping well. The recent events have had me a little frazzled lately. Although I must say, the funeral turned out better than I could have imagined. I think Mama would have appreciated it. What did you think of it?"

"I don't mean to sound insensitive, but that was the best funeral I have ever been to."

"I know what you mean, I actually had fun. How's that for inappropriate? Come on, let's try to get some sleep." I dragged him off to the music room.

* * *

I was alone when I woke the next morning; a sense of abandonment filled me. Irrational as it was because I wanted to get my friends as far away from me as possible. I cared too much for them to let anything happen to them. And then I noticed a wonderful smell wafting through to the music room; the smell of eggs and bacon and toast. My stomach growled at me and I had to laugh. I knew that Mike was in the kitchen cooking breakfast for all of us. I was grateful to have my friends close; it was a confusing rush of emotions that were conflicting inside of me. I sat up onto my elbows feeling the carpet squish beneath me. My shoulder throbbed, reminding me of the strange events of the previous night. I shivered a little at the thought of it, shook it off and took a deep breath, I would try to make today as normal as any other day. At the moment, normal sounded like a beautiful word.

"Smells great Mike, did you make enough for me too?" I asked as I walked into the kitchen.

The voice that responded took me by surprise. It was Katie standing at the stove dishing a pile of eggs and bacon onto a plate as I walked in. "There's plenty considering it's just you and me this morning." She handed me the plate and dished her own up. We sat in silence for a few minutes at the bar. All of the blinds on the windows were drawn close so I stared at the bright yellow walls and the happy sunflower boarder of the kitchen while I enjoyed the food. It would have been better if Mike had cooked it but I didn't want to hurt her feelings, so I shied away from making comments on the food.

"Where is everyone this morning?" I looked at her and realized I must have asked the wrong question. She tried to keep a straight face, but she wasn't succeeding.

"Sami and Jenny went home to pack a few things. We all agreed that we are not leaving you alone until this thing blows over, so we're moving in for now." She smiled but it didn't reach her eyes. I also noticed that she didn't mention the guys.

". . . . and?" I prompted her.

"And what?" She really wasn't any good at hiding things. It wasn't her nature; she has always been such an outspoken kind of person. A little more pushing and she would sing like a bird.

"And . . . . Where are the guys?" I could hear the hysteria break in my voice when I asked.

"I told them I wouldn't tell you, but I think it's a bad idea to keep secrets from you. You're not going to like this, but . . . . don't get mad at the messenger, okay." She paused awaiting my acknowledgement so I nodded my head. "The guys went out into the woods to do some surveillance, just to make sure that we're safe for now."

"When did they leave? How long have they been gone?" My heart started to thrum in my chest. I didn't need this kind of anxiety. What were they thinking?

"They left about a half hour before dawn. It was Ryan's idea to get into the woods before day light. They were going to sit in the tree stands that you and Jesse have out in the woods. Don't worry, they have their two- ways with them and I have one too. They will call if anything happens."

I started mumbling incoherently "Rambo, GI Joe, and Conan the barbarian."

"Oh, get a grip Annie. They know how to handle themselves if they need to."

She was right and I knew it. Worse, she knew that I knew and she gave me that smug little smile that I wasn't in the mood for. I didn't mean to be so blunt, I was actually hoping to build up to this conversation gradually, but that smile pushed me over the edge. "So, what's going on with you and Mike?" I sounded so cynical that I wanted to slap myself across the face for saying it like that. It worked though; the smugness disappeared instantly and was replaced by shock.

"You noticed? I . . . I . . ." she stammered. "With everything that you've had to deal with I didn't think you would notice."

I decided to play the over observant friend roll instead of throwing Mike to the wolves. She might not appreciate Mike discussing their love life to me. "How could I not? The tension between you two is so thick. What's going on?"

She sighed, "I kissed him. It was incredible!"

"So what's with all the tension?"

"You're going to think I've gone mental." She laughed out of nervousness.

"I just told you that I'm an immortal. How much more mental can you get?" It was a rhetorical question, but Katie felt the need to answer it anyways.

"It's worse. Don't laugh, okay."

"I won't laugh, I promise. No matter what it is, I'm here for you, for better or worse." I braced myself, at the least I could do is freeze my facial expression, so that if I did have the urge to laugh, she wouldn't notice.

Katie turned her eyes to the floor and mumbled, "I think I'm turning into a cat."

Promise or no promise, how could I not laugh at that, it wasn't even a soft chuckle. It was the type of laugh that got worse when you try to control it. I was doubled over and holding my hand over my mouth to try to stifle it. It didn't help. I just had to let it out until it subsided.

"Are you done yet?" Katie snapped. "I'm being serious. Could you please try to control yourself?"

"I'm sorry Katie; that was rude of me." I managed to get out between spasms of giggles. I took a deep breath to try to compose myself. I counted to ten silently before I asked, "Why do you think you are turning into a cat." A few more snickers escaped as she glared at me.

"Do you really want to know, or are you going to laugh some more?" Her evil stare sobered me up finally.

"Please forgive me Katie; you just took me by surprise. Please go on."

She glared at me for a few more seconds, before her expression softened. "Fine!" she sounded sarcastic but continued. "Two nights ago, our last night in San Miguel, I took a shower and went straight to bed. I had the strangest dream that I was running through the jungle, hunting. I heard myself scream, but it sounded like a jaguar or a cougar or something. The way the jungle looked, it was so real, it was bright as day even though it was at night. And the smells, I could smell everything very distinctly, the moist dirt, the decaying leaves, the sap from the trees. I could hear everything clearly too. All the animals in the leaf litter, I could hear their heartbeats. It was the most vivid dream I ever had. When I woke up, I was covered in dirt, my pajamas were torn to shreds lying on the floor and I had leaves in my hair."

I was speechless, what could I say about that? 'Wow, and I thought I had it bad' just didn't seem appropriate. Katie looked like she was going to start hyperventilating, desperate to get a response out of me, but all I could do was gawk at her. "Well?" she demanded.

"I always wanted a cat?"

If looks could kill, I'd be dead. "What do you want me to say? I'm happy for you? Or, Sorry about you luck? I'm your friend; I love you with or without a tail." I tried to say it seriously, but I couldn't help snorting through my nose. Finally I broke through her defenses and she started laughing too.

"So you don't think I'm insane?"

"No, I think we all need to accept the fact that crazy is our new normal." I tried to comfort her.

I had a thought cross my mind and blurted out. " Oh!"

"Oh, What?" Katie glared at me curiously.

"Um . . . . Katie, don't hate me, but I think this might be my fault. Kai said we have profound effects on the people nearest to us. He didn't go into details, but this seems pretty darn profound to me."

She remained silent for a moment and then smirked. "That figures, it's always your fault." She was teasing me now. "That's alright, this could be really cool. I just hope I don't get fleas or something."

Katie got up from the bar and picked up the dirty plates to take to the sink. "So what about you and Mike?" I finally managed to get out with an appropriate tone.

"What am I supposed to tell him? 'Hey Mike, guess what, I'm a giant cat.' I'm not sure that will go over so well."

"Katie, if Mike truly loves you, he will love all of you. I don't think he's the type to run away screaming." I walked over to Katie and helped her with the dishes.

"How can you be so sure about that?" She questioned my assessment.

"He didn't run when I told him I'm an immortal, he's tough, he can handle it."

"What do I say to him though? Do I just come right out and say it or am I supposed to hint at it until he guesses?"

"That's for you to figure out. I'm sure you will come up with something." I nudged her with my shoulder. I smiled when she looked at me. I wanted to convey to her that I would stand beside her no matter what happens.

She understood the message. "Thanks, Annie. You truly are my best friend."

"As a best friend, can I make a request?"

"Anything, anytime."

"Just don't eat me when you're in your cat form." Katie grabbed the soapy sponge out of the sink and threw it at me. Her aim was perfect from years of softball; she hit me right on the side of my face. At least she was laughing about it.

* * *

I headed upstairs for a shower, my mind racing through so many thoughts I couldn't concentrate on the task at hand. The only clue that I had actually spent too much time in the shower was that the water started to run cold. I got dressed and headed back downstairs to clean up the mess in the music room from the sleep over. Just as I was coming down the stairs, I heard a commotion coming from the music room, it sounded like someone screamed as they knocked over the drum set. I grabbed the closest weapon I had available, a samurai sword hanging on the wall in the living room. A cold chill ran down my spine when I heard a male voice saying "Stay down!" I was more afraid for Katie then for myself, so I charged through the kitchen to the music room.

"Get off of her!" Before I could even plant my feet to defend Katie and myself, I saw a blur come at me. Even with the sword in hand and all of my martial arts training, there was no way I could defend myself against the speed in which the man had sprung up from Katie and knocked me to the floor. I was grateful that the carpet was well padded, but I still had the wind knocked out of me. I noted that I wasn't being pinned down, I could still move, but I was completely shielded from head to toe. As I looked into the eyes of my attacker, it all started to make perfect sense.

Chapter 9

ANSWERS

"Hello Kai, nice for you to drop in." I said while gasping for air. The smell of a fresh spring rain permeated the air around me. I closed my eyes and inhaled deeply.

"Anyanka!" He sounded aggravated, apparently his personality hadn't improved in a week.

"Please don't call me that."

"Annie, then, are you hurt?" If it weren't for the angry tone in his voice I would have guessed he was truly concerned for me.

"I'm fine. Katie, you okay?"

"No, I'm not okay. I just got shot at, and your boyfriend just attacked me." She sounded peeved.

"Shot at? Were you hit?" I intentionally ignored the boyfriend comment.

"No, bullet proof glass, remember?" I had forgotten that Mama replaced all the windows in the house with bullet proof glass after a hunter had accidentally shot a Chak Mool carving sitting on the floor in the dining room several years ago. She was grateful that we weren't home when it happened, but immediately took evasive precautions.

"It seems you were right, Annie." Kai's velvety voice broke my reminiscing.

"I usually am, but what about in particular."

"You don't have guardians." His snide comment put me on the defensive.

"I don't know about that. It seems my decoy worked on you." As I said the words, the truth of them hit me. Katie and I were physically very similar, right down to our hair styles. It would be easy to get the two of us mixed up.

The two way radio came to life. "Are you girls alright." It was Mike.

Katie crawled to the piano bench to reach for the radio. "We're fine Mike. And you guys?"

"We're good. Jesse got the sniper! We're bringing him in!" There was so much excitement in his voice. He sounded like he was going to explode with pride.

"My other guardians seem quite capable as well." I was feeling a little smug, and proud of the guys. After all, they were just teenagers that bested a sniper, and probably a well-trained sniper at that.

"Perhaps I was mistaken, but they are not doing a very good job." Kai extricated himself from me and helped me to my feet.

"Why would you say that? I think they are doing quite well. I'm still alive, am I not?" Kai lifted my empty hand (somehow I managed to hang on to the sword when he threw me to the ground) and placed something in it. It was a bullet with a red tip. I looked at the bay window and spotted a tiny hole surrounded by fractures. "You caught a bullet?" My voice went up an octave. I couldn't comprehend the strength or the speed necessary to catch a bullet, my brain wouldn't accept it.

"Happy birthday, Anyanka."

He was intentionally trying to provoke me by calling me Anyanka but I didn't overlook the obvious "How do you know my birthday?"

"The summer solstice. It's your season." I was baffled by how much he knew about me.

He inspected my shoulder still taped up from the night before. "You were hit last night. I had never seen that type of weapon before. I underestimated it." He sounded apologetic.

The moment was interrupted by the boys coming through the front door. I knew they had the sniper with them, and I needed answers. I looked into Kai's eyes, a mistake; I was bewildered by his pure beauty. Everything about him was the epitome of perfection. I felt insignificant next to him. "I . . ." I had to clear my throat before I could continue, "I have work to do." Just as I was turning to leave, he grabbed my hand with the sword in it.

"Where did you get this?" He seemed annoyed that I would have a samurai sword.

"From the living room. Why?"

"No, I mean, where did it come from?" He snapped. It occurred to me then that his lips were moving properly with the words he spoke.

"You're speaking English now. Did you learn the entire language in a week?"

"I am a quick study. The sword?" He was agitated with me for trying to change the subject.

"You had time to cut your hair, too?" Not that I didn't like his hair long, but somehow he looked even more beautiful with his hair short and in disarray.

"Anyanka! The sword?"

"Oh, um . . . Mama said it was a gift from an old friend. Why?" He was so absorbed in looking at the sword that he didn't answer.

"Here, you can have it if you want." I offered the sword to him. He took the sword from my hand and held it reverently. I didn't understand what was so spectacular about it. It was just another trinket collecting dust to me. He was so absorbed in thought that he didn't notice when I left to meet the boys in the kitchen.

The scene in the kitchen was a lot to take in. There were four men all dressed to look like shrubbery. The camouflage was 3-D to help hunters blend in better, but they looked comical standing in my kitchen. Ryan was holding a 9mm pistol to the fourth man's back. I walked around to the front of him to look at his face. I noticed he was holding an arrow. On closer inspection I realized that the arrow was sticking through his hand and blood was oozing out the hole.

"Nice shot Jesse!" I felt so much pride for my boys.

Mike swooshed past me as Katie came into the kitchen. He embraced her in a big bear hug. "If I knew what Ryan was planning, I never would have allowed it. I'm so sorry. Were you hurt?" He sounded sick with worry.

"I'm fine." her response was muffled because Mike refused to let her go. Katie tilted her head back so she could speak louder. "I would have been better if *someone* hadn't thrown me on the floor." There was no response from Kai; he was in the music room, probably still staring at the sword. Mike bent down to kiss her. I didn't know the depth of their emotions until I saw the passion in their kiss. I was happy for them and hoped that their relationship would survive the test of time.

I turned back to the other three standing in the kitchen. "Right, let's get him tied up for starters." Ryan proved quite efficient in tying the sniper to a chair. As an afterthought, I unscrewed the broad head from the shaft protruding from his hand, and pulled the arrow out. It wasn't so much an act of humanity as much as I didn't want him bleeding all over the floor. I'm not a person who normally would condone violence, but considering he tried to shoot me, twice, I wasn't feeling very compassionate towards him. As I worked on wrapping his hand up in a dish cloth, I noticed he had an olive complexion and black eyes. He looked to be of Italian nationality, but I wasn't certain of it.

"Who are you?" I tried to make my voice sound authoritative. The sniper just stared at me silently. He seemed overly calm for a prisoner, not in the slightest bit intimidated by any of us.

"What's your name?" Still no answer.

"Did you kill my mother?" My temper was every bit obvious when I asked. I balled my fist up to hit him. I had never felt so much rage in all my life. I pulled my fist back to strike him, and just as I was half way to his face, a hand came between us. It felt like I had hit a brick wall, it was unyielding and it felt like I might have broken a few of my knuckles in the process. The fury subsided when I looked up and gazed into Kai's eyes.

"A moment of gratification is not worth the eternity of regret you would suffer. I will not allow you to endure that." Kai's velvety voice calmed me back to reason.

"He did not understand the questions you were asking. He does not speak English." Kai tried to explain to me.

"How do you know? He hasn't said a word since he came in."

"I know who sent him. I know who would try to keep you from fulfilling your purpose. There is no need for you to question him."

"Then what are we supposed to do with him?"

"Please, allow me." I stepped back to allow him access. Kai turned to the sniper. Until that moment, the sniper had been calm, too calm considering the situation he was in, but when he looked into Kai's eyes, he started screaming for mercy. With Kai standing next to me, I understood every word he was saying, although it was like one of those cheesy martial arts films again. I had never seen someone so terrified of anything before. His eyes were wide, and he was trembling. I didn't understand his reaction at all.

Kai kept his voice soft, and gently laid his hand on the man's forehead. He murmured one word. "Darkness." The sniper stopped screaming and began sobbing hysterically. "You are not strong enough to endure that pain, but now you understand why I am determined to keep Anyanka safe. She must live. Return to your home and enlighten your masters." Kai lowered his hand and turned to Ryan and Jesse. "Untie him, and take him far from here. He will not give you any trouble."

Ryan and Jesse both turned to me. "It's alright guys; just do what he asks, please." It only took Ryan and Jesse a few minutes to get the sniper untied and out the door. He had finally calmed down to a soft sobbing as Ryan and Jesse practically carried him out of the house.

A cold chill ran down my spine when I looked into Kai's eyes. I knew I was looking into the eyes of the most dangerous creature on Earth. I quickly assessed everything that I knew about him. He has immeasurable strength and speed, and he has the ability to control people by simply saying a word. Worse still, he is so perfectly beautiful that he takes away all my ability to fear him. Perhaps that wasn't his asset as much as my weakness.

My hand was tingling, I had never broken any bones before, but I was under the impression that it would be a painful experience. There was no pain so I deduced that it must not have been broken after all.

Mike and Katie were nowhere to be seen, and I wondered if she was telling him about her feline issues. I hoped Mike would understand. Jenny and Sami were still not back from picking up their stuff to move in, so that left me and Kai alone. That suited me just fine. I had a lot of questions and it seemed that he was the only one that had the answers.

"So, would you like to explain all of this to me?" I put my hands on my hips and glared at him. It was hard to maintain my composure when I looked into his eyes, so I tried to stare at his lips. I wasn't having much success. It appeared that his eyes were glowing brighter than the first time I had seen him. It was like driving past a car accident. I had to look.

Kai walked across the room slowly, he appeared to be gliding, and his steps were fluid, like water rolling onto a beach. Graceful, that was what came to mind as I watched him approach me. He stopped directly in front of me before he began his tirade. "I told you to stay close to your guardians, and you left them in the Mayan territories! I told you there are people trying to kill you, and you spend all week out in public! Are you stupid or just suicidal? Do you care nothing for the future of this world?"

I remembered something my mother had always said to me "*I yell at you only because I love you.*" As I listened to Kai, I realized he was only yelling because he cared. I let him yell and when he was finished I only had one thing to say to him. "I'm sorry."

Kai took a step back. I think he was surprised by my response. He wasn't saying anything in return so I continued to apologize. "You had to save my life yet again because I ignored your warnings. I owe you my life. I am sorry for causing you so much distress."

"You owe me nothing." He bowed his head and closed his eyes. "It is you who has saved me. You have given me a reason to live again. For that I am indebted to you eternally." He whispered. He slowly opened his eyes and stepped towards me again.

I looked up into his eyes, something that I didn't think I would ever grow accustomed to. The ice blue glow was enchanting. I just stared at him, taking in the features of his glorious face, feeling so plain next to him. My self-confidence was waning quickly. As I stared into his eyes, he stared back, it seemed he was doing the same, taking in the features of my face. I felt the blush rise to my cheeks.

"You are more beautiful than I ever imagined possible." he murmured.

He ran his fingers through my hair and set my whole body tingling. He continued to stare into my eyes judging my reaction. My whole body burned with anticipation. He leaned down hesitantly until his lips were close to mine. I could smell his breath, cool and sweet. My head was spinning, the rest of the world disappeared, and nothing else existed outside of his arms. It was my dream coming to life . . . . . including his reaction. I felt him tense up and then he pulled away, but he still held my face in his hands. His eyes were wide in terror.

"What is it?" I whispered.

He seemed to be holding his breath. "Just give me a moment, please." he managed to get out between clenched teeth, though he spoke in a courteous tone. As he stood frozen in place, I could see that his eyes began to soften. Finally, after several long minutes, he relaxed his hold on me. "I am sorry

Annie, I should not have done that. Please forgive me, I will do better to behave myself from now on." He stepped away from me quickly.

Before I could even respond, I caught a glimpse of movement behind him, although it was obscured through a thick haze that surrounded us. Kai didn't take his eyes off of me as he spoke. "Hello Ariel. You are late. You missed all of the excitement." He had a smile on his face, as if he was teasing someone.

"So it begins again, I see." A woman standing in the doorway waved her hand in front of her to dispel the haze; it seemed to blow out of the room as on a stiff breeze.

Several things occurred to me all at once. "We are the four elements, aren't we?"

He cocked his head to the side with a quizzical look. "Of course we are, but how did you know?"

"Fire and water create steam." I pointed to myself and Kai. "That was the haze in here when you touched me. Ariel blew it out of the room with her hand, she can control the air. That is three of the four basic elements. That means the forth immortal, or whatever it is that we are, is the last element, earth."

"And you are aware of all of this only now?" Ariel stepped closer as she spoke. She looked confused. "Why didn't Lilith tell you all of this?"

It was aggravating for me, not knowing. I didn't mean to be rude, but I gritted my teeth and stared Ariel down. "Who's Lilith?" As I glared at her, a small part of my brain registered that she was the most beautiful woman I had ever seen. She was obviously Egyptian. Long black hair that shimmered as it swayed with her movements, a golden hue to her skin, slender but muscular build and her eyes were deep black pools that glowed. She was wearing khaki shorts and a brown spaghetti strap tank top that complimented her skin tone and figure perfectly.

Kai led me to the living room avoiding all physical contact with me. "Lilith is a long story, perhaps you would prefer sitting down for this."

Ariel followed behind. "I am impressed brother that you would remember humans are more comfortable sitting."

"I may be old, *sister,* but I still have an infallible memory." Kai seemed to have the same sarcastic nature as I did. I couldn't imagine why he would call himself old though, if I had to guess, he looked to be my age. That isn't old.

"How old are you, Kai?" It seemed rude to ask his age, my mother having pounded into me that age can be a sensitive subject for most people, but curiosity got the better of me.

He smiled, despite the awkward question. "I am one hundred four thousand years old less six months, Annie. I was the first created by Lilith." He looked at me to judge my reaction. I kept my emotions in check so that he could not see the disbelief in my facial expressions. "Do you believe me?"

I didn't know how to answer. So I recited his words back to him. "Whether I believe you or not, does not change the truth of your words."

He laughed at my response. It was the most beautiful sound I had ever heard. "I realize this isn't easy for you, but you need to open your mind to all the wonderful possibilities that have been bestowed upon you."

I nodded my head, and took a deep breath. "I will try to be open-minded. Could you start from the beginning; maybe that will answer all my questions."

"From the beginning then. Have you heard of the book of genesis?"

"Of course. It's the first book of the bible. I didn't mean for you to start at the very beginning of the world, just the beginning of Lilith."

"That is where Lilith's story begins. You know of Adam and Eve. What you are probably not aware of is that Eve was not Adam's first wife. Lilith was. God created Lilith and Adam in his image, his exact image. Do you understand what that implies?"

I shook my head no. How could I possibly fathom the extent of God as a being, "Are you telling me that we are gods?"

"No!" He was angry with me for saying it. He took a deep breath. "I apologize, it is just that there is only one God, and we should never assume that we are as much as he is."

"So, what are we then?" It felt strange to include myself in the "we", but I needed to accept the fact that I was different, and I might as well start accepting it now.

Ariel, who had been so quiet that I had forgotten that she was there, answered me. "We are more than human, but less than God. We have been called many names by men, such as the four elements, the four seasons, the four hor . . . ."

"Enough Ariel, what do men know about us anyways." Ariel stuck her tongue out at Kai for interrupting. I could see that they did act like siblings.

And then the worst thought of all hit me. "Am I your sister too?" I was afraid to hear the answer, all of those wonderful dreams about this man, it would be too traumatic to find out he was my brother.

Kai chuckled softly. "No, Annie. Only Ariel and I are, but that is another story. Do you want to hear the rest of Lilith's story?"

"Yes, I will try not to interrupt again. Please, go on."

"God created Lilith and Adam, they were husband and wife. They were the caretakers of the Earth. They watched over the Earth through countless evolutions. They were created as equals, both having the same strength and intelligence. This caused many arguments between them. They were not compatible as companions. Adam complained to God that he should rule over Lilith as he did over all of the plants and animals of the Earth. Lilith would never agree to this. God annulled their marriage. He put Adam into a deep sleep and removed a rib. He used the rib and the earth in the Garden of Eden to create Eve. Eve was not as strong or as intelligent as Adam, so Adam was able to rule over Eve. What Adam did not understand was that in removing his rib to create Eve, he was no longer an exact image of God. He was mortal, as was Eve, just human. Lilith, however, was still immortal, with all of her strength, speed and intelligence, Lilith remained the caretaker, not only of the Earth, but of Adam and Eve as well. She became known as Mother Nature. Lilith did not interfere with Adam and Eve for the most part, although it annoyed her to see how Adam treated Eve, not that Eve minded. She loved Adam, and did everything he ever asked of her. When Eve was pregnant with her first child, Lilith realized that as the population grew, she would need help in maintaining the balances of nature. God granted Lilith permission to create four offspring, but only during times that the world became unbalanced. I was created shortly before Eve gave birth to her first son, Able. He and I were as brothers." Kai stopped for a moment. It seemed that this story brought up bad memories.

"Wasn't Cain the first born son?" Not that I was a Biblical historian, but I thought I knew that story fairly well.

He averted his eyes and softly whispered, "Yes, I was." I wasn't sure I heard him correctly, but before I could ask another question, he continued. "Please understand that the books of the Old Testament were written by men thousands of years after the events took place. Stories that are handed down from one generation to the next tend to be altered. Although the story is true, it has been altered enough to distort the facts." He took a deep breath and began again. "Lilith saw the inequality between Adam and Eve as unbalanced. To even the scales, Lilith offered Eve the fruit of knowledge. If Adam were to be stronger than Eve, then Eve should be smarter than Adam. It would allow men and women to be equals, as God had originally intended. Lilith underestimated Eve's love for Adam, because Eve shared the fruit of knowledge with him, instead of becoming his equal, she remained inferior to Adam."

It took a moment for me to grasp what he was telling me. "Lilith is Satan?"

"If you mean, is Lilith the serpent in the Garden of Eden, then, yes she is. But Lilith is not the Satan you are meant to believe she is. There is nothing evil about Lilith. She is the kindest, most loving being that God has ever created. Like

I said before, the book of Genesis was written thousands of years later. Lilith was portrayed as an evil being so that mankind would fear her, not trust in her. I never did like that name, it never fit her persona."

"So, Lilith is a snake?"

"Only when she wants to be. We all have an alternate ego, if you will. Lilith thought snakes were amazing creatures. In truth, they are more in tune with their environment than any other creature. Not to mention how beautiful they are, or how cunning and capable they are when hunting."

"So what is your alter ego?"

"I thought we were discussing Lilith? Do you want me to continue, or are you going to keep interrupting." He snapped at me, his bad mood surfacing again.

I glared at him, but instead of snapping back with sarcasm, I decided to play the good girl "Fine, I promise not to interrupt again, please, continue." He waited a few moments to ensure I was going to remain silent.

"Good, now I will continue. Adam and Eve were not thrown out of Eden; they left of their own free will to explore the world. Lilith and I followed. As their children and grandchildren grew, they began to separate and form tribes. Lilith and I separated as well, to watch over these tribes. As the population grew, Lilith and I became aware of a disturbing trend. Mankind was becoming nothing more than godless creatures, rodents that were infesting the Earth. Rape, murder, steeling, mankind had lost its' humanity. God asked us to start over. We found a family that seemed untouched by the norm of society, a man named Noah, his wife and their children. When he was prepared, Lilith called the animals to board his ark, and then we flooded the Earth, wiping out the rest of mankind."

I raised my hand to speak; of course I was going to have questions. How could he expect me not to. "No Anyanka, you promised not to interrupt. A word of advice, never break a promise." I lowered my hand without speaking, but stuck my tongue out at him in defiance. My head was flooded with so many questions, how was I going to remember them all.

"We begged God to never ask anything like that of us again. He could see the pain it caused us. As if the screams were not bad enough to endure, the silence that followed was deafening. God vowed to spare us that pain. As a sign of his peace and love, he gave us a rainbow. It was another twenty millennia before Lilith created Ariel. Mankind began worshiping idols and false Gods. In the midst of all of that, the different tribes were constantly at war with each other. I built the tower of Babble in hopes that if men could understand one another, they could learn to live in harmony. But even though I could help them understand, I was not able to make them listen. The warring only increased, it seemed hopeless. Lilith knew we had to do something quickly before God intervened again. She created Ariel in Egypt. The city of Giza was built for her, and at a very young age she was made queen. It was Ariel that swayed mankind back into believing that there was only one God, and she did an amazing job of bringing peace and order back to the human race. She did all of this before her transformation. Quite an amazing feat, considering that men generally thought of women to be nothing more than a commodity, as if they were just cattle. Lilith stayed with Ariel, and helped her to understand what needed to be accomplished to reestablish the natural balance again. Unfortunately, there was a tribe known as the Hittites that claimed to have a prophet among them, a prophet that had a vision of four immortals bringing about the end of the Earth. They recognized Ariel as one of the immortals and made several attempts to end her life before she became immortal. Lilith feared for Ariel and devised a plan to fake her death and get her out of Egypt." I pried my eyes away from Kai to look at Ariel. I was so involved with Kai's story that I hadn't realized that she had left the room. I looked back at Kai, trying my hardest not to say anything. He read the look on my face and answered my unspoken question. "She stepped out to call for Buddy. He should have been here by now. He is not coming; he will head to Valhalla in search of answers."

Keeping my mouth shut was becoming unbearable. I just wanted to bombard him with so many questions. He laughed at me. "I know this is hard for you, Annie, but bear with me, it will all make sense soon enough." I tried to believe him, but how could a story like this ever make sense?

He continued with his story, "Buddy was created over two millennium ago. He has sacrificed so much of himself to keep the world at peace. He has managed to accomplish more than Ariel and me put together, although he is modest and will never take credit for his accomplishments. He truly is the best of us." He paused and sighed. "And then Lilith created you fourteen hundred years later. Again the world was a mess, the church of God was corrupt, and the Earth's population had exploded. The four of us could not keep up with mankind, even with our superior strength, speed, and intelligence. Lilith feared for your life, having protected Ariel and Buddy both from many assassination attempts, and would not allow you to be known before your transformation. The Hittites that had prophesized the end of the world had passed on their beliefs to others. Around the turn of the first century, this tribe became known as the Illuminati, or the enlightened ones. They knew there would be a fourth, they knew the signs, and watched and waited. I underestimated the danger you were in, I thought that your anonymity would be enough to keep you safe. It was the simple act of coming to visit with you that gave your identity away. Lilith had warned us to stay away, but I was curious, and once I had met you, I was intrigued by you. You were so flamboyant, whimsical, humorous, inquisitive, intelligent and beautiful. Everything about you was attractive to me. I couldn't get enough of your companionship. It was my visits that lead the Illuminati to you; it was my fault that you were killed."

"Please stop, Kai." This was too much to take in. The realist in me was not about to accept Kai's story without some form of proof. "You make it sound like I am the same person you once knew, but I am not. I have no memories of that life; I don't feel any connection with this other person. And I'm not convinced that any of this is true. Can't you see the flaw in your story? You say Lilith and my mother are one in the same, but that is impossible because Lilith is immortal and my mother is dead." It was painful to say the words, but Kai needed to hear it.

"Precisely!" He exulted. He started speaking quickly, apparently overly excited about a revelation he had. "The samurai sword, Lilith is the only one who could have taken it, aside from myself and it's maker, Lilith is the only one that knew what that sword is capable of. She hid it from me to keep me here. The fact that Lilith has passed on explains why Ariel has not been able to sense her presence anymore."

"So what is so special about the sword?"

"That sword is the only thing on this Earth that can penetrate our skin. It is made from a rare ore from a meteorite. Nothing of this Earth can harm us, but this sword is not of this Earth. Not long after you were gone, I asked an old friend to forge the sword for me. It was stolen before I could collect it. Lilith had taken the sword, she never gave up hope of recreating you, and she would not allow me to give up either." Kai sat silent for a moment before he continued. "The only thing that does not make sense is why would Lilith give up immortality? She loved being here, she loved this world, and she loved being a part of life. What reason did she have to become mortal?"

I knew he wasn't expecting an answer, so I just stared into his eyes. It was so easy to become oblivious to the rest of the world when doing so, but my mind had so much information to process. And then it clicked. "Were you trying to kill yourself? Is that what that sword is for?" My voice went up two octaves as I screamed at him. "Suicide, Is that what you were going to do?" I stood up to storm out of the room. In my book, suicide was a coward's choice. Only those who are too afraid to live would take their own lives.

Chapter 10

LILITH

Just as I was about to make a dramatic exit, the doorbell rang. I knew it wasn't any of my friends (guardians) because they would all punch in the code and let themselves in. I was still fuming when I grabbed the door handle, so when I yanked the door open, I startled the man on the other side. My rage dissipated quickly and I managed to get out a polite greeting.

"Anyanka Cain?" The man standing at the door was short in stature, slightly shorter than me. He had a bald shiny head with dark brown hair that wrapped around the sides. He wore thick glasses that seemed permanently imbedded on the bridge of his bulbous nose. And he wore the most boring, drab, nondescript suit I had ever seen.

I was only slightly aware of Kai standing beside me and Ariel standing behind the man on the front porch. Sentinels to keep me safe; but this man before me was no threat. I could read that in his eyes. I had the sense that he had spent too many years behind a desk with no excitement. He looked sad, like he had just lost his best friend.

The moments of silence were becoming awkward. He was waiting for me to confirm my identity. "Yes, I am Anne Cain."

He stepped back and pushed a dolly forward with a large package on it. It took him some effort to move it. "I am Sean Byron, your mother's attorney. She requested that I deliver this package to you today. I also have a copy of your mother's will for you." Kai picked up the package off of the dolly with the incredulous Sean Byron looking at him. Sean shook his head and reached into an inside pocket of his jacket and pulled out an envelope. "When you have time, I will need you to come by my office to sign papers; my card is in the envelope." He paused for a moment. "I . . . I'm sorry for your loss. Your mother was a magnificent woman." He looked as if he was about to tear up. He turned quickly to leave and almost ran into Ariel.

I looked to Kai, forgetting for the moment that I was angry with him. He had a smug look on his face and he was holding the package up with one hand like a serving tray. It seemed light as a feather, though it was hard to judge the weight knowing that Kai has some kind of super strength. He turned and headed for the dining room table without saying a word. I was about to follow when Ariel grabbed me by the arm and held me back. "Don't judge him for what you do not understand." She whispered in my ear. "It wasn't about killing himself; it was about giving up immortality." I looked at her questioningly. She wasn't in the house for the last part of the conversation, how could she have heard anything that was said?

Before I could ask her, Kai yelled from the dining room. "Ariel' it is not your story to tell." he snapped.

Ariel bowed her head in defeat. "Well, his hearing is still perfect." She shrugged, "I wonder how the rest of his senses are?"

"Yes, that one is still perfect as well. And the answer is yes." He had walked back to us and was leaning against the wall looking like a male model, relaxed and smiling like he had just heard a good joke.

"What did I miss?" I looked to Ariel for an answer.

"Kai can hear people's thoughts, but only if the thought is meant for him."

"So, what did you ask him?"

"I asked him if his feelings are the same." Ariel shrugged, as if she knew the answer already.

She grabbed my hand and led me around Kai towards the dining room before I could ask for clarification. "Come, open your package, I just love surprises, even if they aren't for me." She was practically bouncing with excitement. I had to admit, I was curious myself, so I followed willingly.

I wondered to myself if this was a birthday present, or just something that was to be delivered if my mother was dead. There was only one way to find out, so I peeled back the tape that was holding the flaps of the cardboard box closed. To my surprise, there was a pair of eyes looking back at me. It was my face but with blue eyes, not green. A painted canvass laid flat in the box, it appeared to be quite old. The hair style was all wrong, and the clothes were definitely not mine either, but I could not deny that this was a portrait of me.

"So that is what happened to your painting. Lilith must have been saving it for you." Kai said mostly to himself. "You painted this yourself, if you look closely at the eyes, you can see an image in them." As I leaned closer, I could see that he was right. In the center of each eye, was the image of a running horse. The image was so well blended with the coloring of the eye it was hard to discern unless you knew what to look for.

"There is more in the box." Ariel chimed in.

I set the painting down on the table gently and turned my attention back to the box. Inside the box was a large golden tablet covered in strange hieroglyphs. I didn't recognize the hieroglyphs for they were neither Egyptian nor Mayan. Kai stepped in next to me. "How did Lilith get this?" He ran his fingers down the length of the tablet caressing it.

"What language is this?" I looked to Kai for answers since he seemed to be the linguist in the group.

He whispered softly, almost reverently. "These are the markings of the original language. The first language created by Lilith and Adam. This is one of the four tablets given to us by God. They were done in gold to ensure that the tablets would survive the weathering of time. These tablets were given to Lilith the day God granted her permission to create us."

"What does it say?"

Kai gave me a half smile. "This is your tablet." He said while carefully picking it up out of the box and placing it on the table. The table creaked in protest. "Lilith must have taken it out of Chichen Itza before the city was rediscovered. She knew if anyone found this mass of gold, it would be stolen. It says the fourth child of Lilith will be called Anyanka, the Voice of Fire. Anyanka will be given the power to control the fire in the rocks and the sun in the sky, and fire will dance to her song."

"What? Am I supposed to sing to fire?" I was feeling a little incredulous. It sounded absolutely ridiculous. "Are you saying God made this tablet himself? God gave me this ridiculous name?"

"At least you know your real name." Ariel retorted. "Kai never bothered to read my tablet for me." She glared at Kai for a moment and then looked back to me completely calm. "In a roundabout way, God did make this tablet. God uses his devoted followers to do certain tasks here on Earth. He speaks to them, whether it is in a dream or some other form of communication. That is how the pyramids of Giza, Chichen Itza, and Valhalla were created." Ariel looked satisfied as if she just answered every question I had asked. She seemed completely oblivious to the fact that I was still in the dark.

"There is a purpose in everything God does." she continued. "We may not understand the purpose, but we need to believe that God knows what he is doing. He will help us just enough for us to help ourselves."

Kai interrupted Ariel. "We are not certain what is going to happen. We only know when: December twenty-first, in the year of Christ two-thousand-twelve. Six months from today. God did not give us any specific details. This is a test. If we can figure this out and save ourselves, then we are worthy of being saved, if not, then we have saved God the trouble of destroying the world himself."

"God is planning on destroying the world in six months? Why would he do that?" I tried to sound sarcastic, but my voice trembled, I was terrified.

Ariel took my hand as she spoke, "He is not pleased with mankind. They have lost their humanity as a whole. War, murder, rape, stealing, overpopulation, inequality . . . the more advanced mankind becomes, the worse they get. Mankind has been on a downward spiral for millennium." She paused for a moment, then looked to Kai. "Lilith has given us two pieces of the puzzle, Anyanka and the tablet. It seems to me, she kept quite busy as a mortal. I wonder if there is anything else she has managed to do?"

"There is a letter in the box, perhaps it is an explanation." Kai picked up a thick envelope and handed it to me. Before I could open it, the front door opened. I jumped at the sound. Kai put his arm around me and whispered in my ear. "Nothing will hurt you as long as I am here, you have nothing to fear."

I heard Sami call out, "Hey, we're back. Where are you at Annie?" Just the sound of her voice was uplifting. I left Kai's side to meet her at the front door.

Jenny was with her as well. "You look like you need a group hug." Jenny grabbed me and Sami up in a bear hug and almost tripped over the luggage that was lying on the floor.

Ariel cleared her throat behind me, demanding an introduction. "Sami, Jenny, this is Kai and Ariel. Kai, Ariel, Sami, and Jenny" Jenny and Sami stared speechless for a long moment. It was probably their eyes that made people stare, but for Sami and Jenny, it was more than just glowing eyes that kept them captivated. It was Sami that found her voice first. "It is him! Wow, the man of your dreams in the flesh." I felt my face turn flush red, I hadn't shared that bit of information with Kai and I was feeling a bit self-conscious about him knowing.

"The man of your dreams?" He was intrigued, and yet he sounded relieved.

"That is a story for another time. We still have a letter that needs to be read." Without fail, when dealing with uncomfortable emotional moments, I still felt the need to change the subject. Kai glared at me, but let it drop for the moment.

I headed for the kitchen to sit at the bar when Mike and Katie came in from the music room. I hadn't realized where they had gone, but I should have figured that they hadn't gone far. Ryan and Jesse were still not back from dropping off the sniper somewhere in the middle of nowhere. We would have to fill them in when they got back.

"Who's the letter from?" Jenny asked as she was reaching into the refrigerator for a drink. "Want anything while I'm in here?"

"Pepsi please; Kai, Ariel, would you like anything to drink?" What a horrible host I am, they had been here for hours and I hadn't offered them anything.

Kai and Ariel looked at each other and laughed, "Nothing for us, but thanks for asking." Ariel managed to get out between giggles.

"What did I miss this time? What's so funny?"

Kai smiled at me, "That is a story for another time. We have a letter to read, remember?" It felt like we were having a battle of wits and I was losing miserably.

"Right, the letter is from Mama, to answer your question Jenny." I looked at the front of the envelope; there was one word on it scrawled in Mama's beautiful script.

Anyanka

I felt a lump rise up in my throat. I knew I wouldn't be able to read this so I handed the letter to Ariel. "Would you do the honors, please." I would have asked Kai (any reason to listen to his voice) but since he had just learned the English language I wasn't certain he would have learned to read it as well.

"Yes, of course I will, dear." Ariel took the letter from my hand and stood next to Jenny who was leaning on the bar. Sami, Mike, and Katie sat on the bar stools next to me, and Kai remained standing behind me. He put his hand on my shoulder; it was cool to the touch but comforting just the same.

Ariel began.

"June 9, 2012. My darling daughter, as I write this, I know my time is near an end. I do not fear death, I welcome it. I

only hope that my death will buy you enough time to find 'him'. When I last saw 'him', he was called Kai, but he might be using the name Jora. Regardless of his name, you will recognize him, and with your gifts developing so quickly, it will not be hard for him to sense your presence. Stay near him, he will keep you safe. You must survive as the world is depending on you.

'There is so much I should have told you. Please forgive me for keeping my silence. I wanted you to have a normal childhood, to make friends and go to school, and not carry the weight of the world on your shoulders. I enjoyed watching you grow up, watching you discover new things. Childhood is something I never had, so I lived vicariously through you. I wanted you to experience the world through the eyes of a child, before the burden of your destiny comes crashing down on you.

'I know I never mentioned my past, I didn't want to lie to you, so I chose to say nothing at all. I let you come to your own conclusions. The truth is, I was created at the beginning of time. You always asked me how old I am, well, I am over four billion years old. (And you wondered why I was so sensitive about my age). God created me, as he did my husband Adam in the Garden of Eden. After three and a half billion years, Adam and I were no longer compatible, so we divorced and God created Eve out of Adams rib. I am the first of the immortals. My purpose was to take care of mother Earth and all that live here. There was so much to do that I asked God if I could create others to help me. He allowed me to create four offspring. Kai was my first creation. Then there was Tari, (Ariel pointed to herself) and David . . .

"That would be Buddy" Ariel added.

'. . . and then there was you. You were created in twelve-ninety-one. You grew up in Ireland in a place called Glenfinian. Because of what Tari and David had to endure, I chose to keep your identity a secret; only a few people knew your true identity. I even ordered the other three to keep their distance

from you, to avoid any unwanted attention. When you became of age, you were sent to England for your education. You studied art and music and you had an uncanny understanding of math and science. When you were sixteen, there was an accident. The place where you were staying caught fire. Kai was concerned that your identity had been compromised and went to protect you. The fire was just an accident, but it only took one meeting and Kai was enamored by you. I don't know what had happened between you two, a gentleman never kisses and tells, but Kai couldn't help but to visit with you often . . . (I turned to look at Kai, he was standing over me like a protective brick wall.) . . . *The illuminati, an ancient tribe, believed that we existed only to bring about the end of the world. They believed that if they could kill one of you while you were still vulnerable, the other three would not have the power to destroy the Earth. The illuminati had it wrong though, without the strength of the four of you, the Earth is doomed. They had made many attempts to kill Tari and David when they were vulnerable, but they failed. They discovered your identity, and waited for a time when Kai was away. As soon as we knew you were in trouble, we all came, but it was too late. We tried to save you, but you were already gone. Tari and David both went their separate ways to make the best of the time that was left for us. Kai and I tried to recreate you, but God would not allow it. We had our chance and failed.*

'I didn't lose all hope though, I continued to search and research for clues to what the end might bring. It wasn't until twenty years ago that I discovered that the ancient cities created for the four of you, were aligning to the four corners of the world. I suppose I should mention that Chichen Itza was built for you, long before you were ever created. It should make more sense to you now, the feeling that you always belonged there. All four cities were built by the hand of God. I believe that these cities play an important role in saving this world. Unfortunately, I still do not know what is coming, only when: December twenty-first, two thousand twelve. You only have six months to figure it out.

'I asked God one last time to allow me to create you. He asked me a question, "What would I be willing to give to save this world?" My answer was 'anything'. I love this world, it is my home, even with all of its flaws, it is still worth saving. I hope you feel the same. I had to give up my immortality. That was the condition. It took over a year for my body to transform into a human. You were conceived soon after. It is important for you to understand that you were born, not created. You are my biological daughter, not molded Earth that I breathed life into like the other three. I wasn't certain if you would be the same as before, I am still not certain that you will ever become immortal, all I know is that you are developing the gifts you once had. I hope that is enough for the task you are being asked to do. Your destiny is to save the world. I know this may seem overwhelming, but I have faith in you.

'I saved the painting of you. I thought it might be easier for you to accept all of this if you had some memorabilia from your past. I had to keep it hidden so that the Illuminati would not have a way to identify you. Up until your graduation, your anonymity has kept you safe. Now, I am counting on your guardians and Kai to protect you.

Good luck my darling daughter; all of my faith, hope and love to you.

Lilith

Everyone was silent for several long minutes, lost in their own thoughts. It was Kai that broke the silence. "No Ariel" he snapped, "I will not make that mistake again! Nor will I allow you to either." Kai got up and stormed out the back door.

I couldn't speak, I had tears in my eyes, but when I looked to Ariel, she understood my unspoken question. "Vampires," she said it nonchalantly as if that explained everything.

"We can create vampires. Or should I say, I can, but we do not know if Kai has that ability. Kai's one attempt failed. I discovered this fact when my friend Anok offered himself to me. I needed the energy but I didn't want to kill him, so I only drank a little of his blood. Three days later he had transformed into what is now known as a vampire, an immortal. We are genetically superior to humans. Any amount of our genetic material introduced into a human will forever alter them. Vampires are not entirely like us, but they are no longer human either. Unfortunately, I could no longer tolerate being near him, once we have tasted someone's blood, we tend to crave that flavor." Ariel shrugged, "No great loss, once he was a vampire, his personality became less than desirable. Anyways, when you were dying, Kai tried to change you into a vampire. Obviously it didn't work; you had lost too much blood by the time he reached you. I'm surprised that he can tolerate being near you, you smell exactly the same. He is in excruciating pain, denying himself the taste of your blood. Oddly enough, Katie smells just like you."

"You drink blood to survive?" The words were thick in my throat. I didn't really want to know the answer, but it would drive me insane not to know.

Ariel was very casual about answering. "Yes, of course we do. Humans are best, but when they are not available, we settle for animal blood."

Just when I thought I couldn't take anymore, Ariel had to tell me this. Well, I'm still human, so I suppose my reaction wasn't out of place. I ran straight to the bathroom to throw up. I was hugging the porcelain bowl when Sami came in.

"Wow that is so cool." Leave it to Sami to be unimpeded by anything. "It's like a soap opera, only better; Immortals, vampires, and saving the world while the man of your dreams wants to kill you. What more could you ask for?"

Chapter 11

DEALS

Sami helped me out of the bathroom and upstairs to my room. It was early evening, but I was exhausted, I curled up on my bed in a fetal position holding a pillow. Sami covered me with my comforter and sat on the edge of my bed. "What's really bothering you?"

"Oh, I don't know, maybe it's that my entire life has been a lie, or that my mother died to save my life, or maybe it's the fact that the man I have loved my whole life has turned out to be a blood sucking murderer. Pick one! And to top it all off, I may become a blood sucking murderer myself, and if I don't, that's all right, because the world is going to end anyways if I don't figure out how to save it. Why should I be bothered by anything?"

Sami didn't shy away from my tirade. She always saw a silver lining in everything and she was determined to make me see it too. "Tell me something, I'm curious, do you think you had a good childhood?"

"Of course, I had a great childhood. I have no complaints about that."

Sami persisted, "And do you think your mother would have complained about giving her life to save you?

"No, you're right on that point, but it doesn't mean I have to be happy about it."

"True, but I think it's safe to say that your mother thought it was an honorable way to go." Sami stopped for a moment. "What was the other complaints? Oh yeah, blood sucking murderer. You hunt, don't you?"

"Yes, but not humans."

"I know that. My point is, what's the difference if you kill a deer to eat the meat, or drink its blood? The deer is dead regardless. My point is, some people are more of an animal than the deer you hunt. Why would it be so horrible if Kai hunted them?

"That's a lovely thought, Sami, but you don't know if he picks and chooses his victims or if he kills randomly."

"True, but perhaps you should ask him before you judge." Sami knew she had me on that one, so she didn't give me a chance to respond. "And as far as saving the world, well, look at it this way, if you succeed, you will be a hero, and if you fail, no one will be around to complain about it." I had to laugh at her absolutely perfect logic. It all seems so simple through Sami's eyes.

"Thank you, Sami. You are wise beyond your years. If we live past December, you should seriously think about becoming a psychiatrist."

"Yeah, crazy people, it takes one to know one. Your right, I could see myself doing that, and you can be my first patient." We both laughed. "Get some sleep so you can have a clear head later. I think we have a lot of work to do."

Before Sami left, she closed the curtains and shut off the lights. I was alone in the darkness with nothing but my thoughts, and even those were moving in slow motion. It wasn't long before I drifted off to sleep.

I wasn't certain why I was running through the forest, a feeling of danger, a sound, or perhaps a smell that triggered my self-preservation mode. I didn't slow down when the briars cut me, or the branches tangled my hair. I knew that if I stopped, that would be the end of my life. He jumped down from a high branch and landed in front of me, he didn't make a sound when he landed. I couldn't climb a tree, or out run him, all I could do was make a stand and fight. He crouched down into a stalking pose and lithely moved closer. I took my fighting stance, bracing myself for anything. As he came closer he bore his teeth and growled. His movements were so graceful, even with terror gripping me; I could still appreciate the beauty that was before me. In a blurred movement he leapt towards me and tackled me to the ground. I must have been dead, because when I looked up, I saw the face of an angel. He started laughing at me, light and humorous. "Anyanka, you have a lot to learn about fighting." He leaned down and kissed me gently on the lips, I didn't resist. I reached up and tangled my fingers into his hair pulling him in so I could kiss him more fiercely. He pulled away, as he always did when I got carried away. "You know this is not wise." He jumped up and disappeared before I could respond.

I woke up when the dream ended. My room was dark, but I sensed that I wasn't alone. I reached out to turn on the lamp at the side of my bed. It came on before I could touch it. Kai was standing by my bed, watching me. "What time is it?" I croaked as I stretched.

"Two-twenty-six a.m., you have been asleep for five hours, thirteen minutes and thirty-nine seconds."

"And you have been here watching me for how long?" I thought it was strange how he answered so precisely, but I decided to play along.

"Five hours, twelve minutes, and fifty-nine seconds."

I sat up in bed, but kept the blankets wrapped around me. "Wow, you waited a whole forty seconds before you came to spy on me?" I had a hint of sarcasm in my voice, and I wondered briefly if it was wasted on Kai.

"No, I waited a whole two seconds before coming to watch you sleep. Ariel stopped me for the other thirty-eight seconds." I was under the impression that sarcasm was completely lost to him.

"The man of your dreams?" He mused. "I thought that was a figure of speech, I am relieved, I thought my mind had snapped."

"You heard that?" I was embarrassed, especially about the last part of the dream.

He laughed softly. "Anyanka, you have a lot to learn about fighting." He even used the same intonation. I could feel my cheeks turn bright red. Kai didn't seem to notice. "I am flattered that you remember me." He whispered. His thoughts were not on the content of the dream, but on what the dream meant.

I needed to change the subject before he started to analyze the dream and embarrass me even more. So without speaking I said to him, *Kai, please sit with me awhile.* He smiled and sat down on the edge of my bed. "I guess the big question is why do I remember you from my previous life, and nothing else?"

"I have a few theories about that, but nothing that I can be certain of."

Continue please, I thought to him.

He smiled, "You are enjoying this gift of mine, that is fine, but I would prefer to hear your voice. I have missed it, and you."

"Alright then, I will speak to you unless it is necessary to keep quite. What are your theories?"

"My first theory is that when I tried to save you, a part of you did become immortal, your chi (as the Japanese call it). You only survived for a few minutes after, and I was all you saw. I held you in my arms as you slipped away. The last words you spoke to me were 'Our love can never die.' and then you were gone." Kai sat still for a moment, lost in his thoughts. When he looked up at me, he smiled. His white teeth glistened in the lamp light, and his smile touched his beautiful eyes. "My other theory is that not even death can overcome love. It is the purist emotion, so powerful that it can manifest into energy. Distance, time, not even death can destroy this energy."

"You love me?" I lowered my head so I wouldn't have to look him in the eyes.

"With all that I am." Kai reached out and put his hand under my chin, lifting my head. "But you do not love me." He voiced my unspoken thought.

"I don't know you, not really. Sure, I know your face, but your personality, I may think you are the same as my dreams, but you were never angry in my dreams. And be honest with yourself, I am not the same person you fell in love with seven hundred years ago. You don't know me either."

"Stop me if I get anything wrong." He sounded sure of himself. "Your birthday is June twenty-first; your favorite season is summer. Your favorite color is green. You love music, art, science and sports. You enjoy horseback riding, swimming, and reading. You love lightning storms, hate snow, love playing practical jokes, and honestly believe that the secret to life is to be able to laugh every day. The one thing that terrifies you is being up high, you like to keep your feet on the ground . Did I get anything wrong?"

"O.K. so you do know me, but that isn't all of me, there is so much about me you couldn't possibly know. And honestly, you are barely more than a complete stranger to me."

"What would you like to know? You can ask me anything, and I promise I will answer openly and honestly."

"Anything?" Kai nodded his head. "Well, my biggest concern is your diet."

"That is not a question. Ask me the question, Annie." He said in a soothing voice.

"Fine . . . . . . Do you kill people and drink their blood?" I blurted out, I was afraid that if I didn't do it quickly, I would chicken out.

"Was that really so hard to ask?" He didn't wait for me to answer. "Technically, I drink human blood and then they die. It is better if the heart is still beating." He said it casually. I didn't want to panic just yet so I mustered up the courage to ask the next question.

"How do you decide who your next meal is going to be? Are you choosy about whom you eat, or is it just a random thing?"

Kai started laughing, a beautiful sound of musical chimes. "So you are wondering if I kill on a whim or if I am more selective showing a preference to a certain blood type?"

"Yes, but not blood types, it's more like good people versus evil people."

"I assure you that I have never fed from someone unless they have offered themselves to me. I believe you would call that a human sacrifice. The practice has been abandoned for many centuries so I must make do with animal blood. I hope that is ethical enough for you."

"I suppose it could be worse, but how do I know you are telling the truth, or just lying to me so I won't run off screaming?"

"I cannot tell a lie. If I were to lie to you or anyone else, I would suffer a hundred years of fiery torment. I have no choice but to be honest."

"A noble quality, I can respect that. Mama and I always had a policy, we called it painfully honest. I think I see why she called it that now. Tell me, do you want to drink my blood?" I was feeling more comfortable with him. Not that I thought he was ordinary or weak, I could never think that, just that he seemed to honestly want me to know him.

"Your blood calls out to me; it is a temptation that is easily denied. It is a minor irritation compared to the pain of living without you for the past seven-hundred years. I think it is a gift to have you back, it makes me happy to suffer the torment of denying myself your blood."

"You're happy that you're in pain? What are you, a masochist?"

"Perhaps I am, but you have no reason to fear me, I could never hurt you". He looked at me with a hint of sadness in his eyes. "Do I frighten you?"

"I haven't decided yet, mostly you just aggravate me. I think I just need more time to get to know you. Ask me again in a couple of weeks."

"Fine, I will remember that. Is there anything else you would like to know about me?"

I only took a moment to come up with my next question. "What other names have you been called? Have I heard of you before?"

"I am most certain that you have heard of me before. Would you like for me to list all of my names."

"How many names do you have?"

"I only have Five hundred twenty-seven."

"Only, why don't you just give me one or two? "

"Very well then, I have been called Moses by the Jews in Egypt, and Chak by the Mayans."

"You mean Moses, as in the man that led the slaves out of Egypt and parted the Red Sea?"

"Yes. I did that."

"And Chak, the Mayan God of Rain?"

"Yes, but please do not refer to us as gods. We are not worthy of that title." He sounded adamant in his request.

"Where did you get the name Kai Jora?"

"The man that created the samurai sword named me Kai. It means 'Ocean' in Japanese. He said the pain I suffered could overflow the oceans. Jora was a nickname given to me in the Middle East. It means 'Autumn Rain' in Hebrew. I was in Iran just before I met you, helping the farmers with their crops. Jora is the name you knew me by when we first met. It is mankind's responsibility to name us. Each society has a name for us, but it is rare that a name means anything to us. A rose by any other name would smell just as sweet."

"You're quoting Shakespeare?"

"No, I was quoting Lilith. That is what she said to me when she was given the name Satan. I do not know who this Shakespeare is." I chuckled when I realized old William Shakespeare was a plagiarist.

"So tell me some of the things that you have done."

"I created the tropical rain forest, the Great Lakes, and barriers reefs. I created the Tower of Babble, I mentioned that before. I freed the slaves from Egypt, but that does not absolve me from the guilt of annihilating the entire Egyptian army. Like most of my accomplishments, there is a darkness that equals the light."

"Do you consider yourself good or evil, then?"

He chuckled softly, "I do not consider myself either, I am neutral, I am just doing my job."

"Why do you think it would be a mistake to turn me into a vampire? Would I become evil and you won't like me anymore?"

"Nothing can change the way I feel about you. You would not become evil, but you would never be able to reach your full potential as a vampire. I was desperate in trying to save you, but after you were gone I realized it would have been a mistake to change you. There are other options if you do not transform. I will not let anything happen to you, I will protect you, but I need you to do as I tell you. To start with, I want you out of this house tomorrow."

"Where are we going?"

"I am still deciding on the destination, Giza, Chichen Itza, or Valhalla. Atlantis is out of the question."

"Atlantis and Valhalla are real?"

"Of course they are real, as with most myths and legends. Atlantis is the only city built by God himself. It was built before the dawn of man. It is the most perfect city in the world, the city that all other great cities were designed after. And Valhalla is barely more than a myth because the people that live there rarely ever leave. Only once did a couple leave and never return, that is how the legend started."

"Why can't we go to Atlantis?"

"That environment is not suitable for you or your guardians."

"Why? Where is it?"

"It is in the Arctic Ocean."

"We can dress warm, that's not a problem." I really wanted to see Atlantis, my curiosity was peeked.

"No, what I mean by "In" the Arctic Ocean is that it is three kilometers below sea level."

"Oh, I guess that would be a problem."

"We are going to be quite busy today. You should try to get more sleep."

"I'm not tired. I would much rather hear more about you."

"What more could you possibly want to know?" Could he possibly think that his life was uninteresting?

"Everything!" He opened the proverbial door and I was taking advantage. "Why are you so cold all the time? Why do your eyes glow? How old were you when you transformed? What other gifts do you have? Where is the garden . . . .?" Kai put his finger over my lips to shush me.

"I will make a deal with you. If you lie down and close your eyes, I will answer your questions. Do we have a deal?"

It sounded reasonable. I was willing to agree to that. It gave me an idea. "Fine, but I would like to make a deal with you as well."

"What would you like?" He sounded willing so I pressed on.

"I promise not to do anything reckless like getting myself hurt or killed if you promise to calm down and stop yelling at everyone."

He bowed his head in shame before responding. "I promise I will try to be more civilized. That is the best that I can do. Is that acceptable?"

"I'll take what I can get."

"Good, now lie down and close your eyes." Kai took the chair from my desk and sat in it as far from the bed as my room would allow. "Good, now I suppose it is best to explain to you the physiology of an immortal. We are like a living stone. On the outside we appear to have skin, muscles, and skeletal structure, but it is harder, unbreakable, and impenetrable like diamonds. On the inside we are completely different. Where you have organs, heart, lungs, stomach, we immortals have pure energy; it is this energy that makes our eyes glow."

I was trying hard to pay attention but I was more tired than I realized and my mind started to drift off to sleep. I fought to hear what Kai was saying.

"I was eighteen when I transformed, but it has not been the same for all of us. Ariel was twenty-six, and Buddy was twenty-three."

I drifted out of consciousness again and then forcing myself awake to listen to him again. He was humming a song. I recognized it as the song I played on the piano the night I returned from Mexico. "Where did you hear this song before?" I mumbled, even my speech was slurred from exhaustion.

"It is your song, this is the song your soul sings."

"I played this song on the piano last week. It just came to me and I started playing it."

"You can hear your soul? Maybe that is how you remember me." He started humming again. I was about to ask him another question, but he stopped me. "No more for tonight, sleep my beautiful Annie." He stood up and crossed the room so he could run his fingers down my face and across my eyes. There was no more fight in me. I fell asleep quickly, without dreams.

Chapter 12

LEAVING

The next morning the house was buzzing with life. Ryan and Jesse had returned while I was asleep. Ariel had filled them in on all the information we had learned in their absence. I had the distinct impression that Jesse was enamored with Ariel. He was beginning to take on the personality of a Labrador retriever. How cute. What I found to be odd was that Ariel was flirting with him. I would have to make it a point to warn Jesse about the whole vampire issue when dealing with Ariel. Kai didn't want me more than two feet from his side, I had to remind him that I am still human and I needed a few moments to myself. So I had some issues to work out with my neurotic, over protective personal knight in shining rock hard body.

Everyone agreed that staying at this house was a bad idea. All the debates were over where to go and how to get there. We all had our passports, aside from Kai that is (who seems to have been completely out of touch with reality for the past seven-hundred years), but Ryan said it was a bad idea to use them. If the illuminati knew where I lived they would also know my full name, friend's names, favorite places to hang out, and a general layout of the entire town of New London and the outlying areas.

I had heard enough, and I was seriously disturbed by what little I did hear. "Whoa! Wait just one minute! You guys can't go with us."

It was Ryan that rebutted me. "Who's going to stop us? You?"

"Don't think for one second that you intimidate me, Mr. Second Degree Black Belt. I can still take you." I snapped back at him.

"Bring it on little girl." He knew better than to call me that, he was trying to provoke me.

"Have you lost your mind? You guys can't come. You have families, college, and obligations that you can't ignore."

It was Jesse that became the voice of reason. "Annie, we are eighteen and can do what we want. Besides, you're going to need our help to succeed. Our job and obligation is to protect you. Until we save the world, nothing else matters."

Jenny jumped into the conversation. "Are we going to vote on this, because if we do, I vote we duct tape Annie's mouth shut so we don't have to listen to her whine."

I knew Jenny was joking, but Kai didn't know any better. He turned on Jenny with a fierce growl. I caught a glance at Jenny's face as I stepped between them. She was terrified. "Kai, stop! She didn't mean anything by it. It's o.k."

Kai backed down, but the tension in the room still had not subsided. Unfortunately I had no time to deal with it. "I have to head into town. Mike, would you come with me?"

Kai was put off by my request. "Am I not allowed to accompany you as well?"

"Sorry Kai, but it's not like you could blend into the scenery. I don't want to draw any unwanted attention to us, and you do stand out."

"If you are referring to his eyes," Ariel interjected, "I can fix that." Ariel took a pair of dark sunglasses off the top of her head and handed them to Kai. "Put these on."

Other than a slight glow that could be mistaken as reflective light, Kai almost looked normal. Well, not entirely normal, he could put every male super model to shame.

I must have been ogling, because Kai laughed to himself. "Is this acceptable for you, Annie?"

What could I say? "WOW!" Yep, that summed it all up. "Alright then, you can go." I was grateful not to leave him behind. It's not just his beauty that I was finding attractive, I was enjoying his companionship too, at least when he wasn't yelling. There was so much mystery about him, so much to learn. None of this added up to love, but what do I know, I had never loved anyone in that way before. How was I supposed to know what love is?

As we headed into town, I let Mike drive and Kai sit in the passenger seat. Kai was intrigued by all of the buttons and dials on the dashboard. He turned the radio up full volume on one of those pop rock stations that I love so much. He had to cover his ears until Mike turned the volume back down for him. "What is that?" He asked.

"It's a radio." Mike explained. "Music is transmitted from radio stations and the sound is picked up by the antenna." Mike was acting like a big brother to Kai, showing him all the gadgets in the car and explaining things in detail.

"What does this button do?" He turned the air conditioner on and a blast of cold air hit his face. He didn't seem to mind that one so much. He was like a big kid with a new toy, playing with all the buttons just to see what would happen.

We stopped at the lawyer's office first. The secretary ushered us into a small boring office that matched my impression of Sean Byron to a tee. As we waited for the lawyer to arrive, Kai entertained himself with one of those silly desk ornaments that worked by using kinetic energy to move the swinging balls back and forth. Sean walked into the office a few minutes after we arrived, carrying a stack of papers held together by paper clips with a lot of little yellow arrows sticking out the side. It occurred to me just then that I had not read my mother's will and had no idea what I was signing. When Sean handed me a key, I had to ask what it was for. Sean berated me for not reading things before I signed.

"Had you read the will, you would have known that this is the key for a safety deposit box at National City Bank."

"Oh! Is there anything else for me, or are we done?"

"Yes, we are finished here. Again, I am deeply sorry for your loss. If there is anything you need, feel free to call upon me."

I managed to get out a "Thank you." as we were walking out the door. I was in a hurry to leave. The office was so drab that I was about to fall asleep.

My hand was cramping from all the signing that I had finally finished. I hadn't made a scene about it, but Kai took my hand and began massaging it. He sat in the back seat with me for the short drive to the bank just so he could continue to massage my hand. "Better?" He looked into my eyes and I lost all train of thought. I couldn't help but stare at him. "Annie?"

"I'm sorry, what were you saying?" I shook my head to make myself focus on what he was saying.

"Your hand, does that feel better?" He asked again.

I looked down at my hand that he still held in his own. There was steam rising off of it. "It feels fine now, thank you, but is this normal?"

He laughed. I looked into his eyes again; there was so much life in them. He was so different from the first time I met him. There was so much happiness in him that I couldn't imagine him ever being sad. "How would I know what normal is? You are the only woman I have ever loved. This is normal for us, but I do not know about anyone else."

Before I could get out the next barrage of questions, we pulled into the parking lot at the bank. As we were getting out of the car, I had to remind Kai to put the sunglasses back on. He didn't like to have them on, he said they clouded his vision, so whenever we were not in public, the sunglasses were on top of his head.

I steered us clear of the teller's counter and headed for a small office at the back of the bank. I showed the key to a woman behind the desk and she led us to a huge bank vault. The clicking of her high heel shoes echoed off the walls making the vault feel more like a crypt. "I will give you some privacy to open the box. There is a table and chairs in the next room where you can view the contents. If you need me, just hit the button on the wall."

"Thank you." I called out to her as she left us alone in the giant vault.

"I'm becoming desensitized by all the surprises that Mama has left for us." I looked to Mike; he seemed unsurprised by any of this, as if he was expecting everything that has happened. "What is with you, Mike?"

"What do you mean?" He looked so innocent; it was hard for me to be annoyed with him.

"You, you're acting like this is just a normal day in the neighborhood. Like you knew this was all going to happen."

"Would you be mad if I said I did?"

I'm sure my face was turning red with anger. "What did you know, Mike?" I asked through gritted teeth.

"I knew that I was born to be your guardian. I knew there was something special about you. And I also knew that one day I would be in charge of keeping you alive."

I was at my wits end. I couldn't even phrase a coherent question. I stared Mike down, until he continued talking.

"I told you, it's just an instinct. I don't know how I know, I just know. Your mother knew too. She called us your guardians in her letter, or hadn't you noticed?" There was no point in denying it, I hadn't noticed. I also had to admit, there was no point in being angry with him. I took a deep breath to calm down.

Kai put his hand on my shoulder. "Let us be done with this business and get back to the others. There is still much to do." I nodded my head, I knew he was right.

Instead of inspecting the contents of the safety deposit box, I took a green canvas bag off of the table and dumped all of the contents into the bag without looking. There would be time to look when we were back at the house.

"Okay, let us get out of here." I didn't want to admit, even to myself that I was feeling uncomfortable being out in public. This could be a problem considering we were about to travel to God knows where.

The house was buzzing with excitement when we arrived. Katie came bounding up to Mike as soon as we walked through the door and jumped into his waiting arms. The sappiness was going to take some getting used to. Jenny came in right behind Katie. She grabbed my hand and dragged me through the house to Mama's room. "Come, I've got something to show you." It couldn't be a bad surprise; she was too excited for this to be bad.

I allowed myself to be dragged into Mama's bedroom, a room that I had hardly ever stepped foot in before. Sami was sitting on the bed pouting, and Ariel, Jesse, and Ryan were at the desk, staring at the computer. Ariel started speaking as soon as we were in the room. "Lilith documented the entire layout of Chichen Itza. Every glyph is categorized with its location, and translations. We just have to go through the information to find some connection with December twenty-first, two-thousand-twelve. Do you know what this means?"

Was she really expecting me to answer? It was Kai that answered for me. "It means that we do not need to go to Chichen Itza. Buddy is going to Valhalla to search. That leaves us with Giza. This simplifies our search, most helpful considering what little time we have."

"Kai?" Ariel was trying to be soothing. "You know you will have to go to Atlantis sooner or later. You're the only one that can go."

"I know, but it does not feel like the appropriate time." He said through gritted teeth.

I looked to Sami, who was still pouting. "What's wrong with you? Aren't you happy about going to Egypt?"

"It's not that, I'm just mad because they won't let me near the computer." I had to laugh, Sami's electrifying personality tended to destroy electronic equipment. It was probably best to keep her away from the computer.

"Well, you can help me go through this stuff." I lifted up the bank bag I still had in my hand. "Come on. We can do this in the dining room. Let us know if you find anything interesting, guys." No one replied, they were all absorbed in the information on the computer.

In the dining room, I dumped the bag out on the table. Kai and Sami just stared in amazement. I was beginning to think nothing would ever surprise me again. On the table were several dozen passports, debit cards, bank account books, cash from several different countries and an envelope with Kai's name on it. Kai picked up the envelope and turned away from the table. When he turned back a minute later, I realized he had already read the letter, "Anything good?"

"A warning about travel. We should travel in smaller groups of two's and three's out of separate airports; avoid using the debit cards too often; no cell phones; and change passports frequently."

"Is there anything else in the letter?" I asked out of curiosity.

"That depends. Do you know anyone by the name of Cavin?"

"No, none that I know," I shrugged.

"Well then, no, there is nothing else of importance. Now, would you be so kind as to explain to me all of Lilith's suggestions?" It was obvious he wasn't joking, he truly was confused.

"Wow, you really have been cut off from the world for a while, haven't you?"

"Just the past six-hundred-eighty years. I did not think mankind would evolve so quickly."

"Alright, a quick lesson in modern technology. This is a cell phone." I pulled my phone out of my back pocket, a habit of always putting it there since Mama insisted on me having it whenever I went somewhere. "This is how we communicate over distances, unfortunately, it is traceable. If someone were watching for me to use my phone, they would be able to triangulate my position, so, no cell phones." I tossed the phone on the table and picked up a passport. It was for Jesse, at least it was his picture, but the name in it was James Wilson. "This is a passport. It allows us to travel from one country to the next without any hassle at the airport. Airplanes fly in the air like really big birds, we ride in them to get from one place to the next. Debit cards are a form of currency, sort of. Money is put in the bank and we can access that money electronically by using a debit card. Do you understand any of it?"

"I'm a quick learner. Lilith thinks the Illuminati will be tracking us and these travel tips are a way of throwing them off of our trail, correct?" He smiled that charming devilish smile and I had to catch my breath before I could answer.

"You are an impressive man, Kai." I was aiming for flirtatious, but I didn't quite accomplish it. I felt awkward, not only because he was the most beautiful man I have ever seen, but also because I had absolutely no experience in relationships.

I must have been sending my thoughts to him because he responded to my agitation. "Do not fret Annie; you will always be perfect in my eyes." As if I wasn't embarrassed enough, I turned three shades of red. He took my face in his hands. "Beautiful, absolute perfection."

Sami cleared her throat. "Um, guys, we have work to do, remember?" With that we divided up the pile, Sami was to sort the cash by nationality, Kai sorted the passports, and I had to match bank books with debit cards. It wasn't long before Kai found a passport for himself.

"Where did this picture come from?" I took the passport out of his hands to study the picture closer. The name on the passport said David McMaster. I liked the sound of it. The image was a low grade pixel; it was slightly fuzzy and obviously digitally enhanced. It must have been taken in the last week because he had short hair in it. The only thing that looked different was his eyes. In the picture, they weren't glowing.

"It looks like this was taken with a cheap camera and then altered with the computer. I think the lawyer might have taken this?" I offered. Kai didn't have a better theory so we were sticking with mine.

It was obvious that we had what we needed to book our flights to Cairo, Egypt. It was already afternoon and Kai wanted us out of the house before dark. "Ryan! We need to get our flights scheduled. Can you handle that?" I called into the other room. I jumped when he answered from behind me. He laughed and reached around me to pick up several bank books with corresponding credit cards.

"Yeah, I think I can handle that, but it's going to take some time, and I need to borrow the car." I looked at him questioningly. "I don't want to use the same server when I schedule the different flights. It would look suspicious. I'll schedule you, Kai and Sami for one flight, Mike, Katie and Jenny together, and Jesse, Ariel and myself. I need the passports so I have the names correct too."

"Don't tell me, this feels like natural instincts to you. You just know what needs to be done?" I sounded cynical, so I was surprised by his response.

Very nonchalantly he responded, "Yep." He turned and left the house without another word.

Jenny came out of Mama's room. "There's so much information it's going to take a while to go through it all. We're backing it up on flash drives so we can take it with us. So, now all we need to do is get packed. By the way, you should thank Jesse for taking the horses to the boarding farm for you while you were gone."

* * *

We spent the rest of the afternoon packing, trying to figure out what we might need. After packing for every conceivable possibility, I realized, we all over packed. To simplify the dilemma, we decided to pack as little as possible and buy what we needed when we needed it. It was late evening before Ryan returned with the travel arrangements.

"Kai, Annie and Sami, you three will need to leave in the next hour. You will be flying out of Lexington, Kentucky in the morning. Jenny, Katie, and Mike, you will be flying out of Columbus tomorrow afternoon. And Ariel, Jesse and I will be flying out of Cleveland tomorrow night. We will meet up at the Atlanta airport in two days for the flight to Egypt." Ryan started handing schedules out along with passports and bank account books.

Kai didn't want to linger too long, so I grabbed my carryon bag and a purse and headed out to the car. I didn't want to look back at the house, I was certain I would break down into tears if I tried to say goodbye. Sami read my mood, and as always wanted to cheer me up. "It's not goodbye, Annie. It's more of a 'See ya later'. We'll be back, you'll see."

"What would I do without you guys?"

Sami started laughing, "Probably starve. I've tasted your cooking." With that, even Kai was laughing.

"I cooked for you guys one time! Are you ever going to let me live it down?"

"Nope," She managed to get out between giggles. As always, she was able to cheer me up.

Kai was right behind us, "I will drive."

I stopped dead in my tracks and turned on him. "What? Do you even know how?"

"No, but I will figure it out on the way. How hard can it be?" He walked pass me, straight to the car.

"I thought you were trying to keep me alive, not kill me."

Chapter 13

DREAMS

To my utter amazement, Kai turned out to be an excellent driver. Navigating was a snap too; all I had to do was look at a map and then think it to him. We had an uneventful trip all the way to Lexington. Sami and I slept most of the five hour drive, and we made it in plenty of time to make our seven a.m. flight. It was a good thing we arrived early, Sami set off the metal detectors again, so it took extra time getting through security. Kai had to take his sunglasses off, I thought the gig was up, but when he turned to look at me, his eyes were a soft, almost undistinguishable glow.

After we made it through security and out of ear shot of other people, I had to ask. "What happened with your eyes?"

"Ariel gave me two little discs to put on them, she called them contacts. Extremely annoying, but it would be best if I leave them in until after our flight."

"Tell me about Ariel. Why is she your sister, but I'm not?"

He chuckled softly. Sami moved in so she could hear the story as well. "Do you know what happens when you mix wind and water?"

Sami answered, "Yeah, it's called a storm, why?"

"When Ariel and I first met, we did not get along. The truth of it is, we almost wiped out an entire civilization from the fighting. Lilith had to intercede. She bound us together with the web of a spider and made us work together to create something. What we came up with was a violation of nature, but just the same, it survived and flourished. It showed us that even though we are so diverse, we can still coexist. Instead of untying the web that bound us, Lilith dissolved it into our skin. We are now bound eternally as brother and sister."

"What did you two create?" This had to be good; a violation of nature, my interest was piqued.

"It was a duck-billed platypus. Part duck, part beaver, lays eggs and nurses it young. I was aiming more for an aquatic mammal, but Ariel loves birds."

"Finally, one of the great mysteries of our world has been explained!" Sami exasperated.

The three of us couldn't stop laughing the whole time waiting for boarding call.

* * *

The flight to Atlanta was uneventful. For the first time in my life, I was grateful for being bored. Sami and I spent the long hours cooped up in a hotel room updating Kai on the technological revolution. Televisions, phones, radios, cameras, MP3 players, computers and satellite dishes were among the many lessons. Kai liked the MP3 player the most. After listening to mine for several hours, he commented that my choice in music hadn't changed, I still liked *all* music. By night fall, Sami and I got ready for bed just for something to do. Kai looked wide awake still, even after driving all the night before. I silently asked him, *"Don't you ever sleep?"*

He looked into my eyes before responding, "Sleep is a luxury I have not enjoyed since the transformation. I do not get tired."

"Really?! You never sleep?"

"No, never, I envy you, to be able to close your eyes and escape reality, if only for a brief time, to live in a whole other world. The best I can do is meditation, but that is not the same. I am still completely aware of reality when I meditate. Enough about me, you two need to sleep."

Sami asked a strange question. "Do we get a choice this time?" I wasn't aware that Kai had put her to sleep before.

"No, now good night," with that, he put Sami to sleep, and tucked her in. Then it was my turn.

"What's the urgency, we're going to be on a plane for fifteen hours, I'd rather sleep then."

"I know, but I want to try something and I can only do it while you sleep. Now, no more arguments, off to bed with you."

"Are you going to tuck me in too?"

"Of course, now into bed," He murmured softly. I stopped arguing with him and crawled into bed, he ran his fingers across my eyes and I was sound asleep. I thought I felt him kiss my forehead, but I couldn't be certain. My dreams came quickly.

I was lying in a field of wildflowers; the smell of them permeated the air. The sun was warming my face. I turned my head to the side. I knew he would be there. He reached out and took my hand.

"Come; let me show you my city." He stood up in a movement so quick, I flinched. He realized his mistake and very slowly helped me to my feet. "Welcome to Atlantis."

I looked passed him and saw a city glimmering in the sunlight. It was the most beautiful place I had ever seen. On the edge of the city was a ring of stone statues, they apparently went all the way around the city spread out one hundred yards apart. They looked familiar to me, I was certain I had seen these statues before. As we walked nearer to them, I knew they were exact replicas of the statues of Easter Island; only these were in much better condition. We walked pass the statues and into the city, in the center was an enormous black pyramid, surrounding the pyramid were hundreds of buildings made up of marble and black obsidian. These must have been the homes of the people roaming the streets. I looked to Kai.

Kai didn't open his mouth, but I could still hear him clearly. "These are Atlantians, my people. They no longer exist, wiped out by the great flood which left the city under water. Ariel tells me that raising it would be a bad idea, satellites would see it, and there would be a hoard of anthropologists on the island in a matter of days. Raising Atlantis will have to wait until it is time. I am the only one that can search the city for clues, but that would mean I will have to leave you."

I continued our silent conversation as we walked through the busy streets, "Is this just a dream?"

"No, this is a memory. One of my memories. If you remember, I theorized that when I tried to turn you into an immortal, I altered your chi. I think you have the same gift as I do, or at least very similar, that you can hear other people's thoughts if they are meant for you. The night you spent in Chichen Itza you had a dream. I heard that dream. Do you remember it?"

"Yes, I remember it. I dreamt that you were giving me a tour of the pyramid." I was too embarrassed to go into details.

"Yes, that is the dream I am referring to. You had asked me a question about how the pyramid looked in the past. I am certain that it was not one of your memories because you had not been there. I showed you that, it was one of my memories."

"You brought me here to help you search the city?"

"Yes, with any luck you will see something out of place that I always accepted as normal. If we can find the clues we need this way, I will not have to leave you to search Atlantis myself."

"If you don't raise the city, how are you going to search it? Can you breathe under water?"

He laughed softly, "I do not need to breath. It is only necessary to breath if I want to smell my surroundings."

I broke the silent conversation and blurted out, "You don't need to breath?!"

Kai remained silent; he sensed that I was a little terrified by the revelation. I saw the concern in his eyes, and calmed myself before speaking again. "Sorry, it's just a lot to accept, I'm ok with it though. It's just a little hard to wrap my head around that kind of knowledge. What do you smell here?"

"I smell you and Sami, cheap linens, soaps and lotions in the bathroom, bleached towels, and sand." I had forgotten that this was just a dream, and we were in Atlanta not Atlantis.

I slipped back into silent conversation, there was a certain amount of intimacy in sharing each other's thoughts that I was enjoying. "Why don't you want to come here? It's such a beautiful city."

"It is not about coming here that bothers me. It's leaving you for any length of time that has me anxious."

"I'll be fine. I have my guardians and Ariel to look out for me. What could happen?"

"I know they are quite capable of taking care of you. I am anxious about leaving you because it will be the hardest thing I will ever have to do. I am not sure that I am able to leave you, even if only for a short time."

We finally reached the inner circle of homes. As I gazed towards the pyramid, several structures caught my eye. In what looked to be a town square, sat an exact replica of Stonehenge, only this one was completely intact. Stonehenge was aligned with the north corner of the pyramid. Lined up with the west corner of the pyramid looked like the Roman Coliseum. The pyramid itself looked to be twice the size of the one in Chichen Itza. It looked to be carved out of one piece of obsidian, there were no seems. Going up the center of each face of the pyramid were steps that lead up to a platform with a temple and a capstone on top of it. Running down both sides of the steps were hieroglyphs imbedded into the obsidian and painted in gold covering every square inch of the pyramid.

Kai saw that I was incredulous, and gave me even more reasons to be amazed. "This city was built by God himself, before mankind roamed out of Eden. This was once the greatest city in the world, until the great flood. Since then, Atlantis has become nothing more than a myth, a treasure to inspire man's imagination."

"How did the legend survive after all the people were wiped out? Who would have recreated Stonehenge, and the Roman Coliseum?"

"The answer is so simple, you have overlooked it."

"You mean to tell me that Noah and his family were Atlantians?"

"Of Course; after the water retreated, Noah and his sons went their own ways, and with them, they carried the knowledge of Atlantis to be handed down from one generation to the next. On the other side of the pyramid are the Pantheon of Greece and a statue . . . well, let us just say that a friend of mine was trying to be humorous when he carved the statue."

He had me curious, "Can we go see it?"

"Soon, I want to show you the temple first. If there is anything of use to us, it will most likely be in the temple."

As we ascended the pyramid, Kai was pensive. I hadn't realized until then that some of the scenery was incomplete, as if a painter had not used the entire canvass to create his masterpiece. In the places where the scenery was missing, it was a bright light, like light shining off of polished metal. I silently asked Kai, "What is that?" as I pointed to a place on the pyramid that should have had hieroglyphs.

"Something that I never paid any attention to, if I do not know what is there, then I cannot imagine it for you to see."

"What language is this? I don't recognize it."

"This is the original language, the first language created by Lilith and Adam. Adam gave up a lot more than a rib to create Eve; he also gave up his ability to speak the language that he himself helped create. It was only Lilith and I that had the ability to speak this language. Lilith is gone and I . . ."

". . . have the gift of babble and cannot pass the language on to anyone." I finished his thought for him. "The language died with my mother."

"Yes, but I can translate for you if you would like."

"It looks like that might take a while. Can you sum it up for me?"

"It is the history of the Earth. The North steps describe how God created this planet and the solar system that contains it. Stonehenge is a representation of the solar system and how it works. The south steps describe the process of creating life and the balances needed to maintain life. The East and West are dedicated to evolution, the path that shows that all living things are bound by a common beginning." He finished his editorial as we reached the platform. Lucky for me, this was just a dream, otherwise that climb would have killed me.

"I definitely want to hear the unedited version of that sometime."

I took in the scenery around us as we walked around the temple to the entrance on the opposite side. I could see inside the Roman coliseum, it looked like the ball court at Chichen Itza. The field was in the shape of a capital "I" and it looked like the hoops were up on the walls for scoring. As we rounded the corner, I saw the statue that Kai had mentioned, it was huge and obviously it was a depiction of a merman with a trident in his hand surrounded by the seven heads of a sea creature that stood behind him. The last turn on the platform revealed the Pantheon from Greece. It was a majestic building, pristine in white marble. It was exactly as I imagined it, had it not been touched by the sands of time. I looked out over the city, the layout of it was perfectly symmetrical, and sat in the center of a huge island. The houses with their red terra cotta roofs formed a maze around the pyramid which reminded me of the Chinese lattice common on the architecture.

We stepped inside the temple, it should have been dark, there was no light source, but I could see perfectly. I had to remind myself that I was seeing things through Kai's eyes. It was like walking through a snow covered forest during a full moon. I could see everything very clearly. In the center of the room was an octagon shaped pedestal. On top of it sat the largest ruby I had ever seen. It was the size of a bowling *ball, light glimmered off of the thousands of facets and threw red sparkles on the walls like a disco ball. There were more hieroglyphs running down each side of the pedestal. Without taking my eyes off of the ruby, I asked, "What does all of this mean?"*

"It tells the story of the four basic elements. It says that God was lonely. He decided to create a heavenly body, a child of his own. He called this child Earth. He breathed life into this child, and called it air. His child was cold, so God created fire to warm the child's heart, but then the child became thirsty and God cried because he had nothing to give the child to ease its discomfort. God's tears fell on the Earth and the Earth was quenched, he called it water. God knew that the Earth could not live without Air, Fire and Water so he bound them together as elements."

"What does that have to do with us?"

"The power of the world lies with its elements, and we can control those elements. We have been given limitless power to protect the Earth; we just don't know what we are protecting it from."

"And the ruby?"

"You have not figured that out yet? I thought you were smarter than that?" He goaded me. "It is the heart of the Earth, part of the reason I have kept Atlantis hidden, to protect the heart." I reached out to touch it, but my hand went through it. Another reminder that this was just a dream.

I turned a full circle where I stood to take in the details of the temple. On the wall embedded into the obsidian were a golden tablet, and three empty recesses of the same size. The ruby shimmered brightly on the first symbol on the tablet and coinciding spots on the empty recesses. The tablet looked almost identical to mine. Without turning around I asked Kai, "What does this one say?"

"It is the tablet with my given name on it, just like the one you have." He was avoiding the question.

"I didn't ask what it was about; I asked you what it says."

He was reluctant to read the tablet to me, but I pleaded enough that he gave in. He muddled through it in hopes that I wouldn't catch all that he said. "It says Cainivus, the water of life, the most powerful force of nature to be wielded in the name of God."

He paused and then added, "Like I said, this is a job. I do it without pride or complaint. The other tablets were removed before the flood and placed on rafts outside the city. When the floods came, the tablets drifted off to determine the locations of the other cities. You are seeing Atlantis as it looked the last time it saw the sun.

"Cainivus? That's an awful name." I teased.

"That is enough out of you Anyanka." He teased me back.

* * *

"Awaken, Annie." I felt Kai's lips brush my cheek as he whispered.

I sat up in bed instantly and almost knock my head on Kai's. Luckily, Kai moved out of the way in time. "WOW! Was that real?"

"As real as a memory can be, now get up, we have to be at the airport in an hour." I jumped out of bed and headed for the shower just as Kai was waking Sami. Before I closed the door, I thought I heard Kai asking Sami a question. "You did not bite anyone last night, did you?" I was certain I misheard him.

Chapter 14

OASIS

We met up with the rest of the gang at the airport, although we did not acknowledge each other as part of the plan to look inconspicuous. Still, it was good to see them again. I felt edgy not knowing if they were alright. Once on the plane, Ariel whispered to us that she guaranteed a smooth flight and clear skies all the way to Egypt. She didn't help to conquer my fear of flying though.

I remembered to bring a sweatshirt for the long flight; airplanes tend to get chilly at thirty-thousand feet. I put my sweatshirt on and pulled the sleeves over my hands so that I could hold on to Kai without filling the entire cabin up with steam. He looked down at me and smiled, I hadn't realized until then that his mind had been elsewhere until I took his hand. His eyes looked a little crazed. "Is something bothering you?"

"Yes, I have not eaten in a few days, and you smell so good. I think it might be best if I switch seats with someone."

I had forgotten that the smell of my blood calls for him. It was something that he had not mentioned more than once. I didn't want him to suffer, but I was disappointed that he wouldn't be near me for the entire flight. "Oh, if you think that's best, I understand." I tried not to pout, but it was a wasted effort, I was beginning to think that he could hear my mind whether I wanted him to or not.

"I could put you to sleep, you can dream the whole way if you would like." He offered.

"I might take you up on that offer later. I think I'll spend some time with my buddies for now. I'll call you when I'm ready."

Kai nodded his head and walked to the back of the plane where Ariel, Jesse, and Ryan were sitting. I shouldn't have been surprised when Ariel came up to sit with us, Kai wouldn't be happy unless I was fully protected by an immortal. I was grateful that he sent her. I hadn't really gotten the chance to know her yet anyways. I sent Kai a silent thank you.

My impression of Ariel is that she has more energy than Sami, because she managed to keep up a conversation the entire flight. Sitting between the two of them was a little uncomfortable because neither one of them could stop bouncing the whole way. I did discover several things about Ariel. She helped establish the Underground Railroad during the Civil War, she was a key factor in the woman's movement in America in the nineteen-twenties and thirties, and she was a good friend to Martin Luther King. I was so absorbed in her stories that the sixteen hour flight felt like a quick drive to the grocery store. I had to wonder why Ariel and Kai didn't get along when they first met. Ariel seemed like an absolute sweetheart, it was so easy to get along with her.

As we were exiting the plane, Ariel whispered in my ear, "Penguins." I turned my head to look her in the eyes, and she finished the statement. "You were wondering why Kai and I didn't get along at first, the answer is penguins. A bird that lives in water, he said I was invading on his territory and he wanted to destroy my birds." I was stunned into silence, how could anyone fight over birds? Worse, how could anyone fight over birds and almost destroy an entire civilization over it?

I heard Sami respond from behind Ariel, "Good for you, I like penguins, they're so cute."

* * *

We left the airport in separate groups. I had assumed that we would meet up at a hotel. I was surprised when the taxi dropped us off at the edge of the city among some dilapidated shacks that were barely standing. We only had to wait a few minutes before the whole gang was together again. Kai was the last one to arrive, one moment I was about to ask where he was, and the next, he was standing next to me.

It was Jenny who asked the all-important question. "Are we there yet?" She even had that hint of whining in her voice like a little kid sitting in the back seat on a really long trip.

Kai was all business, "No, we have to go ten kilometers to a small oasis in the desert. We will stay there during the day and search the pyramids at night. I do not want anyone seeing us."

"We should get some food and water to take with us before we leave the city." Ryan suggested, as if he had experience in desert survival.

Ariel turned to him, "That won't be necessary, Ryan." She didn't explain herself, but I figured that if Kai wasn't objecting then she must be correct.

"Are we hiking or are we driving?" Jesse asked.

Ariel laughed, I was beginning to think it was a bad sign. Every time she laughed, we were about to get a big surprise. "Neither, we are swishing. I don't want to leave tracks for anyone to follow, and this will be much faster anyways."

I wasn't sure I heard her correctly, "Did you say *swishing*?"

"Yes, swishing, I can't explain it, it's better to just show you." Ariel turned to Kai, "All better, or should I carry Annie?"

"I am much better now, I can take her." I wasn't certain, but I was under the impression that he just ate. I had a morbid thought to ask him what he had for dinner, but I refrained, I decided it would be best not to know.

Swishing turned out to be exactly as it sounded, one moment Kai was picking me up in his arms, and swish, I was in an oasis where the tops of the pyramids were barely discernable with the drab brown surroundings. Kai set me down gently on my own two feet, I swayed and almost fell, but Kai kept his arms around me until I felt stable. I had never had vertigo before, but I was certain this is what it felt like. Ariel had brought Jesse with her. It was a strange sight to see such a refined woman cradling a large man in her arms. His weight was nothing for her insurmountable strength, she didn't even strain when she bent down to set his feet on the ground. Jesse seems a little embarrassed by the change of gender roles, but at least he didn't seem to be suffering from vertigo like I was.

Kai insisted on staying with me and Jesse and sent Ariel back to get the rest of the gang. After she left for the third time, I decided to take advantage of her absence to talk to Jesse. "Jesse, Wow! How do I say this?"

"Just say what's on your mind Annie, whatever it is, I can take it."

"I hope so, o.k., here it is. I wouldn't get too friendly with Ariel, if I were you. She might turn you into a vampire."

Jesse tried to keep a straight face, but he started laughing at me. "I know that, silly. You don't have to worry about me; she won't bite unless I ask her to."

"Oh, how did you know? About Ariel, I mean."

"Kai warned me, we had a chance to talk on the plane. He really is a decent guy, I was a little leery at first, but that's probably because I have some natural instinct to protect you."

"You too, huh?"

Just like Mike and Ryan, he was smug when he answered, "Yep!"

The whole gang had been brought to the oasis within twenty minutes. The place was amazing. The palm trees formed a thick canopy overhead that kept the sun from sweltering us. There was a small stream with plenty of fish and fresh water, and a clearing for setting up camp, which consisted of nothing more than what little we brought with us, a few changes of clothes and toiletries. After spending several hours exploring the one square kilometers of the oasis, and gathering food for dinner from the trees, Ariel called our attention to discuss the trip to the pyramids. She kept us busy through the afternoon going over key areas of the pyramids that might hold the secrets we were looking for. She said there was a secret entrance to the largest pyramid through the sphinx. As I sat on the soft grass quietly listening to her, I remembered that the sphinx had been buried under sand until the nineteen-thirties, and I wondered if my mother had anything to do with its' discovery.

I was so absorbed in Ariel's planning that I hadn't realized Kai was gone. I heard a truck disturb the quiet melody of the breeze rustling the palm fronds. I wasn't the only one to notice the sound, Mike, Jesse and Ryan all jumped to their feet simultaneously and surrounded me. Katie came to stand near me, and Sami and Jenny both took off to hide in the trees. Ariel closed her eyes and stretched her hands out to her side. A moment later she lowered her hands and began speaking, but she kept her eyes closed. "It's just Kai returning from the city. Since Annie didn't do so well with swishing, he didn't want to put her through that again. He is bringing a truck to take us back and forth to the city. I will have to cover the tracks afterwards." I was relieved by the news, I really didn't like swishing one bit, but it turned out that I was the only one that didn't like it. The guys relaxed and went back to their spots on the ground.

Kai came into the clearing moments after the sound of the truck was silenced. Sami and Jenny returned right behind Kai, they didn't make a sound, trying to sneak up on him, but Kai sensed that they were there and turned on them just as Sami was about to pounce on him. She pounced anyways in a playful attempt to knock him over, but Kai grabbed her up in his arms and flipped her onto his shoulder and carried her like a sack of potatoes. He set her down next to me, and with a big grin on his face he asked, "Is this yours?"

* * *

We stayed in the oasis until an hour after sunset. There was a full moon so navigating through the oasis to the truck was a simple matter of following Kai. He had the truck parked at the edge of the oasis and covered with palm fronds to keep it hidden. We removed the palm fronds to discover that Kai had managed to get a Hummer. It was a huge blue beast with polished chrome all over, not something that would be called inconspicuous. Kai must have sensed the negative reaction to the vehicle and defended his choice. "You are all wrong, this is a very common vehicle in and around the city, and it will blend in. Also, this thing has a lot of safety features and it is almost as indestructible as Ariel and I are. It is exactly the vehicle we need here."

Ryan was weighing the pros and cons of having such an obvious vehicle. "I suppose being obvious has its' advantages. We will look less suspicious if we are more visible, and this baby has a ten cylinder hemi so we won't have any problem outrunning any pursuers. It is also one of the few vehicles made that can handle seating all nine of us comfortably. I like it."

"Me too!" Jenny said as she was popping the hood to take a look at the motor.

Ariel rolled her eyes, an easy movement to see without the contacts to cover up the glow. "Alright, brother, you win this one."

"Why, Ariel, I am surprised you admitted defeat so quickly." Kai said mockingly. "Everyone load up, I am driving." Kai announced. Jenny and Ryan both looked crushed, but neither one argued with Kai.

"Shotgun!" I managed to get out before anyone else thought to call it.

Kai drove through the desert with the lights off until we hit the main road running north and south along the Nile River. The only light for miles was the glow of the moon and the lights of the gauges on the dashboard. The glow cast a shadow on Kai's chin. There was something there that I hadn't noticed before, a small curved scar in the shape of a crescent moon. I reached over to feel it, Kai didn't react to my touch, he held still so I could investigate this discovery.

"I thought there was nothing but the sword that can penetrate your skin. How did you get this scar?" I whispered softly to him. The hum of the motor was louder than my voice, and when he didn't answer immediately, I wasn't sure that he heard me. *Kai*, I thought to him.

He took his eyes off of the road to look at me. He was somber, and I lost the courage to ask again. I didn't need to, though, he answered the question. "I wasn't always an immortal. This scar is my reminder to always keep my temper in check. It is from the fight I had with Able. He hit me and cut my chin open. It was then that I lost my temper, it was only a moment, but that is all it took. I hit him back and broke his neck. I have since been able to keep my anger from controlling my actions, but there have been times that I have come close to losing control. I am not a perfect being. It is hard work for me to keep my self- control."

I could tell that it was hard for him to talk about it, as if it was a weakness that he didn't want revealed, and yet he held nothing back because he wanted me to know him, all of him. I still thought of him as a mysterious being, someone that would take years to get to know, and yet I felt like I knew him completely in that moment. My heart skipped a beat and I inhaled deeply. He heard my heart beat with his perfect hearing and misinterpreted it as fear. He bowed his head in shame. "I'm sorry I am such a monster, I didn't mean to frighten you."

It was just a little thing to notice, silly really, but it was the first time he used a contraction when speaking, a sign that he was still learning, still evolving. When I retorted his statement, it was the truth as I saw it. "You are not a monster, Kai. You were young, you didn't know your own strength, but you accepted the responsibility for your actions, you learned from your mistakes." I was annoyed that he was always so hard on himself; he took the blame for everything, including my own death. I didn't mean to yell at him, but I wanted to get my point across and it seemed the only way to do it. "To err is human, forgiveness is divine. Why can't you forgive yourself for what was clearly an accident?"

I heard Ariel snicker in the back seat, everyone else remained silent. I thought I heard Ariel make a comment about a head stuck in an orifice, but before I could hear the ending, everyone else was laughing. Kai remained silent, I think he was stunned, or maybe just processing what I had said. I remained quiet the rest of the trip to let him think. We pulled down a side street several blocks away from the pyramids and the sphinx. Kai held my hand and waited for everyone else to exit the hummer before he said anything. "Thank you Annie. You have saved me again. I will forever be in your debt."

"I didn't do anything. Why are you thanking me?"

"You have lifted a tremendous weight off of my shoulders, for the first time in my life I don't feel the guilt that has burdened me since the beginning of time." He lifted my hand and kissed it. I didn't know what to say, so I bowed my head and remained quiet. He put his hand under my chin and lifted so I would look him in the eyes. There was a genuine smile on his face, the look of a man that had been reborn. "Come, we have much to do. Let's go have us an adventure."

The streets of Cairo were quiet. We had only walked a few blocks when I realized that we were on the wrong side of the Nile from the pyramids. The Nile River was at least a half mile wide at this point. My friends and I were good swimmers, but swimming that distance with a current, not to mention crocodiles, I was a little skeptical. "Kai, you don't really expect us to swim do you?"

"I was thinking about it. Do you object?"

"Very much so; isn't there another way?"

"We could swish you all over there." There was a hint of humor in his voice.

"I think I'd prefer swimming with the crocodiles. What else have you got?"

"How about this?" Kai raised his hands out in front of him. It only took a moment before we could all see what he was doing. Directly in front of us, the water began separating. There was no great thunderous sound; it was all very peaceful and quiet. Within a few minutes, the water had made two perfect walls on either side of a perfectly dry walkway through the river bed.

Mike came up behind me and whispered in my ear. "Who does he think he is, Moses?"

It felt a little bit like payback when I answered him, "Yep."

Ariel led the way down into the river bed, she acted as if this was something she had seen before, and she wasn't dumbfounded like the rest of us. It felt like walking through an aquarium, but it was too dark to see through the walls, it was probably best not to know what was staring at us. I looked back to find Kai, he was still standing on the bank of the river. Ariel, who had been pushing us at a fast pace, realized I had stopped. She was by my side in a second, grabbed my arm and started pulling me along. "Don't worry Annie; he will be with us in a minute." She didn't say anything more. We reached the opposite bank in less than five minutes. As soon as we were all out of the river bed, the water flowed back to its place without a sound.

I was going to ask Ariel how Kai was going to get across, but before I could, he was standing next to me, completely dry. "Did you like that?" He whispered in my ear. He had a hint of bragging in his tone.

I was about to tell him I was impressed, but when I looked into his beautiful, glowing eyes, I forgot what I was going to say. It's possible that I also forgot my own name, fortunately, he reminded me. "Annie?"

I shook my head and snapped back into reality. "Yes, that was very impressive." He was probably beginning to think that I had some mental deficiency. It was just so hard to keep my train of thought when I looked into those eyes.

It was a short walk to the sphinx from the river, but it was all open. Ariel told us to lay flat on the ground while Kai went ahead to take care of the security guards patrolling the area. He was back in thirty seconds. I didn't want to think poorly of him, but I had to ask, "You didn't kill anyone, did you?"

"No, they're just taking a nap. Alright everyone, let's go." We were all chatting casually until we stood between the enormous front legs of the sphinx. It wasn't out of awe for the great sculpture that silenced us, it was Kai. He stiffened, smelling the air and looking through the darkness for something. He didn't whisper when he spoke, it only took a moment for me to realize that it was pointless to whisper. "Ariel, get them inside, Now!" I looked to the direction that Kai was staring, and out of the darkness I could see two ghostly white figures moving towards us. They moved like animals, but walked like humans. Their eyes had a sinister red glow to them. That was all I saw of them, Kai charged towards them and someone was pulling me backwards into a dark passageway. As the door closed, I screamed. "No! We can't leave him! He needs us, we have to help him." I felt my heart rise up into my throat. For the first time in my life, I felt sick, weak and helpless as Jesse wrapped his arms around me to keep me from running back out of the passageway. "Let me GO! He needs us!"

It was Ariel's disembodied voice that interrupted my pleading. "Annie, Kai can take care of himself. The only thing that can kill him is the sword that we left back in New London." She paused and then added quietly, ". . . and you." That sobered me up.

Before I could ask what she meant, Ariel continued. "Annie, you have the gift of fire, let's see if you can control it yet." Jesse releases me, and Ariel placed her hands on my shoulders. She turned me around in the pitch black so I had no idea which way I was facing. "Alright, close your eyes and hold your hands a few inches apart out in front of you like you would hold a soccer ball. I want you to feel the energy that flows through you. Control that energy. Make it flow into your hands. Now, build it up, make it hotter."

I did as she asked, although I didn't understand why I had to close my eyes, I couldn't see anyways. I could feel my body heat emanating from my hands. "Good, now circulate that heat between your hands, let it build up." Ariel continued with her tutorial. "Feel the heat rise. Excellent! Do you feel it?"

"Yes."

"Open your eyes." She commanded.

I opened my eyes, and saw a fireball between my hands. Ariel took a sconce off of the wall and lit it with the fire. The passageway behind me opened just then and I lost my concentration dropping the fireball, it dissipated before it hit the ground. "Kai!" It was the strangest feeling of euphoria the moment I knew he was alright. I couldn't help myself. I ran and jumped into his arms and gave him a big hug.

"What were those things?" My voice was muffled because I had buried my face in his neck to hide the tears of relief.

"Vampires! No problem." I felt the vibrations of his silent laughter. "Did you miss me?" He teased. I was too relieved to be embarrassed by my outward show of emotions.

Chapter 15

PROFOUND EFFECTS

"Everyone stay behind me, there are traps in this tunnel." Ariel announced.

I heard Jenny mumble, "Great, how many ways can a person almost die in one day?"

Jesse cautioned her, "You shouldn't ask questions that you don't want to know the answer to."

Ariel lit sconces on the walls with her torch every few yards to light the way. The tunnel sloped downward gradually, cutting deeper into the bedrock. The farther down we went, the colder it got. I was shivering before we were half way to the pyramid. Ariel stopped and pointed to the floor. "This is the first trap. I am going to release the spikes, so step back." When we were all a safe distance, Ariel stepped on a pressure switch and five long bars covered in six inch spikes sprung down in an arc from the ceiling. Ariel caught the middle two spikes before they could hit her. Stuck on the pole closest to the right side of the tunnel was a skull with a six inch spike protruding into the eye socket. Katie screamed.

"Don't worry Katie, I don't think it was anyone you knew." Ryan joked, and then added, "That wasn't appropriate, was it?"

Jenny leaned into him, "That was a whole new level of inappropriate. Strange, I was thinking the same thing."

"Oh, ha-ha, funny guys," Katie responded, "But if you hadn't noticed, the rest of the body is missing, which means there are rats in this tunnel."

Jenny shivered at the thought of rats and Ryan put his arm around Jenny's shoulder and kissed her on the cheek to comfort her. "At least someone appreciates my humor."

"I should have known someone would try to get in here." Ariel complained.

We all edged past the first trap while Ariel held the spikes to the side for us. We were to the second trap in less than a minute. It was a pit in the floor of the tunnel, at least that's what Ariel claimed. I couldn't see it, nor could any of my friends; it must have been perfectly camouflaged with the floor. Ariel jumped across at least twenty-five feet. She lit more sconces on the other side of the pit before she turned back to us, "O.K. Kai, start tossing them over." I didn't even get the chance to object. Kai picked me up by the waist from behind and threw me to Ariel's waiting arms. One by one, he tossed us all across, the only one that was happy about it was Sami. She wanted to do it again.

"Can you give us a little warning before we get to the next trap?" I was a little miffed about being tossed like a bean bag.

Ariel ignored my tone, but answered anyways. "The next trap is a pendulum. As long as we avoid stepping on the fulcrum that set it off, we won't have any problem getting past it." That sounded promisingly easy. I should have known better to think it would be. The fulcrum turned out to be dozens of nearly invisible trip wires just a couple of centimeters off of the floor and the pendulum turned out to be several that looked like giant axes jammed into the corner of the wall and ceiling, each looking very menacing.

My nerves were frayed and I just went off without thinking. "What kind of sick sadistic person would come up with this stuff?"

Ariel started pouting, "You don't like my designs? I worked very hard to keep people out of this tunnel because it is the only one that leads to the secret chamber."

"Well, job well done then, Ariel; I think you succeeded. It will be a miracle if we make it through." Mike complained. He pulled Katie in tighter to make sure she wasn't planning on going first.

"Nonsense! This is the easy part. Just don't step on the wires." Ariel started walking through the wires; it looked more like dancing than walking. Every step was graceful and certain.

"That would be great if the wires were a little more visible!" Ryan added as he started in behind Ariel. I followed behind Ryan. If Kai had his way, he would have carried me. He was having a hard time dealing with my independent nature, but Mama had never coddled me. Just the opposite, she liked dragging me into her adrenaline rush extreme sports. This didn't feel any different to me.

Sami and Kai were the last to come through the minefield. Everyone had made it through without incident until Sami tripped and set off three of the pendulum axes all at once, and she was only halfway through! Everything happened so quickly. I didn't think about what I was doing, I just reacted. Before the axes could make it to the bottom of their arcs, I had formed a fireball and threw it at them. I managed to destroy two of them, shards of metal tinkered to the ground, but the third one was heading straight for Sami. In a blurred motion, Kai swooped down and grabbed Sami in a football hold and had her standing by my side before the Axe could hit her.

Kai looked awed, like I was something special. I didn't feel special though, I felt like a freak, an exhausted freak. "Well done, Annie! Very impressive." He barely finished the compliment before I crashed into his arms. My legs felt like jelly, they wouldn't hold my weight anymore and my arms were like lead weights at my side. Kai picked me up and carried me. It was the last thing I remembered until Kai's voice pulled me back. "Annie? Annie, please answer me." His voice sounded distant but I could still hear the panic in it.

"I'm alright." I mumbled, it sounded garbled to me so I was certain no one else would understand.

"No, you're not!" I heard Ariel's voice a little clearer and she sounded annoyed. "What were you thinking? Are you trying to kill yourself? You're not ready for that kind of energy. You're too young!" Forget annoyed, she was mad.

"Sorry, I didn't know." My speech was sounding better but it was still slurred.

I opened my eyes. It took a moment to comprehend my surroundings. We were all crowded into a small stone room with hieroglyphs covering every available space on the walls. The ceiling was covered in specs, some of which had lines drawn between like connect the dots. "Where are we?" I managed to ask as the last bit of fog left my brain.

"We're in the temple near the top of the pyramid. It is directly over King Khufu's chamber." Kai responded.

"So was this trip worth the effort?" I asked as Kai set me on my own two feet. He held on to me until he was certain I could stand.

Jenny glared at me, "Effort? You were unconscious for the worst of it. Do you have any idea how many steps it takes to get to the top of a Pyramid? No? Well neither do I, but I can tell you there are a whole bunch of them. I'm hot, I'm tired, and I'm feeling a little crabby because we've come all this way for a stinking riddle that no one understands." Her tantrum finally subsided.

"Riddle? That's what all of these hieroglyphs are?"

"Yes and the only one that can read them is Kai, so they must be about the end of times. My golden tablet is missing as well. " Ariel sounded agitated, but she must have gotten over her anger with me, because she didn't have a scowl on her face anymore. I had to admit, for a small woman, she's quite intimidating when she's mad.

"What about the dots on the ceiling? What are those for?"

Everyone looked up at the same time. I was the only one to notice the carvings in the ceiling, one of the many advantages of being cradled in Kai's arms. I was in a good position to look up. "It's the constellations." Sami murmured. "Look, this is Gemini, Cancer, Leo, and Sagittarius . . ." She rattled on.

"She's right!" Ariel exclaimed. "Their positioning is wrong in relation to each other. I wonder if this is part of the riddle."

"We can figure it out later. Let's get these guys out of here before they melt." Kai suggested. I hadn't realized it was hot,

I was comfortable, but Kai made a perfect air conditioner. I looked to Jesse, he was sweating profusely.

We headed out of the room and down the stairs, Jenny was right, there were a lot of them. Going down was much easier than going up, at least according to Jesse. We made it through the tunnel without incident, although I was still annoyed about the prospect of having to be tossed over the invisible pit again. Ryan took a sconce off of the wall that was still burning and dropped it into the pit. When I looked down, my stomach lurched. The pit was at least twenty five feet across and fifty feet deep. If the fall didn't kill you, the long spikes sticking straight up from the bottom would. When Kai picked me up to throw me to Ariel, I was cursing Ryan for being curious. It is true that ignorance is bliss, at least in this instance.

We came to a dead end, or what appeared to be a dead end. Ariel reached out and touched the wall with her hand. What happened was absolutely amazing. A bright blue light arced between her fingers and the wall. The light appeared to be coming from Ariel, it spread out like a lightning bolt when it touched the wall. It continued to grow and form a door out of the stone, the door automatically swung open. The cold night air hit me as we stepped through the doorway to stand once again between the giant front legs of the sphinx.

We looked to the East and saw the predawn light growing on the horizon. "We need to get across the river before the sun comes up." Kai announced. "Sorry Annie, but we need to swish you over; we don't have time for walking." He was trying to be apologetic, but the crooked smile on his face said he wasn't sorry in the least little bit.

He moved so quickly, I didn't see him coming. I was in his arms in an instant, and my stomach was in my throat. "Close your eyes, it will help." I doubted that closing my eyes would do anything for me, but I closed them anyways.

"We're here, Annie. You can open your eyes now." I opened my eyes to see the Hummer. I was grateful that this crazy night was almost over. Kai stayed with me while Ariel brought the rest of the gang across the Nile.

"She's going to get annoyed with you if you keep making her do all of the work." I commented while we waited in the Hummer.

"Maybe, but she gets even more annoyed with me when I have to leave you."

"Why does that bother her?"

"Ariel is sensitive to the emotions around her. To her, emotions are like songs. Everyone sings a different song. She says that when I am away from you, my song sounds like a whale crying, and if you have ever heard a whale crying you would understand why she gets annoyed with me."

"Is that how she found me in Chichen Itza?"

"Yes, she heard your song. Even before, you had a unique song; it was one of her favorites. You have the same song as before, but it's more complicated now."

"Complicated?"

"It's like hearing a song played on one instrument compared to hearing a song played by an entire orchestra. It's the same song, but there is much more to hear with the orchestra. She said she knew the moment she heard you that you are Anyanka."

We returned to the oasis completely exhausted, except for Kai and Ariel of course. No one had said a word on the trip back, and I was too tired to even ask anyone what the riddle said. We arrived just as the sun was making its' appearance on the horizon. Ariel conjured a heavy wind that covered up the tire tracks leading to the oasis. My friends and I fell asleep quickly. It was midday when I finally woke to find that the only one around was Kai.

I didn't have to say a word, Kai answered the question I was about to ask. "They're close by, gathering food for dinner. I was beginning to think you had slipped into a coma. Do you normally sleep that much?"

"What time is it? How long have I been asleep?"

Kai looked up to the sun before answering me. "It's four twenty-six; you have been asleep for ten hours, thirteen minutes and fifty-two seconds."

That was the second time he answered me with that kind of precision. "Are you always so precise on time?"

Ariel walked back into the clearing with an armful of figs, dates and palm hearts. "Yes, he is. Annoying, isn't it? That's why he was nicknamed father time."

"Sorry, it's what I do, that's who I am." He was speaking to Ariel, but he never took his eyes off of me. I think he was judging my reaction, so I held my facial expression. "How do you feel about that?"

I must have kept a good poker face because he couldn't read me. The truth was, I had no idea what to think so I answered him with the first thought that I had. "Wow, you really are an old man, aren't you?"

Ariel started laughing, but the beautiful chimes of her laughter cut off quickly. She looked to Kai with a serious expression, but neither spoke. The three boys burst into the clearing simultaneously and surrounded me like they had before. Ariel dropped the food that was still in her arms and disappeared.

I couldn't raise my voice more than a whisper. "What's going on?"

Ryan answered me, "Someone is coming."

As soon as he answered my question, I heard the cry of a giant cat. The sound sent chills down my spine. It had to be close. I waited silently, surrounded by four men, feeling completely useless.

"Where are the girls?" I whispered to Mike.

"They're taking care of the visitor." He snapped at me. He was even more agitated than I was about that fact.

"It's just a nomad," Kai responded, apparently someone had reported to him. "Katie scared him off."

A few seconds later, Ariel came back to the clearing followed by a large gray wolf. The wolf eyed me and trotted over and put its' front paws on my shoulders. Some guardians I have to allow a wild animal attack me like this. I was terrified, afraid to even breathe. I stood perfectly still until the wolf licked my face with its' giant tongue. The only thing

I could say was, "Ew!" I swore the wolf was laughing at me. Then, right before my eyes, the wolf shimmered like the sun reflecting off of a mirror. Standing before me was no longer a wolf. It was Sami, butt naked. Ariel was prepared. She was holding a robe out for Sami to put on before her tail had shimmered away. "Oh Sami, this is all my fault, I'm so sorry." I gave her a hug.

"Don't be, that was so cool." Leave it to Sami to be happy that my presence turned her into a giant dog.

Just as I let go of Sami, a cheetah and a ferret came into the clearing. "Good work Katie." Mike said as he walked over to the cheetah with a robe. The cheetah shimmered like the wolf had, and in mid stride was walking on two legs and completely Katie. Mike held the robe for her to step into.

"Did you like that?" Katie was beaming with self-satisfaction. "I figured it would be easier to scare him off than to deal with him face to face." Like Sami, Katie was thrilled with having an alter ego.

Ryan walked across the clearing and picked up the ferret. "Don't forget about Jenny, she did an excellent job keeping us informed of what was going on." Ariel handed Ryan a robe. He put the ferret on his chest and draped the robe over it. A moment later, Jenny was standing in his arms. There was something there that I hadn't noticed before. Ryan caressed Jenny's back and kissed her on the forehead. There was so much tenderness in that small act; I just had to wonder if I never noticed before now.

"Well, this just sucks!" Jesse blurted out. "Why do the girls get to change into animals and we don't?" He really sounded upset.

Ariel walked over to Jesse and put her hand on his cheek. "You don't know, do you?" Jesse shook his head no.

"It is the natural order. In every other species on this planet, the females are the hunters and the males are the protectors. It is only because of Adam that men became the hunters of your species. The natural order has been reestablished in this group. Don't worry my love; Annie is having profound effects on you as well."

Jesse's mood improved immediately. "Oh? Anything cool like turning into wild animals?"

"No, but your strength, speed and intelligence should improve."

Jesse's face fell, "That's it, that's all we get?"

"None of you are aging. Is that cool enough for you?" Ariel smacked his face lightly.

Chapter 16

FIGHTING

"When twilight sets across the land and the four corners are shrouded in darkness, the four horsemen will ride out and unleash their wrath upon the Earth. When light returns to the land, the three kings will sit on their thrones and bring balance to the world. The great cycle will begin again." Kai put his hands up, "That's it, that's all that was written in the pyramid."

"What does it mean?" Katie asked for everyone's sake.

"I have no idea. Did you get anything out of it Ariel?" Kai asked.

"No, it doesn't make any sense to me either."

Maybe I missed something, but I had to ask an obvious question. "Where did the date December twenty-first, two-thousand-twelve come from?"

Kai had begun pacing in the clearing, obviously trying to decipher the riddle. Ariel answered for him. "The last line of the riddle, 'the great cycle will begin again.' The Earth goes through a cycle every twenty-six-thousand years. This cycle will end on December twenty-first, and the next cycle is to begin on December twenty-second, two-thousand-twelve, Kai's birthday. This will be the fifth cycle that Kai has witnessed."

Katie jumped into the conversation. "Don't you guys remember? According to the Mayan calendar, there is only four cycles. There is no fifth cycle."

Katie had a valid point, but I was more interested in another important fact. "Your birthday is the winter solstice?" I asked Kai. I hadn't given much thought to it, but I should have known.

"Yes, I am your opposing force. Summer, winter, fire, water. What can I say, opposites attract." He kept his head down and continued pacing while he spoke.

"What happened at the beginning of the first four cycles?" Jenny asked, as she snuggled up closer to Ryan in the cool evening air.

Kai stopped pacing to answer. "The first cycle was the dawn of man. It wasn't just the day I was created; it was also the day Able was born. The second cycle was marked by the great land migration, the third was the great flood, and the fourth cycle was the last ice age."

"Was there anything catastrophic at the beginning of the first cycle?" Sami asked.

"I don't remember; I was an infant. If the second, third and fourth cycle are any indication though, we can expect great turmoil, some will survive but most won't."

Ryan pushed his glasses up on his nose, he was all business. "Kai, is there anything else we can get from the pyramid?"

"No, we have all the information we can get, it's just a matter of deciphering it."

"What about the constellations on the ceiling?" Ryan continued. I was under the impression he was trying to make a point.

"I think they are a part of the riddle. I have it all memorized, I just need to write it down for all of you."

"May I make a request then?" Ryan pushed on.

"Of course."

"Let's get out of here, go find a hotel or something. I have never been in such desperate need of a shower in all my life."

Kai turned away from Ryan; he looked edgy about leaving the safety of the oasis. "Ariel, what do you think?"

She considered the options for a brief moment before answering. "I agree with Ryan, he is in desperate need of a shower."

* * *

We left the serenity of the oasis in the middle of the night. Our destination was Rome. I had never been to Rome; the history was too well documented to ever draw Mama and me to visit. One thing was certain . . . Rome had a lot of history.

I made the mistake of looking at the speedometer while Kai was driving, I about had a heart attack. He was driving well over one-hundred miles per hour and still complaining that it was too slow. He made a comment about getting out and pushing would be faster, and since he wasn't suffering a fiery torment, I had to believe him. We made the one-hundred-fifty mile trip to the port city of El Iskandariya in Northern Egypt in less than two hours. We were all grateful to get hotel rooms and freshen up before the next leg of the journey, a long boat ride across the Mediterranean Sea. Ryan took the opportunity to book passage on a cruise ship for all of us. The boat was to leave by noon that day. Ariel complained that she wouldn't have time to show us around the city. It was just as well, she kept complaining that her favorite library had burned down.

Kai was looking agitated all morning, pacing back and forth across the hotel room. I didn't have the nerve to ask him what was wrong. I jumped out of my skin when Ariel yelled at him. "Just go already, we can take care of her while you're gone."

He stopped pacing and bowed his head in defeat. He kneeled down in front of me at the foot of the bed and took my hand. "Ariel's right, I should hunt before we leave. I won't be gone long, I promise."

I wasn't sure if he was trying to placate me or himself. I knew he must be suffering just by being near me and I hated causing him that kind of pain. "I'll be fine. Go, happy hunting." He gave me that devilish half smile that took my breath away. I couldn't help myself, I leaned towards him without thinking, his lips were so close to mine. Just before our lips met, he pulled away and stood up.

"Fine, I'm going. Stop being so bossy Ariel." He left without another word.

"What was that all about?" I was curious why Ariel was so anxious to get rid of Kai.

"It's nothing for you to worry about. I'm already feeling much better now that he's gone hunting." She buzzed around the room picking up wet towels and putting the dirty clothes back in my luggage. "I think it would be best if you all get a good meal before we leave. I know a place down by the docks, close to the warehouse district, that serves food a little more to your liking than what the local cuisine has to offer."

"Sounds good to me, I'm starving." My stomach growled to confirm my statement.

"Yes, I know." Ariel exasperated.

* * *

We gathered up the gang from their adjoining hotel rooms and piled into the Hummer. Ariel insisted on driving. It was a short distance to the restaurant but it took a while to get there. Driving in Iskandariya was like driving in New York City during rush hour. As we sat in traffic, I wondered who was missing their Hummer by now. I opened the dash board and rummaged through the papers that were stashed in there until I found a registration. The Hummer was registered to Ariel Ramses. I don't believe in coincidences, so instead of asking Ariel, I just stated the facts. "This is your vehicle. I was under the impression Kai stole this from someone."

Ariel laughed, "Kai would never steal from anyone. He doesn't have to. 'Ask and ye shall receive.' That's all he has to do."

"Ramses?" Jesse asked as he leaned forward between the seats. "You took the name of the most beloved king to ever rule Egypt?"

"Of course, he was my husband." Ariel explained. "It is proper for a wife to take the name of the husband."

"You were married? I didn't know you could do that." Jesse sounded pleased, but there was a hint of jealousy in his voice.

"How else would I have become queen of Egypt?" Now that she mentioned it, I remembered Kai had told me that. "I married Ramses at the age of fourteen. He didn't live to be ninety because he took good care of himself, you know. We had seven children before I became an immortal. I still keep tabs on my descendants; most of them live in this area."

"You're Nefertiti?" Ryan asked from the back seat.

"I *was* Nefertiti. Lilith and I had to fake my death so I could get out of Egypt. The Illuminati tried to kill me several times, death was my only option considering the position I was in."

Jenny jumped into the conversation, "Ramses was in power during the Exodus, when Moses led the slaves out of Egypt. Were you and Kai working together on that one?"

"You are very perceptive Jenny. Kai and I met the night before the Exodus. Lilith and I had been trying to convince Ramses to release the people, but he had become obsessed with immortality and insisted on keeping his slaves so his great monuments would be completed. We tried everything we could think of, locusts, frogs, rivers of blood, nothing worked. We decided to try a more direct approach, lead the slaves out of Egypt and kill anyone who tried to follow."

"The direct approach tends to be the most efficient." Jesse interjected.

"Yes, it is, Jesse." Ariel wanted to add something more to the comment, but we finally arrived at the restaurant.

It was a strange site to behold, in the middle of a foreign country, there sat a McDonald's. Sami imbued upon us her profound wisdom. "You want to know who rules the world. There he is, a silly clown wearing a yellow and red jump suit."

After eating palm hearts, dates and figs for the last few days, the food hit the spot. I was so hungry I managed to eat two cheeseburgers and the entire order of fries. That would have been just the first course in a seven course meal for Jesse, Mike, Ryan and Katie. I couldn't believe how much food the four of them were able to consume.

"If you guys are finally done, we need to get back to the hotel to gather up our luggage." Ariel sounded a little agitated, I didn't blame her, after all, she wasn't eating, just waiting. We hurried back out to the Hummer and piled in. Jesse managed to call shotgun before me, and I climbed into the middle row of seats without complaint.

Ariel took a different route back to the hotel, hoping to avoid all the traffic. We were driving through the warehouse district not paying any attention to the boring old buildings that surrounded us. Everything happened so quickly, Ariel started swearing moments before a large black truck t-boned the side of the Hummer. I'm not certain how Ariel managed to keep the Hummer from flipping on its side. Another truck came up from behind us and rammed the Hummer. We were being herded into a warehouse. "Who is it, Ariel?" Ryan remained calm, his military mind assessing the situation and learning as much as he could about the enemy.

"The Illuminati, and they brought hired thugs with them, there's two, maybe three vampires with them. We don't have a choice, we have to fight." Ariel sounded nervous, that wasn't very comforting.

"Are there any weapons that you can smell?"

"No, which means they prefer hand to hand combat or their weapon of choice is the blade."

Brigadier General Ryan already had a plan. "Do your best to protect Annie, they will most likely use the vampires to distract Ariel while the others go in for the kill. Katie, Sami, you know what to do. Jenny, do you have the dagger with you?"

"Right here," Jenny responded and pulled a dagger out of her purse that was way too familiar to me. It was the dagger I had taken from the man that attacked me in San Miguel. I had forgotten about it until I saw the ruby eyes of the dragon on the hilt.

I looked out the window of the Hummer to get my bearings. There was sunlight filtering in through the dingy windows thirty feet up, it was enough so that I could see several men beginning to circle the Hummer seconds after we stopped rolling.

Ryan demanded our attention. "We jump out quick, and we jump out fighting. We need to get the upper hand. Katie and Sami are our element of surprise. On the count of three we all open the doors and jump out. Ready? One . . . Two . . . THREE!"

My heart jumped up into my throat as we all jumped out. I saw immediately that we were outnumbered. There was twelve of them, and only eight of us. Ryan was a madman, he jumped out of the Hummer screaming a battle cry, and he bridged the gap between himself and two of the Illuminati in moments. He did a flying side kick into the first of the men and a round house kick to the second before either one had a chance to bring their swords to bear on him.

The cheetah and the wolf flew out of the Hummer with the same ferocious tenacity as Ryan had. Mike and Jesse stayed no more than two feet in front of me; they didn't want me involved in the fight. Even Jenny was fighting, I had no idea she was capable of fighting, but she was holding her own. I was getting pissed that the guys insisted on coddling me, so I pushed myself between them and ran into the mix. That was the move the Illuminati were waiting for. Two of the vampires stayed on Ariel while the third honed in on me. He came at me with such speed I couldn't defend myself from him. He stopped inches from my face with an evil leer. I threw a punch at him, but he dodged it with ease. I tried several moves to hit him, but I missed him completely. He was toying with me. He grabbed me by the arms and spun me around. He put me in a choke hold so I couldn't breathe. He was going to kill me. I kept trying to fight him off, but that only made the last of the oxygen in my blood burn up faster. I started to see white spots in my vision, my lungs were burning and I was only seconds from passing out. That was it, I was going to die, and my friends would probably die with me.

I looked out into the vast space of the warehouse. I saw Ryan fighting two men and he was barely holding his own. Jenny was covered in blood and exhausted. Mike and Jesse were both fighting, and the most frightening sight was to see the cheetah lying on her side with a dagger in her chest.

With the last bit of consciousness I called for Kai. Even if he wasn't on time to save me, maybe he could save my friends. There was nothing left in me, I lost all hope. I was ready to give up when the arms that were choking me suddenly disappeared. I could breathe again. I collapsed to my hands and knees and gasped for air. I heard the sound of choking, I looked up and saw all of the Illuminati, except the vampires, falling to their knees and gasping for air. Their lips were turning blue and their eyes were glassing over. One by one they collapsed. The Illuminati were all dead within minutes and the vampires were gone.

I saw Ariel walking towards me. "You're late, you missed all the fun." she said mockingly.

Was she talking to me? The answer came to me on a breeze. I could smell a fresh spring rain in the air and knew that Kai was right behind me. He saved my life yet again. Before I could even revel in the fact that I was still alive, my only concern was for my friends. Kai picked me up off of the cold concrete floor and set me on my feet. "Do not fear for Katie, she has a strong heartbeat, she will be fine." Kai held me up as we walked over to the cheetah lying on the floor.

Mike, who was bruised and bleeding, was already with her, whispering in her ear. The wolf came into view from the other side of the Hummer; she was limping, but looked pleased with herself. Ryan was also limping and holding his arm in an awkward angle, it looked to be dislocated at the elbow. Jesse was unscathed, he was carrying Jenny who had a large cut on her forehead and was bleeding profusely. And then there was Ariel, she looked like she just stepped out of a beauty salon, not a hair on her head was out of place. I was grateful we were all alive, but we all had better days.

"What happened to these men?" I was staring at one of the Illuminati laying five feet from Katie. I was trying to keep myself distracted because Ariel was about to pull the dagger out of Katie's chest. I wasn't sure my stomach could handle it.

Kai took me by the shoulders and turned me so all I could see was him. "They drowned." He said in a matter of fact tone. I looked at him like he was crazy. "I do have control over all of the water, including the moisture in the air. I drowned them."

"What about the vampires? Where did they go?" I needed to keep him talking because the cheetah let out a scream that could curdle blood.

Kai pointed to the floor where I was standing. "You're standing on one of them, compliments of Jenny."

I was in fact standing in a pile of fine silt. "From Ash to Ash and Dust to Dust," Kai explained.

I jumped out of the pile. "Ew!" Kai laughed at me and rolled his eyes.

"Come on, Katie's getting up now." How did he know that I just needed a distraction? "I'll have Jesse help me clean up this mess. You can tend to Jenny. It looks like she needs you." I looked over to the group at the wrong moment. Ariel took Ryan's arm and snapped his elbow back in place. Ryan never made a sound, everyone else flinched.

I took Jenny off of Jesse's hands and tried to staunch the bleeding on her forehead. The cut wasn't deep, but scalp wounds always bleed profusely. While I was patching her up I had the time to ask her about the dagger. I tried to be nonchalant about it. "So, your handy with a knife, I didn't know that about you."

Jenny looked away before answering. "Yes, I found the dagger in your luggage." She answered the question I didn't even bother to ask. "Kai said it might be useful and I should bring it with us. He said it was made from the teeth of a hydra, or something like that. I don't know about all that, but it worked great on the vampires. And since it isn't made of metal, I was able to get it past the metal detectors and onto the plane." I just couldn't picture it: cute, little, innocent Jenny killing a vampire. I shook my head, not that I didn't believe her, it was more of a submission to accept the craziness of my life.

Jesse and Kai picked all of the bodies up and put them in the Hummer. Kai rolled the front windows down and then pushed the Hummer out of the warehouse and into the sea. We split up and took the two trucks back to the hotel to gather our luggage. We did our best to clean up all the blood and bandage the cuts, but we still looked motley.

"You guys look like you were in a train wreck." Ariel assessed. "You might as well claim you know each other when we get to the boat. You can claim you were in a bad car accident together. It's the truth anyways, just not the whole truth."

Chapter 17

GOODBYES

We spent three days on the cruise ship 'Carpe Diem' without a single traumatic event. For the first time in weeks, we were able to let our guards down and just have fun. Kai had to avoid being in close proximity to the other passengers because of his gift of babble, so he only came out of the room at night when most of the passengers were sleeping. On the second day of the voyage, I slipped away from my friends out on the deck to spend some time with Kai.

Kai's face lit up when he opened the door and saw me standing there. "I had a question for you. I hope you don't mind the intrusion." It was a lame excuse, but it was better than telling him I wanted to stare into his beautiful eyes.

"Your company is always welcome. I wanted to ask you something as well, but you first." He stepped aside and let me enter.

I was going to sit down but there were no chairs in his room, only the bed. I opted to stand. "Jenny said you know the story behind the dragon dagger, would you mind telling me?"

"Of course, but might I ask you how you came to be in possession of it before I begin?"

I cringed when he asked me that, he wouldn't be happy when he found out the truth. "Does it matter how I got it?" I tried to avoid answering his question, but it felt like his eyes were burning into my soul and I couldn't keep the truth from him. I looked down at the floor and mumbled quickly. "I took it from a man that tried to kill me with it."

Kai went rigid. I knew he wouldn't take it well. It took him a few moments to thaw, but when he did, he acted as if I had said nothing. "Have you heard the story of a man named Jason and his ship Argo?"

"Of course, that is the epic novel 'Odyssey' by Homer. Jason sailed the seven seas in search of the golden fleece."

"He wasn't searching for a golden fleece." Kai laughed at my historical inaccuracy. "He was searching for his golden tablet, among other things." Kai corrected me.

"Jason is Buddy?" I concluded.

"Yes. On a journey to find his tablet so he could build Valhalla. He was also looking for a weapon to fight against the vampire population that was amassing in Europe. He sailed to what is now Thailand and down the Hades River in search of Hydra, the gate keeper of the underworld. Buddy figured if the beast was meant to keep the lost souls in Hades, then maybe it could recapture the souls that evaded death. The hydra was an amiable foe and Buddy had no choice but to slay the beast. Buddy removed four of her canine teeth and fashioned them into daggers. He used them quite successfully to keep the vampire population under control. He was still human through all of this. He is quite the charismatic adventurer."

"I have one question then. Why would someone try to use the dagger to kill me?"

Kai cringed again, "Because the Illuminati have no way of knowing how far along you are in your transformation. Your skin will harden like mine and will become impenetrable." He raised his hand and brushed the side of my neck with his cold fingers. He gently traced the bruises left from being choked two days prior. "Apparently you are not as far along as they suspected." I could see a storm brewing in his eyes. I could only imagine what he was thinking and it made me shiver with fear.

"Enough about that," Kai's eyes softened instantly. "I have a question to ask you. It has been two weeks, are you frightened by me still?" There was a hint of sadness in his voice.

I became aware just then that the idea of hurting me, hurting my feelings even, caused him pain. At that precise moment I had absolute faith that Kai would never, could never hurt me. And although it would take me a lifetime or more to get to know this wonderful, beautiful man, I knew I had nothing to fear. My answer was simple and confident. "No." I took a step to stand toe to toe in front of him so I could look him directly in the eyes. "I may not know you very well, but I know you would never do anything to hurt me."

"I would rather burn in hell for eternity than harm one hair on your head." He put his arms around my back, and gently pulled me to him. I put my hands on his arms and leaned my head on his muscular chest. "Can I ask you another question?" He murmured.

"Yes." I whispered.

"Do you love me?"

He took me completely off guard; it was a question that I could not answer. I pushed away from him to look him in the eyes again. There was a hint of pain in them, and it felt like I was being stabbed in the heart. "I . . . I . . ." I had to take a deep breath and try again.

Kai put his finger to my lips. "You do not have to answer if you do not want to." He looked crushed.

"Kai, I'm sorry, it's just that I have no idea what love is, this is all brand new to me."

He smiled again. "I suppose I had that one coming to me." He mused.

"What do you mean?"

"I was one-hundred-three thousand years old and I could not answer that very question when you asked me. It was not until I was losing you that I was able to admit my feelings. I swore that if I had the chance to do it all again, I would not be afraid to tell you how I feel. I love you, Anyanka. You are the only woman that has ever touched my heart." He said it with such intense emotions, there was no room to doubt his feelings for me.

"Will you be patient with me?" I kept my head down. I didn't think I could handle the intensity of his eyes.

"I will wait all eternity for you, as long as I have you in my life."

"Can I ask you a personal question?"

"You can ask me anything, I will not hold anything back from you."

"You said I was the only woman you ever loved." I could feel my face flush bright red; it was harder than I thought to ask the question. I had to turn away before I managed to blurt it out. "Are you a virgin?"

"Yes, I am untouched." He said nonchalantly. "Believe me it is not from a lack of potential mates. I never had an interest in joining with a woman. I was complete, not wanting for anything."

I'm sure I was pouting, but I couldn't help myself. "You don't have any desire for me?"

"How did you come to that conclusion?" He didn't let me answer. "You are the only woman I have ever, since the beginning of time, had any desire for. From the time I met you, even though I was denying it to myself, I wanted to be with you in every possible way. I could not stay away from you, even when I was ordered to stay away. I will wait for you though, and if you decide I am not the one for you, I will respect your decision."

Just listening to him proclaim his undying love for me set my entire being on fire. My heart was pounding and my skin was tingling. I desperately wanted to kiss him, I needed to kiss him. I must have been sending my thoughts to him, because he bridged the gap between us and whispered in my ear. "May I kiss you, Annie?"

I turned back around to face him before I answered. "Yes."

He leaned down slowly, just inches between us. The smell of fresh spring rain permeated the air around us. The anticipation was unbearable, all I had to do was go up on tiptoes to get what I wanted, but I waited, remembering that he was in pain from denying himself my blood. I let him make the move. He was looking into my eyes, judging my reactions. Just as he was about to bridge the final gap, he stopped and pulled away.

"She has the absolute worst timing." He mumbled through gritted teeth. "Come in Ariel." I looked to the door, but I couldn't see it through the thick haze in the room.

Ariel opened the door, I could just make out her silhouette in the doorway. "What have you two been doing?" She accused. She waved her arm to dispel the steam from the room. I could feel my face turn bright red. "Never mind, I don't want to know. You two need to come with me, we found something interesting from the data Lilith left us."

We followed Ariel down the hall to her room. Jesse and Mike were sitting on the bed with Sami in between them, pouting. Katie was sitting across the room with the laptop sitting on a dresser. I wanted to ask where Ryan and Jenny were, but decided that was none of my business. Kai walked over to Katie, and I hopped on the bed behind the other three.

"What did you find Katie?" Kai was all business. I wondered how he could switch modes so quickly. I was still in steamy mode and hoped no one else noticed.

"Look here," Katie pointed to the screen. "Lillian had this section of the pyramid enlarged and computer enhanced. It was weathered badly but some of it is still visible."

Kai leaned over Katie's shoulder to get a good look at the computer screen. "It says 'in order to move forward to the next era, the wise will look to the past for answers. History will repeat itself.'"

Ariel walked over to Kai and put a hand on his shoulder. "You have to go to Atlantis, Kai. You can't avoid it."

Kai snapped at Ariel, "I know! Why do you think I am taking all of you to Vatican City?"

"Don't get pissy with me mister." Ariel snapped back at him. It looked like a sibling argument was about to ensue.

"I'm sorry." Kai backed down immediately. "You know I trust you, it is just so hard to leave her."

"Why do you have to go to Atlantis?" Katie asked.

"The pyramid in Atlantis has the entire history of the Earth written on it, even before mankind. It will have the history of every new beginning on it. Unfortunately, I never read all of it."

"Vatican City?" Sami asked. "Does that mean the Catholics have it right?"

"Yes and No," Kai answered vaguely.

"What's that supposed to mean?" Mike responded.

"It means they are neither right nor wrong. Any religion that can lead a person to live a good life and follow the guidelines set forth by God, has it right, but not everything they preach is correct."

"What about Christianity verses Judaism?" Jesse asked.

"What about them?"

Jesse wasn't sure how to ask the question, so he simplified. "Do you believe in Christianity?"

Kai and Ariel looked at each other. I was under the impression that Ariel was telling him how to answer. "I am more Christian than Jesus Christ himself. I will say no more on the subject." Kai left the room without another word.

"What's that supposed to mean?" Ryan asked no one in particular.

Since Kai had already left the room, Ariel explained for him. "He only meant that Jesus was Jewish, not Christian."

"That's comforting." Ryan responded.

I wanted to follow after Kai, but Ariel stopped me before I could leave. "Oh, no you don't."

"Why?" I felt like the defiant child standing in front of her.

"You shouldn't ask questions that you don't want answered. I need you to go take a cold shower." I would have argued with her, but I was under the impression Ariel was the type that you didn't want to make an enemy. Without so much as an argument, I bowed my head and then marched to my room to take a shower. I wasn't planning on taking a cold shower, but as soon as I got under the spray, it turned cold. I was shivering when I got out, and that seemed to make Ariel very happy.

We waited until the rest of the passengers exited the cruise ship before we left our rooms to venture out into the busy streets of Rome. Jesse and Mike were at my sides, Ryan and Ariel took point, and Kai took the back. The girls stayed loosely to the sides. Everyone kept the formation casual so that anyone walking by wouldn't notice, but I felt like it was overkill.

As we walked up the hill from the dock, Ariel started pointing out some of the historical sites like a tour guide. I don't think anyone had ever had a tour like this, though. "This is the Temple of Venus and Rome. It was dedicated to me in 629A.D."

Jesse sounded jealous. "It should have been bigger."

Ariel turned around as we were walking to give Jesse a kiss. "You are so adorable. I could just eat you up." I cringed. Even though I adore Ariel, I was still feeling overprotective of my hunting buddy.

Ariel changed the subject quickly. I think she was feeling my tension. She pointed to a giant arch, "That is the arch of Constantine. He was the Emperor that changed religion forever. During his reign as Emperor, the city was almost completely destroyed from the pagans and the Christians warring. It was Constantine's decision to unite all under one religion. He formed a counsel that decided which books were to be admitted into the Bible and which ones were to be ignored. Little known fact, Constantine wasn't Christian until he had a "vision" (she used her fingers to make quotations) on his death bed." She was about to say something more, but thought better of it.

"Alright Kai, we will get taxis to take us to Vatican City." All eyes turned on Ariel. "He doesn't like having Annie exposed like this. He's feeling anxious."

We split up into three groups to take taxis up to Vatican City. Kai and Ariel rode with me. I enjoyed having Ariel with us because so much of the ancient city was dedicated to her, Lilith and Kai. It was like being in Rome when Rome was the greatest city on Earth. "There's the obelisk that Alexander the Great brought back from Egypt as a shrine to me. Oh, and how he loved women." I got the impression Ariel was fascinated by the man.

She continued the tour guide speech. "There's the pyramid he built for me as well. It's kind of small but it was the thought that counts."

Kai didn't say much as we drove through the busy streets until we drove by the Coliseum. "Do you remember this from Atlantis? The sole purpose of the arena is to encourage men to become greater than they are by challenging them to defy the boundaries set in their own minds. Some men died while others were elevated to legends. Unfortunately, it is better known for the persecution of Christians."

Ariel didn't approve of Kai's assessment, "Barbarians? Rome is better known for the great thinkers of history. Over there is the Forum, not much is left of it, but on those very steps men like Plato, Socrates and Aristotle preached their wisdom to the masses. They were brilliant men, I enjoyed their company greatly."

Ariel and Kai argued back and forth as we drove through the crowded streets and up the hill to Vatican City. I could never doubt for a second that these two were siblings. The taxi dropped us off at the entrance to a huge square that was blocked off so no traffic could enter. I paid the driver while Ariel gathered up the rest of the gang as they arrived minutes after us.

"Where do we go from here?" Katie asked as she slipped her arm through Mike's.

"I think we should follow the crowd." Kai pointed to the general direction of a huge crowd. "I've never been here so I'm just guessing, but I would say, where there's a crowd, we are likely to find the Pope." Kai looked nervous as he looked out into the crowd.

Ariel put her hand on his shoulder. "Don't worry brother, they're Catholics, they will most likely consider it a miracle and not even consider that you are the cause.

He chuckled softly, "You're right, they are a superstitious bunch."

Again, the gang gathered around me as we headed towards the crowd. I saw what appeared to be guards scattered throughout the crowd. They were easy to spot with their bright blue and yellow vertical stripes and splash of red on their sleeves topped off with black berets with red plumage and swords hanging at their sides. "Who are they?" I asked no one in particular.

"That is the Swiss Guard." Ariel replied, "It means we are headed in the right direction."

"Why are we here in the first place?" Jesse asked.

"The Pope owes Kai a favor and it's time to pay up. Brilliant if you ask me, even the Illuminati wouldn't dare desecrate this sacred ground." Ariel paused and then added, "Not unless they are desperate."

"Are you trying to make us feel better?" Katie asked sarcastically.

"Come on, and try to stick together." Ryan said as he started to push his way through the crowd. Ryan was easy to follow with his long red hair. We made it to the bottom of the stairs of St. Peter's Basilica where the Pope himself was seated twenty feet from where we stood.

"What is the name of this pope?" Kai asked.

"Pope Benedict the sixteenth, I believe." Ryan replied. I nudged him. I was amazed that he would know the answer to that. "What? I'm Catholic, what did you expect?" He turned back to Kai. "How do you propose we get past the guards?"

"We don't need to. Ariel?" Ariel wiggled in next to Kai, and when the Pope was looking in their general direction, they both removed their sunglasses for a brief moment.

That must have been enough, because the Pope immediately called a member of his guard over. There was a brief conversation, and then we watched and waited while the Pope continued with the Papal Audience. Moments later, a member of the Swiss Guard came and escorted us out of St. Peter's Square.

"Where are you taking us?" Sami asked.

"To the Pope's apartment," The guard replied, but his lips were speaking a different language. "He is obligated to keep his schedule. He will meet with you in one hour. He asked that you make yourselves comfortable while you wait." The guard led us to a building adjacent to the Basilica. We took an elevator to the top floor; the guard had to use a key just to push the button. As the elevator opened, the guard stepped aside to let us pass.

All nine of us stared in utter amazement at the apartment. It was enormous, and filled with works of art from one end of the room to the other. It wasn't gaudy or extravagant, which made it that much more spectacular. There was a marble statue of a woman wearing a tunic, a bow in one hand and the other reaching for an arrow from the quiver on her back, and a dog by her side. I looked closer. The face belonged to my mother. I pointed at it, but I couldn't find my voice.

Kai took my hand and gently rubbed it. "Yes, that is Lilith; this statue represents her role as Diana, the Deity of the hunt. And look over here." He led me across the room to a statue near a palm tree. "This is Ariel, also known in this region as Venus." I looked into the blank eyes of the statue, it was definitely Ariel.

I had an epiphany. "The Kuklukan pyramid in Chichen Itza is Lilith's pyramid? Lilith . . . . my mother, is the plumed serpent god of the ancient Mayans?"

Kai answered gently, "Yes, remember Lilith's alter ego is the snake."

"Yes, I remember. If Ariel is Venus, then the inner pyramid is hers?"

"Yes, and I am represented as Chak, the Deity of Rain."

"What about Buddy? Is he represented in Chichen Itza?"

"Of course he is. Can you not guess?"

"Buddy is the bearded man in the Temple of the South at the ball court." I stated, it was so simple like it was something I should have known my whole life. Suddenly, the great mysteries of Chichen Itza were all explained as a moment of revelation. "He sits opposite of Venus in the Temple of the North. Ariel and Buddy are opposing forces. Earth and Air, Spring and Fall." Kai nodded his head in confirmation.

There was a statue at the far end of the room that I recognized. It was the statue of Atlas, the man that held the weight of the world on his shoulders. I walked over to it with Kai silently behind me. I wasn't at all surprised when I looked at the face and saw Kai. The body was definitely his as well. He leaned down to whisper in my ear. "This is who we are, myths and legends. We are creatures of great power that men fear and honor. Some call us gods or angels; others call us demons and devils. We are none of these. We are the keepers of the Earth, we are the witnesses of time, and we are the hand that passes judgment when God orders us to do so." Kai pointed to a painting at the opposite end of the room from Atlas.

I walked slowly towards it, understanding for the first time what Kai had said. I heard the words he said to me the night before our journey began, 'I am neutral, I am just doing my job.' On the wall, in a large gilded frame was a painting of the four horsemen. I felt like I was being pulled to it by a giant magnet. My heart was in my throat and I couldn't say a word. I stood staring at the painting for a long time. I could see the faces of three of the horsemen, Kai, Ariel, and the third that must be Buddy. The forth horseman's face was obscured by long flowing hair, but I knew it was me. I stood there staring, not thinking, not feeling, just accepting as I took in all the details of the painting.

I snapped out of my stupor when I heard the elevator doors open. I turned to see the Pope step out. Kai was the first to greet him; he didn't bow or kiss the Pope's ring like they did in movies. Kai held his hand out and waited for the Pope to do the same, a simple hand shake. I stayed back, feeling a bit awkward.

"I ask that the rest of you make yourselves comfortable." The Pope said, he was obviously speaking in a different language. "Cain, we can speak in my office." The Pope held his hand towards a door to my left waiting for Kai to lead the way.

"Anyanka comes with us." Kai announced. The Pope's eyes lit up in acknowledgement.

"Very well," The Pope nodded his head to Ariel, "Nefertiti." Ariel nodded back without a word.

Kai took my hand and lead me into the Pope's office. There was a large mahogany desk sitting in the center of the room facing the door with a giant red velvet chair with gold trim sitting behind it. Kai sat me in one of the two smaller chairs facing the desk and stood behind me as the Pope walked around to sit in his chair.

The Pope opened a desk drawer and pulled out an old scroll. "I have been the pope for just under seven years; this letter has been handed down from one pope to the next for seven-hundred and five years, always with the message that as the pope, this obligation must be fulfilled." He patted the scroll. "I have read the contents of this scroll, I was under the impression that Anyanka," He held his open hand towards me, "no longer existed, though I had recently heard a rumor stating otherwise. I would venture a guess that Lilith was allowed to reincarnate her?"

"Yes, but at the expense of her own mortality. Lilith is gone." As Kai said the words, the hole in my chest burned, I missed my mother. I had to wipe a tear that was running down my cheek.

"May I ask where you heard this rumor?" Kai questioned the Pope.

"From an acquaintance of Anyanka's, Father Jack, the pastor from her home town." I was surprised to hear the name, but it made sense that Father Jack would come here to report to the pope after the incident at the graduation ceremony. That's why he wasn't in town for my mother's funeral.

"May I ask you a question in return?" The Pope's face went rigid. "What of the secret that you are bound to keep?" The Pope's voice rose in volume slightly, he seemed agitated.

"I am bound by my word." Kai responded calmly. "I have not spoken of it."

"Does she know?" The Pope asked sharply.

"No, but if she figures it out, I will make her vow to never speak of it, she will be bound to silence as well." I had no idea what they were talking about, but it sounded intriguing.

"We need to speak in private, Cain." The Pope turned his eyes towards me.

Kai walked to the front of my chair and kneeled down in front of me. "Don't panic, my love, this is just temporary." Kai reached up and touched both of my ears, "Silence." I could see his lips moving but I couldn't hear anything he was saying. As a matter of fact, I could no longer hear anything, the birds singing, the cars on the streets down below the open window, the rustle of the curtains as the swayed when a breeze came in through the window, nothing. I was completely deaf. What annoyed me most was that I couldn't even read the Pope's lips as he spoke because he was speaking in Italian.

I decided not to cause any trouble and sat still while Kai and the Pope spoke privately. I tried to keep occupied by looking at the décor of the office, but my eyes kept wandering back to Kai, so I admired his perfect physique instead. I had a sudden urge to reach out and grab his perfect . . . . Kai moved away from me mid thought. I must have been distracting him so he removed the temptation. Five minutes of total deafness before Kai finally kneeled in front of me and touched my ears again.

"I'm sorry I had to do that to you, but it was necessary." He looked up at me with those beautiful eyes under his long lashes. I started to lean down as if to kiss him, but he stood up quickly to return to his post standing behind me.

"Anyanka," The Pope greeted me like an old friend. "I am thrilled to see that you are alive and well. I had believed my term as Pope would be served only to prepare as many souls for the kingdom as I could. Now that you are here, there is hope that not all will be lost." He looked up to Kai. "What can I do for you, Cain?"

"I need for you to repay the debt. I want you to give Anyanka and her guards asylum here in Vatican City until I return." He was demanding more than asking.

"Of course, they may stay in the apartments on the lower floors. I will put my best guards on their detail, but I can only protect them if they remain in the Vatican." He looked me in the eyes as if to warn me to stay put. "Is there nothing more you will ask of me? We owe you a terrible debt; this is a small price to pay."

"Keep her alive, and the debt will be paid in full. I will leave tonight, but I will not guess at my return. There is much that needs to be done." Kai took my hand and pulled me up out of the chair. He reached his hand across the desk, "Goodbye and God bless."

The Pope stood up and shook Kai's hand. "Goodbye and God speed to you. Anyanka, I look forward to spending time with you."

"Thank you." I wasn't sure if I should shake his hand as well or bow to him, so I opted to nod my head.

We gathered up the gang and headed to the floor below to the apartments we were to call home for an indefinite amount of time. There were four separate apartments, nothing as grand as the Pope's but still very nice. There were two guards that arrived minutes after we did that would be stationed in the hallway, and four more guards in the lobby at all times to escort us throughout the city.

Kai stayed with me all afternoon, even though Ariel begged him to go hunt. He hadn't been hunting since Iskandariya four days prior, and that didn't turn out so well.

I had the feeling that Kai wanted to talk. He practically booted Ariel out of the apartment that she and I were to share. I didn't need Ariel to tell me that Kai was feeling anxious. I could see it for myself.

"What is wrong with you, Kai," I grabbed two handfuls of his tight fitting t-shirt.

I don't think I intimidated him. He took my hands and pried them off of his shirt so that he could kiss the backs of them. "I told you, this is the hardest thing I will ever have to do. I can't bear the thought of leaving you." He paused and dropped his eyes. "Why do you think you can't admit that you love me?"

It was strange how he worded his question, insinuating that I did love him, but I was afraid to admit it. He hit that nail on the head. "I keep waiting for you to realize that I am not the same person you fell in love with seven-hundred years ago. I have this feeling that you are waiting for me to become something I'm not."

"You still doubt your true identity? Even after the fireball you created in Giza, or turning your guardians into animals? You are the only one that doubts your identity." I knew he was right, but I still didn't feel a connection to the first Anyanka.

"Why do you love me? What happened at our first meeting?"

Kai's eyes seemed to be looking beyond the scenery, out into the past. "There was an accident at the residence where you were staying. I was nearby, in case of emergency, when I smelled the smoke in the air, I feared the worst. I went to save you, but you ended up saving me." He paused a moment, I could tell he would say no more on the subject. "Come with me." Kai lead me out of the apartment and down the hall to doors that led to a balcony. There was a nice breeze and the weather was perfect. We sat and talked all afternoon until evening. He asked me a lot of questions about my childhood and my mother, and friends that I had. When the sun disappeared over the horizon he stood up and helped me to my feet.

"Dance with me." He murmured softly.

"But there is no music to dance to." I retorted.

"Listen to the song of the night." He said in a seductive tone.

I listened intently until I understood what he was saying. The songs of the katydids and the frogs and many other creatures filled the quiet of the night. Kai took my hand in his and wrapped his other arm around my waist, it seemed old fashion to me, but to Kai this was the proper way to dance. He hummed a happy tune that complimented the song of the night as we twirled around on the balcony. At that moment, it felt like the world slowed down just for us. Lightning bugs filled the night sky like a million twinkle lights, their sole purpose for existing was to make this moment unforgettable. The moon was glowing almost as bright as Kai's eyes, but it wasn't nearly as beautiful. We danced and twirled and laughed, our bodies were in perfect rhythm with each other. It was a magical moment, and then it was over.

"Where did you learn to dance?" I asked him, trying to hang on to the moment a little longer.

"From you; until I met you, this was just a job. You taught me how to live, that's how you saved me." Kai sighed deeply, "I shouldn't delay anymore. I must be going." He took my chin in his hand so I would look directly into his deep icy blue pools. "I love you, all of you, the past and the present. Promise me you will be careful, I can't live without you again." He kissed my forehead, and stroked my hair. "I am missing you already."

I wanted to see him smile one more time before he left. "I will see you in my dreams."

"I wish that were true, but that gift doesn't work underwater." He stepped back. "I will be back soon." And then he was gone.

Chapter 18

FRIDAY OCTOBER 13TH

We spent several weeks in the Vatican without incident and without word from Kai. I was beginning to worry that something might have happened to him. Ariel said I was just being silly. What could happen to an immortal? I suppose she was right, but I missed having him around.

The Swiss guards that were assigned to watch us turned out to be quiet friendly. When we needed a break from researching and trying to decipher all the clues we had gathered, they took us on tours of Vatican City and told us some of its' amazing history. On a tour of the Basilica, one of the guards pointed to the gold trim on the altar at the front of the church and then rattled on in Italian. When he was finished, Ariel explained, "The gold on the altar was a gift from Christopher Columbus when he returned from the New World." She sighed, I think she was having a good memory flashback, but she shook it off and moved on.

Later on in the tour, the guard pointed to a statue. Ariel translated. "This is Moses, created by Michelangelo." She turned to us and winked.

I'm glad the Swiss Guards didn't speak English, because I spoke before thinking about what I was saying. "He has a beard? Yuck, I hope he keeps it shaved off, he looks much better without it." Ariel nudged me with a stern look on her face, but she couldn't help but snicker.

"No, but most artisans believed that great men were old and wise, and great women were young and beautiful. Sexist people if you ask me." She sounded annoyed.

It was then that I heard someone calling my name behind me. "Annie! Thank God, you are safe. I feared the worst when I heard about your mother." It was father Jack from the Catholic Church in New London.

"Father Jack!" Ryan, Katie and I said simultaneously. I walked forward to greet him. "I had heard you were here. It is a pleasant surprise."

"Yes, but there is no time for pleasantries. I found something in the Archives that might be of interest to you." Father Jack lead the way out of the Basilica and out across the busy square at a fast pace. We came upon a building that was the length of two football fields and three stories high. "This is the Archives." Father Jack interrupted the silent march across the square. "This building holds some of the oldest documents ever written. I was already planning this trip to do research when I saw the sign at the graduation ceremony."

I managed to catch up to Father Jack and walked beside him. "How did you know the sign, Father?"

"I am a theologian, I have studied many religions." He stated, he must have thought that was enough explanation because he didn't bother to say anything else until we were inside and going through security. We had to put on lab coats and booties over our shoes to protect the ancient books and scrolls among other ancient artifacts. The Archives were more impressive than any museum that I had ever seen.

There were shelves as far as the eye could see, covered with books and scrolls. I stood in awe at the amount of history represented here. Father Jack interrupted my ogling. "This is the main floor. We need to go to the basement level. Follow me please."

We all followed in silence, except for Ariel. "This place is puny compared to the library at Alexandria."

Father Jack led us to a stairwell that took us down one level. There were no shelves on this level, only crates. I couldn't guess at how many crates were on this level, tens of thousands, more? Sami looked like a kid on Christmas morning waiting to open her presents. "What is all of this stuff?" She asked in awe.

Father Jack responded with a most appropriate of answers. "Only God Knows." He led us half way down the long aisle before he turned into a row of neatly stacked crates.

One crate was out of place and lying on the floor. "This is what I wanted to show you." He stood back to allow all of us to look into the crate. Inside was a golden tablet like the one my mother had sent to me.

Ariel whispered softly so that her voice didn't echo in the cavernous basement. "Oh, there it is. I am curious to know how anyone managed to get past my security, though."

Jesse stepped up behind Ariel to look in the crate. "This is yours? What does it say?"

"Don't know." Ariel admitted. "I can't read this language and Kai and Lilith have never read it."

"Why wouldn't they have read the tablets?" Ryan asked.

"It was not engraved until I was created, by then, the city had been created and the tablet was well hidden within the pyramid. I didn't find it until right before the exodus. We were a little busy by then." Ariel retorted sarcastically.

"It's probably for the best, Ariel." I consoled. "You probably have a horrible name like mine and Kai's. It might be best if no one knows it." Everyone was laughing, except for Ariel.

"It's not funny Annie. How would you feel if you had no idea who you really are?" She didn't give me a chance to answer. "We need to make a rubbing of this so Kai can translate it when he gets back." I had obviously upset her with my cajoling, and I did my best to remain silent until we were heading out of the Archives.

"Ariel," I spoke softly so no one else could hear. Ariel leered at me, but said nothing. It took all my courage to say what I needed to say. "I'm sorry I upset you. I do know how you feel, though, not knowing who you really are. It is aggravating that other people know me better than I know myself. Again, I am sorry."

Ariel remained silent for the rest of the walk back to the apartments. Just as we stepped into the elevator she finally thawed out. "You're probably right. It will probably be a hideous name that I will never want repeated again." The tension in the elevator was suddenly lifted and I heard several soft giggles escape from the rear of the elevator.

There was a surprise waiting for us when we returned to the apartments that day, there was a message taped to the door. It was from the Pope's secretary, the Pope would be dining in his apartment at eight o'clock and requested that we would all join him for dinner. I hadn't expected a man as important as him to take time out of his busy schedule for us. I was flattered.

By seven-fifty-five, we were all cleaned up and presentable for our audience with the Pope. I was a little nervous, but not nearly as bad as Ryan. When the doors to the elevator opened on the top floor, the Pope was waiting for us. He was dressed casual, black slacks and shirt with the white collar of a priest and bunny slippers on his feet.

Ariel gave her approval of his footwear. He looked down and wiggled his feet to make the bunny ears flap. "I hope you don't mind the informality, they were a gift from my niece. She said that with a job as important as mine, I need comic relief every now and then. My niece is a very smart woman. Please, come, sit at the table. Dinner will be served in just a few minutes." He seemed like a normal human being with a normal life, it was hard to imagine that this man was the leader of the entire Catholic Church. I was also impressed that he was speaking English, and quite fluently.

We all sat at the table, leaving the head chair for the Pope. The table was just the right size for all nine of us to sit comfortably. The Pope asked us to bow our heads in prayer. "Bless us o Lord, and these thy gifts which we are about to receive, from thy bounty through Christ our Lord. Amen." The pope softly added, "whoever eats the fastest gets the mostest." Two serving women entered the room carrying large bowls of salad and cutting boards with warm bread. They served all of us silently and left quickly. It was like sitting in a five star restaurant. The food was delicious and the service was second to none.

We ate in silence for the first course of the meal, making only brief comments about the taste. The serving women re-entered carrying large trays with plates on them. The main course of dinner consisted of steak covered in caramelized mushrooms and onions, broccoli and baked potato. The pope cleared his throat, "I thought you might like an American meal tonight."

My voice was a little shaky but I managed to get out a polite thank you the same time everyone else did.

"Has Cain told you the story behind this debt that was owed to him?" I wasn't sure if he was just making pleasant conversation or if he was planning on telling us the story.

Everyone looked to me to respond. "No, he hasn't mentioned it."

"Would you like to hear it? It is your story, Anyanka."

I snapped my head to attention, "Yes, I would like to hear it."

"Very well, now, where to begin?" The Pope pondered for a moment.

"The year was thirteen-oh-seven in London England. A young girl named Anyanka had been sent from Ireland to stay in England for her education. Her guardian in England was a Templar Knight. Remember that in the thirteen hundreds, not many of the population were educated except for clergymen. It was very rare that a young girl would be educated at all. This girl was brilliant and had a good understanding of math and science, music and art. She gained the attention of a bishop named Johan von Kamp, the church usually employed the educated and he wanted to assess her for possible employment. Johan went to visit the girl at her home. He knew immediately when he saw her that she was the fourth immortal that the Illuminati had predicted would destroy the Earth. He knew because he was a member of the Illuminati. Being a leader of the church, Johan also knew that if one Templar Knight was her guardian then all Templar Knights were her guardian. He devised a plan to simultaneously attack all the Templar Knights and the girl; it was the largest coordinated attack that spanned across three continents using the church's own guards to do it. He sent scrolls all across the land to the different regiments stating that the Templar Knights were Satan worshipers and Satan himself had manifested in a girl named Anyanka living in England. They were to coordinate their attacks so that the Templar Knights would not have any warning. The attack was set to begin at 8 o'clock on Friday October 13th thirteen-hundred seven. Most of the Templar Knights were killed and Anyanka sustained mortal injuries. Cain and Nefertiti came immediately, but it was too late. Anyanka slipped away within minutes after they arrived. It is one of the darkest histories of the church, one we are ashamed of. Cain wanted his vengeance. He confronted the Pope, Benedict the tenth, ironic, I know. The Pope swore that the church did not condone this heinous act and promised Cain that so long as a Pope was head of the Church, we would make amends for his pain and suffering. This is what he asked of us, to keep you safe while he is gone. I have every intention of doing just that."

I was grateful for my friends, because they asked the questions that I couldn't even think of to ask. Jesse started the barrage. "That's where the myth of Friday the thirteenth came from; Anyanka's death?"

"Yes, to this day, the date Friday, October thirteenth is still considered to be a bad omen."

Sami jumped in with the next question. "What was so special about the Templar Knights, why did all of them have to be killed?"

"The Templar Knights were a special faction of the church sent out to find and protect some of the church's greatest treasures. They had the best military training and experience. They were a close knit group, more like brothers than soldiers. When one of them needed help, they all came. That's why the Illuminati had to kill all of them.

Katie continued with another question, "What did the bishop see in Anyanka? She looks perfectly normal to me." She held her hand out to me.

"I can answer that one." Ariel offered. "Several months before the attack, there was a fire at the residence where Anyanka was staying. Kai thought that she might have been compromised and went to protect her. The fire turned out to be an accident, but the damage was done. Kai had fallen in love. He visited with Anyanka almost every night. We think the Illuminati spotted Kai coming and going every day and assumed the rest, that's what led them to Anyanka. Kai always left Anyanka at seven-thirty every evening, in accordance with her guardians' request. The illuminati must have known this because they planned their attack for half an hour after Kai had left."

"Kai blames himself for Annie's death?" Mike asked. "Wow, that's like adding salt to a wound. Hey your girlfriend is dead and it's your fault. That would be awful. It's no wonder why he's so overly protective of you, Annie." As an afterthought, Mike scooted his chair a little closer to Katie's.

Jenny had a question that I was curious to hear an answer to. "What did Kai do after Anyanka died?"

"Yes, I suppose it's only fair if you know the whole story." Ariel looked uncomfortable answering, but like Kai, she didn't want to hold anything back. "After Anyanka died, Kai went to the Pope for answers. As you already know, the Pope swore to his innocents, so Kai returned to the scene of the crime. He picked up the smell of several men and tracked them to their homes. The one that killed Anyanka was tortured until he told Kai of the orders his regiment had received from the bishop Johan von Kamp. Kai cursed the soldier to suffer the same pain that Kai had to endure. Two days later that man killed himself. Kai hunted down the bishop. That is one man you would not want to be associated with. Kai tortured him with large painful black boils all over his body. He gave the bishop the black plague and told him he would kill anyone he touched. The bishop was to live out the remainder of his life completely alone. The bishop heeded Kai's warning, but Kai forgot to take into account the rats, and by the thirteen-forties, the black plague wiped out two-thirds of the entire

European population, but by that time, Kai was already lost to us. He had been to Japan to have his sword made with the intention of becoming a mortal, but Lilith put a stop to that. Kai wallowed in self-pity for seven-hundred years avoiding all human contact, and avoiding us, until I found you." She was looking me in the eyes when she finished the story, trying to judge my reaction. I wasn't sure how I felt about it, so there was nothing to read from my facial expression.

Sami distracted Ariel with another question. "How does an immortal become mortal?"

"It was Kai's theory, but apparently it worked. Annie's samurai sword is the only weapon that can cut our skin. Kai was going to use it to remove a rib, like God did to Adam to create Eve. The moment Adam's rib was removed, Adam had become mortal. With you mortals, time heals all wounds, but for us immortals, time means nothing, and we forget nothing. Kai was doomed to an eternity of pain and suffering." I realized immediately that this is what Ariel was going to tell me when Kai had interrupted her. He wasn't trying to kill himself; he just wanted to become mortal so he wouldn't have to suffer anymore. This is how my mother became mortal. Finally, we have some answers that didn't create more questions.

The Pope looked up to a clock on the wall, "I am truly sorry to have to end this, it has been a fascinating evening, but I have to get an early start in the morning. I hope we can do this again soon." The Pope stood up and we all followed suit. He said his goodnights to all of us and went to bed. After a meal like that, bed sounded good to me too.

Ariel came into my room after I was ready for bed. "You didn't say much tonight, I thought you would have some questions."

"Yes, I do have a question. I just didn't want to ask it in front of everyone else." I looked directly into her glowing black eyes before I asked. "How can you be certain the Illuminati don't have it right? Maybe we are meant to destroy the world, even if it's not on purpose, we could destroy it."

Ariel laughed, "You still don't know who you are, do you?" She sat down on the bed next to me and wrapped her arm around my shoulder. "You are right, we do have the power to destroy the Earth, but we are not capable of doing it."

"I don't understand, you're saying we can but we can't?"

"Exactly! For us to destroy the Earth, we will destroy ourselves. We are a part of the Earth; we are made of the Earth."

"Correction, you are made of the Earth, I was born into it." I pointed out to her.

"You may have been born into it this time, but you are still Anyanka, and she was made of the Earth." She proclaimed. "That's why you haven't been able to morph into your alter ego, you still haven't accepted your true identity."

"You're not making any sense to me." I had to stifle a yawn before I continued. "Maybe I just need to get some sleep. I'm too tired to discuss the laws of physics with you tonight."

"Alright Annie, get some sleep, maybe this will all make sense to you in the morning." She kissed my forehead and then left the room. I knew she would be back after I fell asleep to watch me. I was beginning to think she was as overly protective as Kai. Perhaps it wasn't so much that she was protecting me as much as keeping Kai from sounding like a weeping whale.

The last thought on my mind before I drifted off to sleep was Kai. I missed him so much it was beginning to feel like a physical pain in my chest every time I thought of him. I curled up on my side clutching a pillow trying to relieve the pain.

* * *

I was sitting on a hearth in front of a huge stone fireplace warming my hands. It was the only light available in the room. I turned around and saw that I was in a large room with wooden floors, stone walls and cathedral ceiling. There was very little furniture in the room, just two chairs and a small table sitting between them with only a candle sitting in the center. A door opened behind me and I was chilled by the cold air that swept into the room. A man came through the door carrying fire wood. He closed the door with his foot and then came towards me.

"Are you still cold, Anyanka?" The man's' voice was gentle and familiar with a heavy English accent.

I answered him in a whisper, "As always. I'm sorry to put you out like this, Corin. I don't mean to be so difficult."

"Nonsense, it is an honor to have you here." He put the firewood on the hearth and threw a few logs into the fire and sat down next to me. "Will Jora be returning tomorrow evening? He is a good man but I fear he is interrupting your studies."

I put my hand on his, "Your concern is appreciated but unnecessary. Jora is helping me with my studies, especially history."

He looked down at my hand and jerked away from me. I didn't understand what I had done wrong, but I was apologizing to him. He was holding his hand like he was in pain. It was then that I noticed my hand print in bright red where I was touching his. "Your powers are coming to you Anyanka, but do not fret, this is nothing."

There was a knock at the door. Corin mouthed the words silently, "Go hide." I got up and quickly left the room, I wanted to see who was at the door, so I stood quietly around the corner in the next room. Corin opened the door.

"Bishop von Kamp, for what do I owe this honor."

I could hear the man enter the house. "I understand you have a boarder here." It was a deep husky voice.

Corin responded politely, "Yes, but she is out for the evening. What matter do you have with the child?"

"I hear she has a brilliant mind, I came to test her. The church is always interested in employing the best minds." He paused, and when he started speaking again he sounded excited. "Well, if she is not here, I will waste no more of your time this evening. Good day Sir Corin."

"Good day Bishop." I heard Corin respond just before he closed the door.

I came back into the room just after Corin closed the door. "What was that about?"

Corin looked concerned. "I do not know, but I will feel better to summon my brothers to stay close by for now."

It must have been days later, I was sitting in a chair in front of the fireplace reading a book by candle light. Corin was not home, so when the door opened, I expected it to be him. I didn't look up from the book I was reading when I greeted him. "Good day Sir Corin. Have you fared well today?" I was answered with silence. I looked up to see a young boy in flowing red robes looking back at me with strange red eyes. "Tell Chak he should have killed me when he had the chance." He looked behind me and nodded. I felt a sharp pain in my back, it was hard to breathe. The boy reached behind me, when his hand returned he was holding a dagger in the shape of a dragon with blood dripping down the blade. The boy licked the blade. "The blood of an immortal is pure power."

I sat up quickly grabbing my chest. I had a sharp pain that made it hard for me to breathe. In the darkness I heard Ariel's disembodied voice, "You're okay Annie. It was just a dream." Ariel sat on the bed next to me and wrapped her arm around my shoulder. I laid my head on her shoulder and tried to catch my breath before I could say anything.

"That was the weirdest dream I have ever had, and that's saying a lot." I tried to explain to her so she wouldn't worry.

"Would you like to tell me about it?" She murmured softly.

"No, it doesn't mean anything anyways. It was just a dream." I yawned, "Will you stay with me until I fall asleep again?"

"Of course, I am here for you."

"Thank you, Ariel." I wanted to tell her how much I appreciated having her here, but I fell asleep quickly.

Chapter 19

LOSSES

The next several days the dream haunted me. I tried not to let it show, but my friends knew me too well. Whenever they would ask what was wrong, I would just say "I'm fine." They weren't buying it. I must have been worse at acting then I thought, because by the third evening, all six of my friends came to mine and Sami's apartment for an intervention.

Ariel was all too eager to let them in. "Do your best guys, she's beginning to sound like fingernails across a blackboard. Bye." She waved and was about to walk out the door.

"Wait, where ya going, beautiful?" Jesse asked. Katie nudged him towards Ariel.

"I'm going hunting. Annie's beginning to smell like a fine wine, its best I take care of business while you are entertaining her."

Jesse inched towards her but there were still several feet between them. "Be careful." I couldn't tell if he was just being shy or if he was intimidated by Ariel's pure beauty. No matter, Ariel took the two steps needed to bridge the gap. She took Jesse's face in her hands and pulled him down so she could kiss him. Jesse wrapped his arms around her waist and pulled her in closer. He murmured in her ear, "Hurry back." He let her go and without another word she left.

"Wow! That took you long enough." Sami said, teasing Jesse.

Ryan played defense on Jesse's behalf. "Hey, older women can be quite intimidating." He paused then added, "Let me rephrase that, women are intimidating, cut the guy some slack."

Sami was on the verge of laughing. Mike jumped into the conversation. "Sam, wipe that wolfish grin off your face, you have no idea what it's like for us guys."

Sami burst out in laughter and the rest of us joined in. It had been a while since we were able to laugh like that, it felt great.

Katie brought in movies and CD's and Mike had bags of junk food, including marshmallows. "What are we going to do with those?" Ryan complained, "We don't have a place to start a bonfire."

Mike pointed to me, "No, we have something better than a bonfire, we have Annie."

"She's not a toy that you can play with, buddy." Ryan was sounding a little too defensive. I stepped in before the tension got too high.

"Thank you Ryan, but I don't mind, it will be good practice for me anyways. Besides, this is supposed to be a fun night, so let's have some fun."

Jenny had been quiet the whole time; she inched her way towards Ryan and took his hand. "What about last time, Annie? You passed out on us. Ariel said you weren't ready to do that kind of stuff yet."

"She was referring to the whole 'sustaining a fireball while throwing it' thing. Just making a fireball seemed fairly easy." I explained to her. "Don't worry, I'll be fine. Come on, let's get this party started."

Katie's timing was perfect, as soon as I finished talking she had the music playing. It took a whole two seconds and everyone was singing and dancing to the music. I wondered briefly what the guards outside the door would make of the racket. A slow song came on next. Katie and Mike started dancing together, and Jenny and Ryan started dancing too. Jesse pulled Sami and me towards him and the three of us swayed to the music together. "I love you guys." Jesse said as he put a big bear hug on Sami and me. Sami, in the true spirit of having fun, licked Jesse on the side of the face like a big dog. "Awe, Sami!" Sami and I couldn't help but laugh. He released Sami to wipe his face off with his sleeve. When she was free of Jesse's hug, she leaned over and licked me straight up the front of my face.

I stopped laughing and Jesse started, "Sami! Is this because I turned you into a giant dog, or are you just being demented?"

"Maybe a little of both, but I really do love being a wolf. There are no colors to see but I can hear and smell everything."

"I know what you mean." Katie said as she was laying her head on Mike's shoulder. "The coloration is off, brighter for me, I can hear everything perfectly clear and the smells in the air are so crisp, it's like having a second set of eyes. I bet I could kick-butt playing Pin-the-Tail-on-the-Donkey or Marco Polo."

"I bet I could beat you." Jenny smiled devilishly. "I may not have gotten the cool vision or hearing, but my sniffer is primo."

"You guys want to find out who's the best? We can test you." Jesse challenged.

All three of them answered together, "Yeah!"

Sami went to her room to get t-shirts to use as makeshift blindfolds and Jesse poked his finger with a kitchen knife to put a speck of blood on a paper towel. Once the girls were blindfolded, Jesse hid the towel in my room between the mattresses on my bed. When Jesse was back in the room we set the girls loose to find the towel leaving the blindfolds on to make it a challenge. It was amazing to watch them. Sami weaved in and out of the furniture without hitting anything. Katie had a different approach; she jumped onto the furniture and went over it instead of around it. Jenny went over the couch, under the table and around the chairs. They were all very lithe in movements, but Katie was the fastest, her cheetah speed gave her the advantage and she found the towel in my bed within twenty seconds.

"Next time you should make it more challenging." Katie was gloating.

"Oh, you're such a cheetah, Katie!" Jenny joked with her.

"And you can be such a weasel, Jenny." Katie responded. They gave each other a high five.

Mike and Ryan rolled their eyes; the puns were a bit too much for their tastes. Mike decided to interrupt before it got any worse. "We still have movies to watch and marshmallows that need roasting."

I jumped on Jesse's back out of spontaneous playfulness. "You get the forks, I've got the fire."

"Sounds good," he replied, but he didn't put me down. He carried me to the kitchen and backed up to the counter to set me down. When he turned around, he had a serious look on his face. "Annie, if you start feeling tired or woozy you need to stop immediately. Okay?" It felt like he wanted to say something else but couldn't get the words out.

"Okay." I agreed quickly. "You okay, Jesse? You're looking a little tense these days."

"You have no idea." He muttered. He took the forks out of the kitchen drawer and handed them to me, then turned around so I could ride on his back again. I wrapped my arms tight around his neck and kissed his cheek. "What's that for?" He asked.

"Just for being you, Ariel's a lucky woman." Jesse snorted but made no further comment as he carried me back into the living room.

The movie was just starting, one of my favorites, it was from the nineteen eighties on dancing and defying authority. The music in it was great, we all sang and danced to the songs. I made a fireball and let everyone roast marshmallows.

Jenny roasted extra marshmallows for the security guards in the hallway. When she came back in she was still holding the marshmallows on the forks. "There are a couple new guys on our security detail. They don't seem to be as friendly as the last two. Wouldn't even look me in the eyes when I offered them marshmallows." She shrugged and then gave one of the marshmallows to Ryan.

By the end of the movie, I was exhausted, and it was only nine o'clock. Jesse gave me a stern look when my eyes started drooping. "That's it, the party is over!" He announced.

There was a lot of moaning, but no one said anything. "No, wait guys. You can stay, have fun. Katie, if you don't mind, I'll sleep in your bed tonight, you can sleep in here."

She answered eagerly. "Yeah, go ahead. I hope you don't mind the smell on the pillow, its Ode-de-Mike. I sprayed it with his cologne."

I could understand why she did it, if I could bottle the smell of Kai, I would spray it on my pillow too. "I'm sure it will be fine. Goodnight guys."

Jesse walked me across the hall to Katie's and Jenny's apartment, he even tucked me into Katie's bed. "You over did it, didn't you?" He meant to berate me, but he was too concerned to sound authoritative.

"Maybe a little, it's not like the last time though, I just feel sleepy, not completely drained."

"Do you want me to stay with you until Ariel gets back?"

He was beginning to annoy me, like I couldn't sleep without someone watching me. I had to remind myself it was my fault my friends were like this, and I was determined not to make it worse by alienating them. "I'm fine. Go have some fun." He leaned down and kissed me on the cheek. "What's that for?"

"Just for being you, Kai's a lucky man." He hesitated. "Are you sure . . .?"

"Go!" I demanded

"Goodnight Annie."

"Night Jesse."

* * *

I fell asleep quickly that night and woke to Ariel barging into the room at five A.M. "There you are! I knew you were here somewhere. I could hear your song."

I was disoriented being woken up so quickly so I didn't understand the importance of what she was saying. "If you're in Katie's bed, where is Katie at?" She paused, and then froze.

I could feel the tension building up in the room. "Get out of bed; we need to wake the others." My head was still in a fog, but I got out of bed to help her wake everyone else.

Ariel was so quick, I didn't have to do anything, I made it to the hallway by the time she rounded everyone up.

"What's going on?" Mike asked while yawning.

Ariel held the door to my apartment open for all of us to gather there. Sami was sitting on the couch curled up in a fetal position holding a pillow. The look on her face was terror. "What's wrong Sami? Are you okay?" I sat on the couch next to her. She leaned towards me and put her head on my shoulder and I wrapped my arm around her to comfort her.

Ariel closed the door and stopped. "Katie is missing."

Chapter 20

SCHEMING

"This is my fault. The Illuminati thought Katie was me." I felt so guilty; it was like my mother dying all over again.

"We have to find her!" Mike demanded.

Ryan tried to be the voice of reason. "We don't know if she is even alive. We can't go risking Annie's life to save her."

I felt awful enough, but that comment just stabbed me in the heart. It got worse when Ariel agreed with Ryan. "He's right; we can't risk Annie's life to save a guardian. Katie understands that she has served her purpose. She has made the ultimate sacrifice, we should be grateful."

"She's not dead! You speak as if she were dead!" Mike was screaming; the panic was evident in his voice. "You said so yourself Ariel, the Illuminati would not desecrate this sacred ground. They would have taken her somewhere else first and realized their mistake before . . . . . Katie is worth more to them alive than dead."

Ryan put his hand on Mike's shoulder. "You're right, she is probably still alive, and they would consider using Katie as bait to lure us out. We can't go. We would be walking straight into a trap. It would be suicide."

"Don't even consider it Annie." Ariel pointed at me. Was she reading my thoughts? I thought only Kai could do that, but I wasn't certain.

I needed to test her, so I played innocent. "Consider what?" I stared her down, I had on my best poker face, and it worked.

"Nothing, I guess. I thought maybe . . . . . nothing." She looked at me questioningly. It was the confirmation I needed, she was just guessing at what I was thinking. I just had to figure how to get away from her, and then figure out how to find Katie and save her. I looked at the faces in the room. They were all sick with worry. Ariel looked the worst, probably because she could feel all of our emotions, but there was no way I could convince her to change her mind. I had to keep her out of this; she would only try to stop us. She broke my concentration when she started talking again. "We wait until Kai returns and then I will go after her."

Mike went from sick with worry to irate in two seconds flat. "Kai's been gone for weeks! We don't even know where he is, or when he's coming back! And you want us to just stand around with our thumbs up our . . .!"

"Mike," Jesse stopped Mike before he got graphically vulgar. "This isn't helping Katie! We need to remain calm and think things through." Jesse was looking at me when he was speaking, and I knew I could count on him. Jenny and Sami were definitely in, Mike of course. The only one I wasn't certain of was Ryan, the one we needed the most.

Sami sat up from being curled up on my lap. "No one has asked the most important question." Everyone turned to look at Sami. "How did the Illuminati know where to find Annie? How did they know which bed she usually slept in?"

No one said a word for several minutes. It was Jenny that finally broke the silence. "The guards in the hall, I didn't recognize the ones on duty last night. They weren't very friendly either. It must have been them."

"You're close Jenny," Ryan complimented, "but you overlooked something. It would have been the usual guards that betrayed us; otherwise the Illuminati would have known Annie was sleeping in Katie's room last night."

"But they were so nice. They took us on tours of the city and showed us the best places to eat." Jenny reminded us.

"They were also exposing us so the other Illuminati could identify me." Ariel noted. "I was so stupid. It's just sheer dumb luck that Annie is still safe." Ariel paced back and forth berating herself.

"We need to do something." Mike complained. "It's stupid to just sit around and wait for them to try again."

"There is something we can do." Ryan was speaking to Ariel. She stopped and leered at him. Ryan wasn't intimidated, "We need to find those guards and question them. They may be persuaded to be helpful. We need to get as much information as we can before Kai returns."

Ariel contemplated Ryan's suggestion for a moment before responding. "I will speak to the captain of the guard, he should be able to give me names and home addresses. I will be back in a moment. No one leaves this room, understood?"

We all nodded are heads, but no one said a word. We waited ten seconds after the door closed before anyone began speaking.

"What's the plan, Annie?" Ryan whispered. I was a little surprised, I wasn't certain he would agree to anything like this, and yet here he was starting the conspiracy to defy Ariel.

"You know me too well. Let's come up with battle plans. Mike and Jesse, we need to be able to get past Ariel and the guards, that's your job. Sami, Jenny and I will keep Ariel occupied while you guys get things together."

Jenny asked the all-important question. "When are we going?"

Jesse had an answer for her. "We have three to four days before Ariel will need to hunt again, we can speed that up if we can get her to use excessive amounts of energy." We all looked at him questioningly. "What? We talk, I was curious about her eating habits. That's all."

"Alright, three to four days, you heard the man." Ryan announced. "We need to be able to communicate with each other without Ariel realizing, any suggestions?"

Sami raised her hand. "Yeah, the bathroom, the one room that Ariel never goes into. We can leave notes in there, she will never notice." That was something I had never noticed before, but Sami did have a point. I had never seen Ariel or Kai take a shower, brush their teeth or use the bathroom. I guess it is not necessary for immortals.

"That's brilliant Sami. Alright we know what needs to be done. Let's be quick about it, Katie is depending on us." Ryan wrapped up the conversation before Ariel returned.

When Ariel returned, we all looked as glum as when she left. "I got the names of the two guards. The captain is having them brought in for us to interrogate." Ariel paused; she turned and looked me directly in the eyes. "I just want to say that I am sorry we can't go after Katie. It would be irresponsible to expose Annie like that. I can't allow anything to happen to her. You understand don't you?"

I never realized that Mike would have made an excellent actor. He put on the most pathetic pouty face I had ever seen. "Your right Ariel, it's best to wait for Kai to return." He was so convincing, I even believed he meant it.

Not wanting to sit around, I looked to Ariel. "How long before we can interrogate the guards?"

"An hour, maybe more; the captain wanted to speak with them first. He will call us when it's time."

"Good, I call first shower." I said to Sami.

Sami played along. "Darn it, you usually use up all the hot water."

I wrapped a notepad and pen in my clothes before heading to the bathroom. I already had several plans to keep Ariel busy for the next few days. The trick was going to be wearing Ariel out without wearing us out in the process. I turned the cold water on and let the shower run while I sat on the edge of the toilet writing my ideas down.

Sami,

You and Jenny are going to have to be my liaisons to coordinate with the guys. Ariel won't be letting me out of her sight.

After the interrogation with these guards, I will convince Ariel that we should interrogate all of our guards. That should take up most of the day.

Tomorrow I think one of us should feign sickness, that way we can send the guys out for 'Research.'. That will give them the chance to get supplies without looking suspicious.

Whoever is stuck in the bedroom all day with the flu can do research on line.

I have a few ideas to wear Ariel out, but I'm not sure if they'll work, if you've got ideas, I'd love to hear them.

When I was done writing, I turned the hot water up and jumped in the shower. I left my note for Sami folded up under her toothbrush. I made a point not to brush my hair so I would have to come back to the bathroom after Sami had her shower.

Ariel had changed clothes as well, which was strange since she didn't carry any luggage with her, she had been wearing the same khaki shorts and brown tank top since I met her. She had changed into a cute yellow sundress with a matching floppy hat, not what I would call appropriate for interrogating men that betrayed us, but she looked dazzling in it. "What's the occasion? I thought we were interrogating the guards not going out on the town."

"Don't you like it?" she asked as she twirled around to show it off.

"I love it, but I don't think it's appropriate for what we are about to do."

"Nonsense, it's perfect for what we are about to do, and I am certain we will get better results doing it my way instead of trying to torture the answers out of them."

"I know better than to doubt you, but it doesn't mean I understand."

Ariel giggled, "I know. Come on, it's time to go to work." Ariel took me by the hand and led me to the elevator, messy wet hair and all.

Sami and Jenny were right behind us. I heard Sami whisper something to Jenny, but I couldn't make it out. Jenny responded with a little more volume. "Oh, this, I have to see."

We didn't have to go far, just two floors down to the first level and down the hall to a large conference room. I recognized the guards immediately, even without their uniforms. Their captain was sitting in a chair next to them. He stood as we walked into the room. He said something, but it sounded like gibberish to me. He must have been speaking Italian. Ariel translated for us. "He said he apologizes for their conduct and assures me that any punishment I request for these men will be delivered."

Ariel responded to the captain in Italian. He bowed and left the room without another word. Ariel sauntered around the giant conference table to stand behind the two men. She put a hand on each of their shoulders. "Now, what would you like to ask these men?" She was looking directly at me, and the men were ogling at her.

"Ask them who took Katie?"

Ariel repeated the question in Italian as she ran her fingers down the side of one of the men's face in a very seductive manner. He started speaking very quickly and he had a lot to say. He spoke to Ariel for ten minutes uninterrupted before he finally fell silent. The other guard only had a few things to add.

Ariel looked back to me. "Is there any other question you would like to ask these men?"

"Yeah, where did they take her? Is she still alive? How many men are holding her? What kind of weapons do they have?" I looked back to Sami, "Am I forgetting anything?"

"Yes, you are." She looked to Ariel. "Ask them if they're planning another extraction since they failed to get Annie the first time."

"They already answered all of that. Were you not listening?" She quickly realized her mistake, "Never mind. Is there anything else you would like to know?"

"Yeah, how did you get them to talk? What did you do to them?" Jenny asked.

Ariel smiled wickedly. "I'm not called Aphrodite for nothing. All men whose hearts belong to no woman belong to me. I just had to ask the one that wasn't married." She picked up the left hand of the talkative guard and pointed. "See, no ring."

I had one more question for Ariel. "Why did you have to get dressed up then?"

"I didn't, I just felt like dressing up." She twirled in her dress behind the men and practically danced her way out of the room.

We were in the elevator on our way back up to the room when Jenny asked, "Are you going to tell us what the guard said?"

Ariel gave a quick response. "Yes."

"Well?" Sami prodded.

"Not until we're all together. The boys need to hear this too."

We got off the elevator and headed straight for the boys' rooms. Once we were all together, Ariel divulged all the information she gathered from the guards. It wasn't much. "The guard was bribed to give the information to a man that spoke Spanish. He was given a million Euros to tell the man where Annie slept. That's all he knows."

"Um, Ariel?" Jenny chimed in. "The man spoke to you for ten minutes. What else did he say?"

"He complimented my beauty." Ariel was holding something back, I could tell by the way she held her eyes just off so she didn't look at any of us directly.

"What are you keeping from us, Ariel?" I demanded.

Ariel swore under her breath. It was so unlike her. "Fine, Katie was kidnapped by an old acquaintance of mine by the name of Chak Mool."

It felt like someone just slapped my face. "Chak Mool? You mean the Chak Mool from Mayan culture?" I wasn't expecting to hear that.

"Yes. Do you remember the story I told you about vampires?" She didn't wait for an answer. "He was the first vampire. His name was Anok. He looked after me when I fled Egypt. He was a good friend, a good soul. When I became immortal, he offered himself to me, but I didn't want to kill him. Even after he became a vampire, he remained a good friend and traveled with me to Chichen Itza. The Mayan's named him Chak Mool, the Blood God. He changed, being respected wasn't enough anymore, he wanted to be feared. He also began hunting humans. He had become the monster of your vampire legends. I could no longer stand to be near him. I was grateful when Kai banished him from the city, and if he tried to return, he would suffer the pain of his victims for all eternity. The idiot returned begging for my forgiveness, now he can't even hunt for himself. He has to drink cold blood, and he's really pissed at Kai for that. Seven hundred years ago he teamed up with the Illuminati to get revenge. He knew all about the Illuminati, I told him everything when he was looking after me. The Illuminati were well funded and well informed, if the fourth immortal had been created, the Illuminati would know. Apparently he is still with the Illuminati and he wants to make Kai suffer all over again."

As Ariel was speaking, I remembered the day I wandered away from my mother in Chichen Itza and curled up on a Chak Mool statue to fall asleep. The look in my mother's eyes, terror and relief, it all made sense now. Chak Mool was the one that killed me seven hundred years ago, and he is back to try to do it again. Suddenly, the Illuminati seemed insignificant.

Ariel continued, "On the positive side, Anok won't kill Katie."

"How can you be certain?" Mike demanded. He was looking for a glimmer of hope.

"It would hurt him too much. Besides, Katie's blood won't appeal to him, it has too much of an animal smell to it now."

"So what do we do now? Where do we find Anok? And how do we defeat him?" Mike was anxious to take action. I could imagine how he felt, not knowing where Katie was. I was feeling the same about Kai.

"We will do nothing," Ariel stated firmly. "We cannot expose Annie like that. We will wait for Kai to return and then I will take care of this matter myself." Ariel was adamant.

I figured this would be a good time to distract Ariel for the rest of the gang. I covered my face with my hands and started to cry. I stood up and ran out of the apartment and up to the roof. I knew Ariel would follow me; she wasn't letting me out of her site. After the run up two flights of stairs I was breathing heavy, I took advantage of that to keep from answering Ariel immediately. The more time out of the apartments, the more time the others could spend planning. "This . . . is . . . all . . . my . . . fault!"

Ariel tried to comfort me. "That is not your burden to bear. This is my fault; I should have taken his life when he offered it to me."

"Katie wouldn't even be in this mess if it weren't for me. We don't even know if she's still alive. If I had kicked everyone out last night, and slept in my own bed, she would still be here!"

I pushed it too far. Ariel was irate with me. "Listen here, young lady! You have a much higher calling than Katie. She knows her place in this world, she has accepted that. You need to accept the fact that if you die, the world is going to be destroyed. If that happens, then none of your friends will survive! Don't you dare get all self-sacrificing. If you sacrifice yourself, you sacrifice everyone. Just remember that." She was pointing her finger at me. It reminded me of the way my mother would yell at me when I did something bad. "Now get your butt back downstairs so we can figure out what we're going to do."

I went willingly but I dragged my feet so it would take longer. I must have been overdoing it because Ariel sighed in aggravation on the way back down.

I went straight to the bathroom when we returned to the apartment. I was hoping the others had left me a note to let me know what was going on. Sitting under the first layer of the roll of toilet paper was a small paper folded up into a little triangle. It took a moment to figure out how to open it.

Annie,

The guys are not sure we can pull this off. Mike suggests you grow a set and tell Ariel we are going after Katie, with or without her. Ryan thinks it's best to get you out of here tonight anyways; it's not safe if the Illuminati know where you are. We'll back you up when you talk to Ariel, but do it soon.

I knew Sami was right. I had to stand up to Ariel. It wasn't going to be easy and Ariel was not going to be pleasant about it. I washed my face, and sucked in a deep breath trying to calm myself. I stepped out of the bathroom with total resolve.

I never had to say a word. Ariel snapped at me. "Fine, we'll go find her, but if anything happens to you, I will never forgive you!"

No one said a word, but Ryan started tapping away on the laptop making travel arrangements.

Chapter 21

STRATEGY

I looked at Ariel suspiciously. "Why did you give in so quickly? I thought I would have to argue with you for hours."

"I chose not to fight a losing battle. You were all determined to go after Katie, with or without me. You have a better chance of surviving if I'm with you." As an afterthought she added, "For the record, I want to reiterate my objection to this whole matter."

"Your objection is dually noted." Jesse smirked. He crossed the room to be near Ariel, but he hesitated to take the final few steps.

"And you!" Ariel pointed her finger at Jesse. "How can you, of all people, defy me?"

Jesse looked her straight in the eyes. "I'm not sorry, Ariel. Katie is like a sister to me, I would do anything for her or any of these guys."

"Yeah, I get the whole family thing. What I want to know is *how* you can defy me? It's never happened before."

"I have my priorities in order. It would be selfish of me to turn away from Katie just to make you happy. I can't do that. Besides, it's easier to ask for forgiveness than to beg for permission."

"Perhaps that is why I find you so attractive, you are very strong minded. A very rare quality indeed," She complimented him. Jesse took the last steps and grabbed Ariel up in a passionate kiss.

The sappiness was a bit much for me at the moment, not only was Kai not here, but we never even kissed yet. I was feeling a little jealous that in the midst of everything that has happened, they could find time for a relationship. I cleared my throat to remind them that they weren't alone. Jesse finally put Ariel back on her feet, his face was beat red.

"So, what's the first move, Ryan?" Mike was anxious to get moving.

"My original plan was to expose Annie, let her be taken and track the Illuminati back to their . . . lair?"

Ariel growled, it was a terrifying guttural sound that made the hair on my arms stand up. "There is no way I will allow something that risky." She snapped at Ryan. "I will allow them to take me instead."

Jesse was shaking his head no. "I'll be fine, Jesse. Like you are to Annie, Anok was my guardian, he won't hurt me." She turned her attention back to Ryan. "How did you plan to get the Illuminati's attention?"

"They're looking for us, so checking into a hotel under Annie's name should do the trick."

"And tracking me from a *safe* distance?" Ariel wanted the full plan, if she wasn't happy with it, we weren't going.

"We can use a GPS tracking device, they're easy to come by. Jenny even came up with a way of hiding it on you so if you're searched, the Illuminati won't find it."

Ariel nodded her head, she was satisfied that the first part of the plan was sound. "What are your plans once you've reached the Illuminati's lair?"

Ryan knew she was testing him, he wasn't about to disappoint her. "We will send Jenny in for reconnaissance. We have to be flexible for any situation. Our main goal now is to have a variety of options. I have a list that we need to fill. I already contacted Sue to ship the samurai sword to us in Madrid. If we have to fight vampires again, I want more than one weapon that can kill them."

"You lost me at 'Sue' and 'Madrid', otherwise the plan is sound."

Ryan was beaming at the compliment. "Sue is Katie's mother. I contacted her via email this morning. Katie told Sue everything that was going on before we left. Sue said if we needed anything, call her. She sent the sword Fed Ex overnight priority. It will be in Madrid by this time tomorrow. I chose Madrid for two reasons. The first, you said Anok was speaking Spanish when he bribed the guards. He's Egyptian, so Spanish is a second language for him, ergo, we are going to Spain. The second reason, as if my first reason isn't good enough, I always wanted to go to Spain." Ryan shrugged; it made perfect sense to him.

"You've already made arrangements?"

"Yep."

"What makes you think we can defeat the Illuminati?"

Ryan was confident, maybe even a little cocky. "We have the perfect military unit. Jesse is a sniper. I've seen him shoot, he never misses no matter what weapon he's using. Mike is a front line grunt. He can handle himself in intense situations, and he fears nothing. Jenny is a perfect spy and she is stealthy on the battlefield, it takes a lot of talent to sneak up on a vampire to kill him." Ryan winked at Jenny before continuing. "Sami has brute strength, reserves of energy, and excellent tactical skills. She separates her opponent from the group before engaging in a fight, just like a wolf. Annie and I both have hand to hand combat training as well as weapons training. And if we can release Katie early in the fight, we can count on her for her speed and agility."

"That's a very thorough assessment of you team Ryan, but why do you need my help?" Ariel pressed on.

"Using Annie as the bait would be a bad idea. They might kill her on the spot and we would never find Katie. But if we use you as the bait, the Illuminati will take you to Anok and that means to Katie as well."

"Why would Anok want to see me?" Ariel found the proverbial weak link in Ryan's plan.

"Because he still loves you, why else?" Ryan questioned Ariel.

Ariel started laughing, that was usually a bad omen.

I flinched instinctively. "Anok wasn't in love with me, we were just friends. Anok was in love with Lilith. He suffered the same male complex that Adam did, that's why he became obsessed with power. He felt he should be more powerful than Lilith if he were ever to be worthy of being joined with her."

Mike butted into the conversation before I could ask Ariel about my mother and Anok. "Why did he go back to Chichen Itza to apologize to you then?"

"Because of his quest for power, he killed the man that I loved. Like I said, we were companions, very close companions. He felt horrible about causing me pain. He wanted me to know how sorry he was."

I just couldn't imagine it. My mother had a boyfriend? I had a strange feeling that I was still missing a piece to the puzzle. Everything fit together but I still wasn't seeing the whole picture. "Will the plan still work? Will he be willing to see you?"

Ariel shook her head no. "He will be suspicious if I show up to talk to him. I was very clear with him that I never wanted to see him again."

"That means I still get to be the bait." I was tired of sitting around, I just wanted a plan that we could use so we could leave.

Ariel turned on me, "No, not just you. We will go together. I will accompany you to keep you alive, not to see Anok."

Sami finally spoke up; she had been quiet since we got back from interrogating the guards. "I'm confused. Do we have a plan that we can use or do we have to keep working on it?"

Ryan stood up and headed for the door. "We have a plan. I want us out of here in one hour, so everyone get packed."

I hadn't realized Mike and Jesse were missing until we were gathered up in the elevator. "Hey, where are the boys?" I asked no one in particular.

Ryan answered me. "They better be sitting just outside the square in a non-descript vehicle if they know what's good for them."

We walked across the empty square in silence. Ariel smelled the air for anything out of place. Ryan was scanning the roof tops and the girls kept me surrounded while scanning ground level. I felt ridiculous but I wasn't about to complain. We rounded the corner where Mike told us to meet him and there he stood leaning up against a bright yellow Hummer.

Ryan snapped at him. "I thought I told you to get a nondescript vehicle! Not a neon blinking sign that says 'Here we are, come and get us'."

Jesse rolled down the window of the passenger seat. "The same rule applies, Ryan. The more obvious we are, the more we will be overlooked. It's kind of like hiding something in plain sight. Besides, name another vehicle that can carry all seven of us in comfort."

Ryan shook his head but didn't say another word. Ariel insisted on driving and Jesse refused to move. I climbed in the third seat by the window, wanting to be alone with my thoughts. The scenery was nothing more than a blur to me as my mind drifted elsewhere. The most distinct of all my thoughts were of Kai, when I started thinking about him it became hard to breathe. I missed him so much. I missed his smile, his laughter, the cool touch of his skin, the rock hard beautiful body . . .

"Annie! Knock it off." Ariel startled me out of my daydream. "I am trying to drive here; you could try not to distract me please."

"What did I do?" I was fairly certain I hadn't moved or made a noise since we got in the Hummer.

Jesse was only slightly calmer than Ariel when he answered. "Whatever feelings you were having are very distracting to Ariel. She almost broke my hand because of you."

"Oh! Sorry Jesse." I stifled a giggle; I would have felt guilty if Ariel did break his hand. Otherwise, I was just slightly embarrassed. I had an epiphany, every time Kai and I almost kissed, Ariel interrupted us. I was beginning to think that it wasn't a coincidence. Why could everyone else be allowed to kiss but me and Kai? Why did that bother Ariel so much? Maybe she didn't approve of me being with her brother. I wasn't about to ask her in the car, but the first chance I got, I was going to find out.

I had to change gears, so I thought about my mother. There was so much mystery about her. I thought I knew her, but the more I heard about Lilith, the more I felt like she was just a stranger that I happened to see every day. I had never known her to have a boyfriend. She didn't seem to mind being alone. I interrupted a conversation to ask a question. "Ariel, did my mother love Anok?"

Ariel answered with a curious tone. "Yes, very much so, in fact, they were going to be joined, but circumstances change and they never did. Where did that question come from?"

"I was just trying to get a sense of who my mother was before she gave everything up for me." I was about to go back to my thoughts when I came up with another question. "What do you mean 'they were going to be joined'? What is that?"

"It's similar to mortals being married, but with a higher level of commitment. Marriage is the union of body and mind. Joining is the union of the souls. Once joined, no force of nature could break the bond, only God could do that."

"My mother was going to marry the vampire that killed me?" No one answered me; I didn't really expect them to. I couldn't imagine my mother being married, let alone, to a monster. I was lost to my thoughts again. I tried to understand what Anok was like. Ariel said he was a good companion with a good soul. He loved my mother, but he became greedy for power so he could be stronger than her. Ariel called it the Adam complex, sounded like a guy thing. He accidentally killed Ariel's love so Kai banished him from Chichen Itza. He was willing to suffer a horrible curse just to get Ariel's forgiveness. From all of that, he didn't sound like such a deplorable creature, he sounded more like a human that made a mistake and tried to make amends no matter what the consequences were. Then he teamed up with the Illuminati so he could take revenge on Kai for kicking him out of the city?

Maybe there was more to the story that I didn't know. "Ariel, did Lilith stay in Chichen Itza after Anok was banned?"

"Yes, she did, she had obligations to fulfill. This all happened during the construction of the pyramids, Lilith had to stay until they were completed. Afterwards, she stayed with me to help me get through the grief of my loss. She never did try to find Anok, I think she didn't want to upset me, I was not very happy with him."

So Kai separated Anok from the woman he loved and Anok wanted revenge for that, not for being banned from the city. That really sounded human. I interrupted another conversation, "Ariel, what are the differences between immortals and vampires?"

"Where are you coming up with these questions?" She sounded like a mother that was tired of hearing the question "Why?" too many times. I remained silent until she answered the question. "Vampires are normally weaker than us, unless they are well fed on human blood, and then, they are only as strong as us. They have a hard time letting go of their human beliefs, and they don't adapt well to change." She sounded slightly annoyed as she answered me.

Jenny added to the conversation. "They're relatively easy to kill too, if you know how to do it." There was another fact that I was having a hard time accepting. Jenny-the-Vampire-Slayer; nope, not ready to deal with that one yet.

I decided to keep quiet the rest of the trip, my questions were annoying Ariel, I didn't need her mad at me right now. I was about to put my life in her hands, I didn't want those hands wrapping around my neck and strangling me.

***

We made it to Madrid in good time. The sun was just coming up behind us as we crested the mountain and looked down on the city. As we drove around the city looking for our hotel, I saw a fountain in the town square. It kind of looked like Moses with the long flowing beard. I broke my pact of silence. "Ariel, is that . . .?"

"Yes, it's Kai as Neptune. He did tell you that one; didn't he?"

"Yeah, but it's still kind of strange seeing his face on statues everywhere we go."

Jesse agreed with me. "I know what you mean. You probably haven't noticed, but Ariel is everywhere too."

Ariel sounded embarrassed. "You'll get used to it eventually."

I had to nudge Jenny, Ryan and Sami awake when we pulled up to the front of the hotel. I couldn't believe they could sleep through all the ups and downs and curves on the road, especially as fast as Ariel drove.

Ryan snapped awake. "I'll take care of check-in while you guys park and bring the luggage in." He took Jenny's hand and they both got out of the Hummer.

We parked around the side of the hotel and met Ryan and Jenny in the lobby. He handed out keys to the rooms and we rode up the elevator in silence. I no sooner dropped my luggage on the floor and fell on the bed when everyone converged on my room.

Ryan was all business. "Alright you two, Jenny has your tracking devices. You are not to take them off for any reason. We can expect the Illuminati to respond quickly. They have had twenty-four hours' notice of our arrival. I predict no later than tonight."

Jenny was changing my earrings. "That's a tracking device?"

"Yes, I put a tracking device in both of them in case you lose one. Ariel, I noticed you don't have your ears pierced so I made a burette for your hair."

"Thank you, Jenny."

After Jenny fitted us with tracking devices, she turned on a hand held GPS the size of a cell phone. "O.K. we're live. We should be good to go as long as the Illuminati make their move and get you guys where you're going within thirty-six hours."

"Why thirty-six hours?" Sami asked for me.

"That's how long the batteries are good for." Jenny turned and left the room quickly and Ryan herded the other three out, leaving me and Ariel alone.

I was not going to waste the opportunity to question Ariel's motives. "You don't approve of me, do you? You think I am a bad match for Kai?"

"What? Why would you say that?" She was genuinely surprised by the question.

"Every time Kai is about to kiss me, you interrupt. You don't think I'm right for him." I concluded.

"Heavens no child, you have it all wrong. I think you are perfect for my brother, and my brother is perfect for you. And I dare say, Lilith thought the two of you were perfect as well. That's why she named you Anyanka Cain. She was calling you Kai's wife. It's the intensity of the emotions you have for each other that I'm having a hard time dealing with. I feel everything; every time you two get close it sets my soul on fire. Poor Jesse, he probably thinks I'm bipolar. Besides, Kai is much easier to listen too when you are with him. His soul has a beautiful song; it compliments your song perfectly."

"Is that it? That's why you keep interrupting?"

"Well, it's not the only reason. You smell delicious. When Kai gets close to you, it feels like an inferno in his throat. I feel that too. It's easier for him to deny the temptation because he remembers all too well the pain of having to live without you. He spared me that pain by going underwater, I can't feel him or hear him unless he is on the surface, in my element."

"How did you contact him then, when you found me?"

"I sent Buddy to bring him. I can't go underwater, I float." She smiled impishly.

"When will I get to meet Buddy?"

"I thought you already did. He was in the jungle with Kai watching over you while I went hunting." She cocked her head to the side in a questioning manner. "He never changed out of his form, did he? All you saw was the wolf. I bet that was an interesting site to see in the jungles of Central America."

"How did Buddy get his name? It's a strange name for a higher being."

Ariel laughed, "He was in New York City about ten years ago, and he stepped out onto a street right in front of a taxi. The driver leaned out the window and screamed. 'Watch where you're walking, Buddy.' And the name stuck."

"That's how we get named? By someone making a comment and the name just sticks to us?"

"Yeah, pretty much, that's it."

"That's good motivation to be nice to people, I guess, or I could end up being called 'Evil Bitch.'" The humor was lost on Ariel.

"So, you and me, are we good?" I wanted complete clarification.

"Annie, you're practically my sister, we are beyond good."

I gave Ariel a big hug. I was so relieved that she approved of me. It was a big weight off of my chest.

After I let her go there was a moment of awkward silence. "What do we do now?"

"We wait, and when the Illuminati show up to kidnap us, we act like helpless women." We both had to laugh at that comment.

***

Ryan predicted the Illuminati's move to a tee. Two men showed up after one o'clock in the morning dressed in hotel uniforms. I don't think they were expecting two of us, and they were definitely not expecting Ariel. Ariel wasn't going to play the victim. She said something to them in Spanish. They set their guns on the floor and then we followed behind them out of the hotel like they were our prisoners, not the other way around.

Chapter 22

OFFENSIVE

"What did you say to them?" I asked her when we were sitting in the back seat of our kidnappers' car.

"I told them to take us to their leader. It does sound kind of silly saying it in English though. It's more ominous in Spanish." She assessed.

I was finally feeling the effects of sleep deprivation. I had been awake for two days, not able to sleep since Katie disappeared. I leaned my head against Ariel's rock hard shoulder and fell asleep. It felt like only minutes had passed when Ariel was nudging me awake, but it was more like hours because the sun was coming up already. "Annie," Ariel whispered in my ear, "We are stopping, I think this is it."

I looked out the window to see a giant castle sitting halfway up a mountain side. I got the cold chills thinking about Katie stuck in there for the past two days. I leaned into Ariel and whispered back, "Can you feel Katie's presence?"

"No, but that doesn't mean anything. She could be in cheetah form right now. I just have to say, you were never this attached to Corin." Ariel was no longer whispering, and I realized that our captors couldn't speak English anyways. She had only whispered so I wasn't startled awake.

I was only paying half attention to her until she said the name Corin. It felt like she just slapped my face. The dream I had after the dinner with the Pope, came flooding back to me. It wasn't just a dream, I was remembering my previous life, and I finally felt the connection that had been missing. At that moment I knew who I was, past and present, but it wasn't the right time for rejoicing.

"What about the others?" I held back the panic waiting for her to answer.

"They are close. Ryan is feeling a bit smug this morning because he guessed right about the Illuminati's lair. I hope he comes down off of his high quickly. This has been the easy part."

Ariel was right and I knew it. This could be a suicide mission. I didn't feel scared, although I should have. I felt annoyed with myself for not saying the things that needed to be said. Life is too short to waste time with doubt and uncertainty. As the captors opened the doors to the car, I thought to Kai. I wasn't sure if he would hear me but I wasn't afraid to say it anymore. *Kai, I do love you, with all of my heart and soul. I'm sorry it took so long to say it. I will love you for all eternity.*

We stepped out of the car and began our long climb up a set of stone stairs carved into the mountain. Our captors lead the way not even bothering to bind our hands or even watch us. The castle loomed above us with its ancient stone walls, turrets and cast iron gates. I was concerned the others would have to take the stairs to reach it, they would be exposed. I looked to Ariel.

"Don't worry, they have climbing gear." Ariel was completely relaxed, of course, what could any of the Illuminati do to an immortal? She had nothing to fear.

We reached the gates at the entrance to the castle. There were four guards watching the gate and they all looked bored out of their wits. After one look at Ariel, they all perked up. They spoke quickly to our captors and stepped out of the way for us to pass. Ariel murmured to me, "They said that the others are in the great hall waiting for our arrival."

That didn't sound good. How many were there? My heart rate spiked, and Ariel took my hand and gave it a squeeze to reassure me. It helped a little, but the thought that I would never see Kai again almost had me in tears. We walked up more steps to huge wooden doors that opened silently inward as we reached the landing. Warm air hit my face from inside. I hadn't realized how cold it was outside from the strenuous climb up. I sucked up my courage and walked through the doors. 'I was doing this for Katie,' I had to remind myself. I held my head up and looked straight ahead, I would not show these men the fear I felt inside. I would not give them the satisfaction of knowing that they defeated me mentally as well as physically. Ariel looked impressed by my stature. She mimicked my stride perfectly, and we walked into the great hall side by side with confidence.

The room was enormous, at least half the size of a football field. One wall was covered in mirrors from floor to ceiling and the opposite wall was nothing but giant windows, making the room appear twice as big. There was a huge wooden table at the center of the room with chairs all the way around with at least thirty men sitting quietly waiting for our arrival. Past the table on the floor was a statue of Chak Mool. I knew I should have thought that was menacing, but I could never fear Chak Mool, the statue anyways.

The man sitting at the head of the table stood up to greet our two captors. He was wearing red velvet robes with gold trim, otherwise he looked like a normal business man; someone I wouldn't pay attention to if I passed him on the streets. As they spoke, I looked around the room for Katie. She wasn't here, it was a huge castle though, and she could be anywhere.

When he was finished speaking with our captors, he looked to Ariel and spoke to her in perfect English. "Nefertiti, you are as beautiful as ever." He sounded quite charming. I had to remember that he wanted me dead. "My name is Zachary DeSanto, but you may call me Zack. I am the leader of the Illuminati."

Ariel got straight to the point. "Cut the crap, Zack. We know why you brought us here. I want to state for the record, again, that your whole organization was based on a crazy man's dream after smoking opium. We are not here to destroy the world; we are here to save it."

"You lie! Hold your tongue, witch, I will not listen to your evil. I know you are here to lead me astray, give me impure thoughts and keep me from fulfilling my destiny!"

My first impression of Zack was completely wrong. This guy was a crazy zealot, the type that could never be reasoned with.

"Anok!" he called and clapped his hands twice to summon the vampire.

The sun was shining through the windows and I watched with curiosity to see if Anok would burst into flames when he stepped into the room. I didn't even hear footsteps coming down the hall to announce him, so when he stepped into the room I jumped at the sight of him. He didn't burst into flames or even start smoking, I was a little disappointed by that. However, he did have a subtle iridescent shimmer to his exposed skin. He was beautiful, not like Ariel, but he was definitely something to look at. His eyes were not what I was expecting either. I was expecting them to be red, sinister, but instead, they were a pretty jade green, like mine. That's when all the pieces finally clicked together, but I didn't have time to say anything.

Anok grabbed Ariel around the arms to hold her while three men came at me. I punched the one in the center right in the nose before the other two grabbed my arms. The third one stepped back and allowed another man to come and grab my feet. I kicked him in the face before he got a good grip on me. They lifted me up and carried me over to the Chak Mool. statue. I struggled as much as I could, I wasn't about to make their jobs any easier. Two more men were waiting by the statue holding chains that were attached to the floor. I got one of my legs free and kicked as hard as I could to make him drop my other leg, when my foot made contact with the man's' face I heard a crack. His cheek split like a piece of rock. He leared at me with bright red eyes, I knew then that he was a vampire. The other two men carrying me dropped me on the statue and held my arms so that the others could put the shackles on me. The vampire put more shackles on my ankles. I couldn't move, I couldn't fight, I was done, and I knew this was the end. I only hoped that the others had enough time to find Katie and get her out safely. I looked to

Ariel, she was still being held by Anok, She looked calm, and I think she was even smiling. My eye sight went blurry and I couldn't see anything clearly, I realized I was crying.

I made one last effort to tell Kai how I felt. *'Kai, if you can hear me, I want you to know that I love you and I'm sorry that I'm going to hurt you again.'*

I took two deep breaths to calm myself down. If I was going to die, I was going to die with dignity. The leader stood over me and chanted in Spanish, I couldn't understand why he was delaying the inevitable. It must have been some kind of ceremony because he droned on and on. Someone brought him a dagger, an ivory dagger in the shape of a dragon with ruby eyes, the same as the one Jenny now has. He took it in both hands and held it above his head as he continued chanting in Spanish.

And then it happened, I saw Zack's lips moving and I understood what he was saying ". . . And rid this world of the abomination and save our race."

I started laughing. It was a quiet chuckle at first, and quickly built into a full blown guffaw. I must have broken Zack's concentration because he stopped chanting to look down at me.

"My boyfriend is going to kick your ass."

Zack's eyes grew wide as he realized what I meant. He rushed to bring the dagger down into my chest, I felt the blade hit my chest, but it didn't penetrate deep. I looked up and saw the eyes of an angel, glowing bright icy blue, and he looked pissed. He pulled the dagger up out of my skin holding Zack's hands to the hilt. Once the dagger was clear he shoved Zack across the room, the dagger went flying with him. Kai broke the shackles holding my ankles and wrists and picked me up off of the statue. We were in a room full of men that wanted me dead, but all I could see was Kai.

He lifted me higher to kiss me, but Ariel interrupted, of course. "Um, guys this is no time for a reunion. We have work to do." She said it in a sing song kind of way.

Kai set me down and stood in front of me. I heard the gurgling, choking sound of the men in the room. I buried my face in Kai's back, I knew he was drowning them; I just didn't want to see it.

There was a loud sound that made me jump. The heavy doors to the hall were forced open. I looked around Kai to see my friends being dragged in by six iridescent skinned vampires. Katie was with them. What was she wearing? A bed sheet?

Ariel was fighting Anok in hand to hand combat. It was a beautiful, lethal dance, what little I could see of it. Most of the movement was so fast it was blurred. The two of them were so graceful. It was hard to take my eyes off of them. My attention was drawn back to my friends when Ryan ordered, "Now!"

Instantly the three girls shimmered into animal form, and right in front of me Kai shimmered too. He transformed into a giant black Jaguar, I wasn't expecting that. I thought he might have turned into a fish or a merman. In one lithe move he sprung across the room to join in the fighting. Ryan had the samurai sword, he seemed to know what he was doing, and I had never seen him move so fast. He destroyed two vampires before Sami and Katie could get into the fight. Jesse and Mike were matching Ryan's speed. Mike was thrown to the ground just before Jesse stabbed a third vampire in the heart with a makeshift wooden stake from a broken chair. Mike didn't move. I ran in to take care of him, but Anok broke off from his fight with Ariel and grabbed me around the waist. Everyone in the room froze. I heard a growl escape from the giant black Jaguar. He was looking for a way to save me. My eyes were still on Mike though. He wasn't moving, I couldn't tell if he was breathing.

Anok whispered in my ear. "Do you see the pain in Cain's eyes? That is what I live for. He took away every other reason I had for living."

"Chak Mool," I gasped because he was holding around my ribcage so tight, it was hard to breath. "I have a message for you from Lilith."

He loosened his grip on me, but he didn't release me. I took it as a sign he was listening to me. "She wanted me to tell you she expects you to continue your roll as my guardian and that she forgives you." He was still for a moment, processing what I had said. He released me completely, and I turned around to face him. As he looked me in the eyes, his facial expression changed. I knew what he saw. He was seeing the same thing I was seeing, my own eyes looking back at me. Realization finally sunk in, he knew what I had only recently figured out myself. I was his daughter.

Kai shimmered back into his human form. I was in sensory overload knowing for certain that my father is a vampire. Kai walked towards me, completely naked. It was the most beautiful sight I had ever seen . . . until Ariel covered him up with a robe she pulled off of Zack's dead body.

Anok hesitated before asking me a question. "Where . . . . Where is Lilith?"

"She's gone. She was killed in a car accident." I wasn't gentle about telling him, I was still a little miffed about him trying to kill me. When I saw the depth of pain in his eyes I regretted not showing him more compassion.

He fell to his knees and bowed his head. "I knew her days were numbered. Kill me, Kill me now." He whispered.

Ryan walked forward carrying the samurai. I put my hand out to stop him. "No!" I knelt down in front of him. He wouldn't look up at me. "Anok, we need your help. We only have five months left before the world is destroyed unless we can find a way to save it. "

"What can I do? I am nothing compared to Lilith."

"Yes, but you knew her best, more than any of us did. Perhaps there is something she told you, that she never told any of us. Please, help us."

"All Lilith told me was to look to the heavens for answers. I thought she was telling me to pray, but perhaps there was more to it than that." He looked up to Kai, "Is this what I did to you? Is this the pain you suffered?"

Kai was cold when he answered. "Yes."

Anok was grabbing at his chest, he looked as if he was crying, but there were no tears. "My brother, I never imagined anyone could feel this much pain. I know I don't deserve forgiveness, but I am sorry."

Kai picked me up and set me on my feet next to him and then reached his hand down to help Anok to his feet. It wasn't a peace offering, just a sign of truce or perhaps a show of sympathy.

I had more important matters to attend to so I shrugged it off and skipped for joy over to the Cheetah. I wrapped my arms around her neck and scratched behind her ears. I heard her purring. My friend was back where she belonged. I retrieved a robe off of another of Kai's victims and draped it over Katie so she could shimmer back to human form. Ryan and Jesse did the same for Jenny and Sami.

Mike moaned, and we all rushed to his side. "Did anyone get the license plate number off of the bus that just ran me over?" He mumbled. We were all laughing, just grateful that we survived.

I stood up and noticed the three remaining vampires left in the room. They were standing at attention waiting for orders like soldiers. One of them caught my attention, his eyes were wild looking. Ariel must have sensed the change in the room and dove into him as he was about to attack me. I realized I was still bleeding profusely from the stab wound in my chest. I looked to Kai as I was starting to feel light headed. My knees began to buckle and Kai grabbed me up in his arms. I could hear the panic in his voice as he called for Ariel. And then there was darkness.

Chapter 23

DARKNESS

I had the strangest sensation that I was floating, I felt nothing. There was no pain or pleasure. Nothing felt cold or warm. I could hear nothing but my own thoughts. I couldn't move or speak, or see or smell anything. There was only darkness, and it was devouring me. I couldn't feel my arms or legs to even fight off the darkness, there was nothing left of me. Time stopped moving, a second felt like eternity, and eternity felt like a second. I had no concept of time. I was trapped in my own mind. I tried to grasp at the last few minutes before the darkness overtook me.

I remembered Mike was going to be alright and Katie was back with us. I remembered seeing Jenny shimmer back into human form, and Ryan holding a robe for her. Jesse was running with a dagger to kill the vampire Ariel had just tackled. Sami shimmered back into human form and picked up the robe that Jesse dropped on the floor. I thought I saw Anok charge Ryan as if he were attacking him. The last thing I remembered was Kai, the look of horror on his face, and the sound of panic in his voice as he called for Ariel.

That was the key that started my heart again. It was racing so fast I thought it was going to pound its way out of my chest. It was the only thing I could feel, but it was better than nothing, at least I knew I was alive. I drifted in and out of consciousness; there was very little difference between the two. Consciousness meant I could feel my heart race, unconsciousness meant I couldn't. I had no idea how long I was trapped inside my head. I remembered reading stories about prisoners being locked in cells with no light. They would only be in there for a day or two, but when they were brought out they could have sworn they were locked away for months. That's what this felt like.

I tried to concentrate on my heartbeats. I felt the pounding. I reached out with my mind to feel my heart hitting my ribs. I found my rib cage. I could feel the movements of my erratic breathing. I could feel the air being drawn down my throat, and back out again. I tried to control my breathing. I took a deep breath and there was a sharp pain. I reveled in the fact that I could feel the pain. I let the air escape my lungs and I took another deep breath. The pain felt sharper the second time, much too sharp. I went back to shallow breathing to avoid that pain again.

I heard a voice whisper softly beside me. "Annie, my love, can you hear me?" I couldn't tell if I was just imagining it or if Kai was actually speaking to me.

I answered anyways," *Yes, I hear you*".

"Good!" I knew then that I wasn't imagining his voice, because he sounded pissed. "How dare you do something so insanely dangerous? What were you thinking? Were you trying to get yourself killed? Do you realize that if I arrived a half second later, you would be dead? You almost died anyways, and I was helpless to save you!"

"*Kai,*" I interrupted his tirade, I knew the only reason why he was mad was because he was afraid of losing me. I would take all the yelling he had to give because I knew he loved me. "*Kai, I am so sorry that I put you through that, but I had to come here. I had no choice.*"

"I know. Ariel explained it all to me." He sounded much calmer, but I could still sense the tension in his voice. "I'm sorry I yelled, you have been through enough, you don't need me adding to your pain."

"*I deserved it. I knew what I was getting into and I came anyways. What did happen to me? I was fine one minute and the next I couldn't hold myself up.*"

"The sword fractured a rib, when I picked you up from kneeling with Anok. It shifted and punctured your lung. You were drowning in your own blood. Ariel called for Buddy, he arrived within a minute after you passed out. He has the ability to heal, did you know that?"

"No, as a matter of fact, you hardly even mention Buddy. Is he still here? I want to meet him."

"No, he had to return to Valhalla, but he promises to meet up with us soon. He told me to keep you perfectly still for several days to make sure your rib doesn't break again. I put you into a coma; I know how hard it is for you to hold still."

"How much longer do I have to lie here?"

"Twelve hours, nineteen minutes and forty-three seconds."

"Are you going to keep me company the whole time?"

"I will stay as long as you let me."

"Good, you aren't going anywhere then."

* * *

Twelve hours, nineteen minutes, and forty-three seconds later, Kai released me from the coma. I opened my eyes to the most beautiful sight, his eyes looking back at me. He was kneeling beside the bed. There was something that I had to say to him, I didn't want to waste any more time. "I love you, Kai."

"I know. I've always known, but I'm glad you finally figured it out." He smirked at me. I wanted to hit him for being so cocky, but he was right.

"And I love you, Anyanka, with all of my heart and soul." For once, I didn't mind being called that name. He leaned down to kiss me, but I put my hand up in between our lips. He pulled back questioningly.

"Ariel, she says it drives her insane when we get too close to each other." I explained

He laughed and beautiful chimes filled the room. "That's why I sent Ariel with Buddy. She's far enough away that we won't affect her, and if we do, she won't make it back in time to stop us." He leaned down again, this time I didn't stop him. He was slow and cautious being very careful not to jostle me as he came closer. I reached my hand up to caress his cheek. I felt his cold, hard skin beneath my burning hand. He was the perfect antidote to the fire raging within me. The anticipation was more than I could bear, until our lips finally met. It was the most incredible moment of my existence, the moment when my dreams finally became reality. Every nerve ending in my body was a live wire. I could feel he was about to pull away so I reached up and grabbed handfuls of his hair to pull him tighter to me. I didn't want the moment to end, but he was so much stronger than me and he pulled away.

He chuckled softly as he reached up to release my grasp of his hair. "I know you think I'm perfect, but I'm not. I have to fight my desires every time I am near you." He kept hold of my hands and kissed the back of each.

I pulled my hands away from him and grabbed a pillow to cover my face. It was then that I realized I had no idea where I was. I was holding a black velvet pillow with gold trim. I didn't recognize it. I looked around the room but I couldn't see anything because of the steam. I was just about to ask Kai where we were when the bedroom door flew open.

"Is something burning in here?" Mike sounded panicky. "There's smoke rolling out from under the door." I think he realized quickly because without missing a beat, he changed the subject. "Hey, Annie, you're awake! Good to see you're still alive." He turned to holler behind him. "Hey guys! She's awake!" Within seconds, the room filled up. My friends were all here.

Sami came in last. I saw that she was trying to sneak up on Kai, still kneeling beside my bed. At the last moment she pounced, Kai turned and grabbed her in mid-air and gently threw her on the bed next to me. "Is this yours?" He asked jokingly.

"Yeah, this is my dog, Sami." I joked back to him.

"Why is it foggy in here?" Katie asked as she looked around the room. "Oh, never mind." She obviously figured it out for herself.

Jenny snuggled up next to Ryan, "So how does it feel to be taken off of the endangered species list?"

Ryan shook his head, "That's not what happened here, Jenny." He sounded ominous. "Those men only represented the separate chapters of the Illuminati. We just stirred up the hornets' nest."

Jenny came to a full understanding. "Oh. Wow, that really . . . ."

"Sucks," I finished for her.

Sami propped herself up on an elbow. "What do we do now?"

"I say we go home." Mike offered. Home sounded like a perfect idea.

"Where are we anyways?" I had to ask. The last of the fog had dissipated out of the room and I could see that the walls and floors were made of stone. I was laying on a king size canopy bed with velvet trim, blankets, and pillows. I pieced it all together quickly. We were still in the castle in Spain

Kai knew I figured it out already, but gave me an answer regardless. "We never left, I was afraid to move you any farther than necessary."

"What happened to my father?" I asked out of curiosity. Kai cringed at my choice of words.

"He's gone. The pain was too much for him to handle." Kai didn't sound sorry about it, in fact, he looked a little pleased.

"Kai, despite the fact that he killed me once and made you suffer seven hundred years of misery, he was my father; couldn't you show a little remorse for him?"

"Remorse for him; Why? Because he wasn't strong enough to endure the darkness?" I had never seen Kai be so insensitive.

"What do you mean by 'darkness'?" I had heard him say it before but he never explained himself.

He took an unsteady breath before he began. "Darkness is not measured by the absence of light, but by the absence of faith, hope and love. We immortals see the world from a different point of view. We are not merely passing through on our way to a better place. This is it for us. This is where we are meant to be for all time. We have an eternity to wait for the perfect person to come along, so we wait. Our love is as eternal as we are. Nothing will ever change the way we feel for someone. To lose that kind of love and commitment is devastating. There is nothing left for us to look forward to, nothing that can fill the emptiness, and nothing that can ease the pain. Ever!"

"Except in your case," Jesse responded optimistically.

"Yes, by a miracle of God, I got Annie back." He gave me that half smile I couldn't resist. I couldn't help myself. I leaned towards him and kissed him right in front of everyone. He wasn't objecting.

I vaguely heard Sami protesting. "Ugh, is it going to steam up every time you two kiss? This is going to play havoc on my hair."

"So what's the game plan?" Jenny asked in an attempt to ignore the public display of affection.

I pulled away from Kai to look into his eyes. "Can we go home?"

"I will take you anywhere your heart desires." He promised.

Chapter 24

DÉJÀ VU

"I thought you said we were going home?" I was finally feeling more alert by the time we were half way across the Atlantic. With nothing better to do, I glanced at my ticket and realized we were heading to Chile.

"There is something I need to see." Kai answered vaguely. As a matter of fact, all of his answers had been vague since we had left Spain. When we asked him what the pyramid said about the previous eras, he said "There isn't much to tell." When we asked him what took so long to get back to us, his response was "There were obstacles." He had become the master of vague.

As I sat in the seat wedge between Jesse and Kai, a feeling of dread came over me. "Kai, be straight with me, how bad is it? What's going to happen?"

Kai looked at me with weary eyes. "I do not want to say anything until I have confirmation. We are going to a small island off of the coast of Chile. It is the only place in the world that the next event can be seen. If I am correct, then we will know with absolute certainty what is coming. We have to be on the island in three days."

"Does this have anything to do with the constellations on the ceiling of the pyramid in Giza?"

"You will have to ask Sami. I gave her the sketches I drew. She has been working on deciphering it."

"What is today's date anyways?" Since we had left home, the days all started blurring together. Time felt like the enemy and I had done the worst thing by ignoring it.

"Today is July eighteenth. We only have five months, three days, and nine hours until the end of this era." Kai looked down at his hands, "I wonder if anyone is aware of how precious their time is."

"Do you really think God will destroy the human race?" Maybe it was naïve to be hopeful, but that was all I had to hold on to at the moment

Kai only laughed softly. It wasn't a humorous laugh. It was more of a cynical laugh. He looked me in the eyes and a cold chill ran down my spine. "The human race has become a plague on this planet. I do not know the mind of God, but if I were in his position, I wouldn't be happy about the way the human race has evolved." Kai released me from his stare and looked straight ahead. "We are not here to decide the fate of the human race. We just have to keep the planet from being destroyed. That is our job."

I couldn't respond to him. I was lost to my own thoughts running through my head. What have we done to deserve being shunned by God? What will happen to us if we fail? What will happen to everyone else if we fail? I knew the answers to those questions and I didn't like it. I had to ask myself a question that I would truly have to consider before answering it. Is this world worth saving? And if it is, what would I be willing to do to save it? My mother asked herself the same question, and she gave the ultimate sacrifice to save this world.

Jesse whispered in my ear, a pointless gesture with Kai so close. "He's been all doom and gloom since he returned from Atlantis. He was hiding it from you so you wouldn't worry while you were healing. If you ask me, I think that's why he sent Ariel away, so she wouldn't have to suffer being near him." Jesse had sad puppy dog eyes just from mentioning her name. He sighed deeply and I could tell his thoughts were elsewhere.

Sitting between Jesse and Kai, a situation I would normally enjoy, became unbearable. I stood up and excused myself. Kai didn't bother to ask where I was going. He probably figured I couldn't escape an airplane in flight. I walked several rows back to where Sami and Katie were sitting. They were going over the clues that we had gathered on this crazy endeavor. "Need any help?" I startled Katie, but she recovered quickly.

"Ah! Fresh meat," Katie exclaimed as she moved to the middle seat to make room for me.

"Where's Mike?" I looked up and down the aisle but I didn't see him anywhere.

"He's playing mediator for Ryan and Jenny. Those two have been fighting for the last two days. I hope Mike can fix this, I hate the tension."

"Can I ask, or is it none of my business."

"You can ask, but we don't have an answer for you." Sami replied as she put down a sketch that looked like a connect-the-dots puzzle.

"Have you two figured any of the clues out yet?" I took a glance at the laptop sitting on Katie's lap.

"Still working on it, but we have a couple of theories." Katie tapped a couple of keys on the computer and pulled up a text file. "I had Kai write down the riddle for us. Here it is. 'When twilight sets across the land . . .' I think that might just be referring to a time of day or maybe even a metaphor for the end of the era. Sami thinks it might be a more figurative message, like the 'Dark Ages'." Katie looked up from the computer. "What do you think it means?"

"I don't know, maybe it is referring to an eclipse." I offered. Katie started tapping away on the computer again. "What is the next line?"

". . . and the great kingdoms are shroud in darkness." Sami didn't even look at the computer. She must have had the riddle memorized. "We got nothing on that, it just sounds redundant from the first line."

"The second line means that the first line is definitely not referring to a time of day." Katie and Sami looked at me questioningly, so I continued to explain. "The 'great kingdoms' are referring to Atlantis, Valhalla, Giza, and Chichen Itza. They are spread out too far apart for them to all be shroud in the darkness of night at the same time. At least two of them will be in daylight at all times. If it is referring to an eclipse then the second line means 'at the peak of the eclipse'."

"That would be one impressive solar eclipse if that's the case." Katie added. "Most solar eclipses are only visible from one place at a time. It would have to be visible from two places for this to be accurate." She typed in a few more notes on the computer. "The next line is '. . . the four horsemen will ride out and unleash their wrath upon the Earth.' I'm not thrilled with the word 'Wrath.' It sounds like you guys are getting revenge for something."

"I agree." Sami added with an accusing tone.

It was a strange sensation that I felt like I had to defend myself for something that I hadn't done yet. "Hey, take it easy on me now. Wrath does not necessarily mean revenge, it could just be a show of power or something like that."

"Fair enough," Katie submitted, "but if you burn everything up because you're mad about something, I will never forgive you."

"Fine, I promise not to burn everything up, scouts honor. What's the next line in the riddle?" I had to change the subject quickly.

Sami spoke up before Katie could. "When light returns to the land, the three kings will sit on their thrones and bring balance to the world."

"O.K., so what are your theories on this one?"

"Well, if we go by your theory, the end of the eclipse will bring about a new world order, and it sounds like the leaders have already been picked. The big question is who?" Katie offered.

Sami chuckled. "It sounds like the Nativity story when the three kings showed up bearing gifts."

I had a strange suspicion that Sami was on to something, so I excused myself and walked up the aisle to speak to Kai. "Kai, the three kings of the Nativity story? Was that you, Ariel and Buddy?" I whispered softly to him.

He had an inquisitive look on his face. "Yeah, that was us. Why?"

"Just curious," I didn't want to explain it to him; he might not deal well with my theory. As I walked back to Sami and Katie, a feeling of dread overcame me. If there are only three kings to bring balance to the world, then chances are I am not destined to survive.

I really didn't want to discuss that with Sami and Katie, so when I returned to my seat I only answered with a cheerful "Yep!" Before either could ask me to explain, I jumped in with another question. "What about the constellations? Have you discovered anything with that?"

"No, the positioning of the stars is completely wrong, so I tried to apply astrology instead of astronomy. I think it might be some kind of 'Rosetta Stone.' If I'm right, then the astrologers have gotten it all wrong."

"What do you mean?" I prodded her to keep from returning to the previous conversation.

Sami took the laptop from Katie and tapped away at the keyboard for a moment. "Your zodiac sign is Cancer, but look at what this says about you." Sami had pulled up a web site that described each zodiac sign in detail. "See, this says you were born under a water sign, but you have the gift of fire. And Kai, he was born under an Earth sign, but he has the gift of water. Now look at this." Sami pulled the sketch out again. "Here is your sign, Cancer, but what is weird is that it is aligned with Sagittarius. That's why I'm having a hard time understanding this stuff, there's no rhyme nor reason to it. All I am certain of is that opposites attract, but I could have gotten that from my daily horoscope." Sami pulled a newspaper out from beside her and handed it to me. She had it folded over to the horoscope page. "See what I mean?"

I no longer heard what Sami was saying. I spotted an article just below the daily horoscopes. It was a continuation of a story from page three. The title caught my eye and pulled me in. It read 'The End is Near' I started scanning the article and saw the key words I was looking for, St. Miguel, Mayan Calendar, and Apocalypse. I stood up and headed back to my seat between Kai and Jesse. I mumbled a "Be right back." to Sami and Katie as I left.

"Kai, look at this." I didn't bother to sit in my seat. I just squatted in the aisle. "Remember I told you that I got the dagger from a man that tried to kill me? Well, this is him." I pointed to a picture on the third page. Kai sat silently for a moment reading the article. It took him much less time than what it would have taken me to read the whole article.

"It says this man is a priest and he is sending out a message to the world that the Four Horsemen of the Apocalypse are here, repent and be saved from their wrath." Kai sat silently for a moment. "If only it were that simple." Again, he sounded so negative.

"What are you hiding from me Kai?" I had him trapped on a plane at thirty thousand feet and I was determined to get an answer.

Kai instantly changed moods. "Have I mentioned that I think you are the most amazing woman I have ever met?" He dazzled me with his gorgeous blue eyes. Even with contacts to cover their glowing sparkle, I was overwhelmed by his stare. I completely forgot what I was asking him, and he wasn't about to remind me any time soon. He stood up to let me back in my seat. The remainder of the flight was lost to me. He must have put me to sleep. When I awoke, the plane was on the ground and the passengers were already debarking.

"That wasn't fair." I mumbled groggily to Kai. I think I heard him chuckle, but I couldn't be certain.

* * *

"We are going to have to find a boat to take us to the island." Kai announced as we were walking down to the docks. I shivered in the cold air. It was winter time in Chile and none of us were dressed for the weather.

"We can get a charter boat to take us to the island." Ryan suggested. He was avoiding be near Jenny and had wedged himself between Mike and Jesse. Jenny looked annoyed but said nothing.

"No, this time of year the sailors won't go anywhere near the island. The waters are treacherous." Kai offered.

"How do you know all of this?" Jesse asked out of curiosity.

"These people are of Mayan decent. They still pray to Chak, the Deity of Water." Kai pointed to himself. "I can hear thoughts if they are meant for me to hear."

"I suggest we split up." Mike offered. "Kai and Annie can go find a boat, while the rest of us can go and get supplies."

"That's a good idea, Mike." Kai complimented. I was surprised that he didn't insist on everyone sticking together, especially out on the crowded streets. He usually made it a point to have everyone in a formation around me. Maybe he was finally easing up a little, or maybe not.

"Jesse, give your hat to Annie." He turned and stopped in front of me. I was startled by his quick movements. He untucked my shirt and tucked my hair up under Jesse's hat and pulled the brim down low. "There, now you are not so noticeable. Let me do the talking." I nodded my head, it wasn't like I was fluent in the local language anyways. "Meet us at the dock gate in three hours." He said to everyone else as they were turning to head to the town market.

Kai leaned down to speak softly in my ear. "I owe Mike for that one."

His comment took me off guard. "What do you owe Mike for?"

"For giving us some time alone." He smiled devilishly as he turned me towards the direction of a huge yacht named 'Pandora's Box'.

"You want to borrow *this* boat? I don't think the owner will appreciate us sailing this into treacherous waters." I was gawking at the sheer magnitude of it, the sleek lines, the two decks above the water line, and the satellite dish mounted on top. This was a yacht that put all other yachts to shame.

"Ariel won't mind, as a matter of fact, she offered it to us already." He read the questioning look on my face and responded quickly. "I said we needed to find a boat to take us to the island, not that we had to buy, rent or steal one." He had a smug look on his face.

"This is Ariel's yacht? What does Ariel need a yacht for?"

"She says it is a luxury that she can't deny herself." He stepped onto the boat and offered his hand to help steady me as I stepped on. The deck was gleaming white with dark cherry wood and polished brass furniture. Kai led me to a sliding glass door that opened into a sitting room that was furnished with a baby grand piano and oversized furniture. I was in awe of my surroundings and didn't notice that he was leading me to a set of stairs that led down to a hallway lined with doors. I looked through an open door and realized that this was the staterooms, though much nicer than the staterooms on the cruise ship.

"What are we doing down here?" I sounded pathetically innocent, which is precisely what I was. My heart started to pound in my chest and the butterflies were swarming in my stomach.

Kai replied in a soothing yet mocking tone. "No need to get worked up, my love. I thought you might like to clean up after our travels, I know how you are about using all the hot water so I thought it would be best if you went before the rest return."

It was a simple gesture, but one I appreciated greatly. I was beginning to think he knew me better than I knew myself. "Thank you, Kai." I replied softly. I turned my head to look at him, but he was gone. I did a full turn, but he had left the room without making a noise. I shrugged it off and headed to the shower. I didn't realize how tense my muscles were until the hot water hit my skin. True to my nature, I stayed in the shower until the hot water ran cold. I wrapped myself up in a fluffy, oversized towel and headed back into the bedroom to raid the closet for clean clothes. Lying on the bed was a pair of artfully faded blue jeans and a plain white turtle neck and heavy red hooded sweatshirt. Kai had thought to set clothes out for me, a tear started to form at the corner of my eye.

As I stood there wrapped in a towel, contemplating how truly perfect Kai was, I sensed he had entered the room. I didn't need to turn to confirm his presence. I sniffed the air and smelled his fresh spring rain scent. My heart started to pound out of my chest as I anticipated his touch. After several long moments, he put his hands on my shoulders, I sighed with relief. He began caressing my shoulders and slowly moved down to my arms that I left hanging at my sides. When his hands reached mine, he intertwined our fingers and pressed up behind me. I shivered as his breath tickled the back of my neck, and then he whispered, "Annie". His voice was soft and melodic. He wrapped his arms around my waist tightly, I could feel him trembling with desire, but his will to resist was stronger than his desire. "Forbidden fruit to torment me and test my will." He murmured softly. My heart was pounding out of my chest; it was becoming unbearable to even breathe. I wanted him more than ever. I could feel the tears welling up in my eyes.

I inhaled deeply and pulled away from him. I turned to see that he was surprised by my reaction but he didn't react. "I'm sorry Kai; I just had the worst case of déjà vu."

"It is best that you pulled away. My will is strong, but perhaps it is best not to test it. What part of this do you remember?"

"All of it. I dreamt this very moment a week before I even met you." I said softly, I was in shock by how exact my dream had been.

"That's amazing; precognition was Lilith's gift, not yours'." He murmured more to himself than to me. "Do you know what this means?"

"Yeah, it means that if I can get control of this gift, I will be able to see what is going to happen."

"Well, yes, there is that too, but it also means that you have probably inherited Lilith's other gifts as well."

"What other gifts did she have?"

"She was able to control magnetic fields and she could hear the truth no matter what was being said to her." Kai bridged the gap between us and began running his fingers through my hair. He sent a shiver of pleasure down my spine.

"Oh!" I was going to make a sarcastic comment about my mother having an extra set of eyes in the back of her head, but before I could, Kai leaned down and kissed me hard on the lips. Instantly, the rest of the world disappeared, all that existed in that moment was the two of us. He wrapped his arms around my waist and pulled me in tight. My hands traced the contours of his muscular arms and chest. His cool skin was a perfect antidote to my scorching body. It was only a moment before he pulled away again.

"You should get dressed now." He turned and disappeared through the thick haze that filled the room.

Chapter 25

CONFIRMATION

Kai avoided any physical contact with me until the rest of the crew showed up, and even then, it was barely more than holding my hand. Apparently his iron will was a little rusty. He mumbled on about not trusting himself.

With the supplies loaded on the yacht, we were on our way to the island of Robinson Crusoe. According to Kai, the island has a Mayan effigy on it that Ariel had built in honor of her lost love, Chief Itzamna from Chichen Itza. His last request was to be honored until the end of times. Ariel visited his memorial every year on the anniversary of his death, which is why she had her yacht at the dock. The anniversary of the chief's death coincided with our graduation present, the trip to Chichen Itza, the day that Ariel heard my song and summoned Kai from the deep blue.

The tension between Ryan and Jenny had gotten unbearable five minutes after leaving the dock. Mike herded me up to the wheel house to avoid the conflict. Katie was at the helm programming the GPS for auto pilot . She looked up but didn't say a word. I think she had expected to see the two of us.

"It's already started." Mike commented. "I thought they had agreed to a truce."

Katie looked out the window for a moment before answering. "I hate to admit it, but it would be best for the team if they left."

"What?" I couldn't believe Katie wanted to break up the team. "What's going on? Why are Ryan and Jenny fighting?"

Katie sighed deeply before standing up and walking over to me. "As if you don't have enough to worry about, but it's pointless to try to keep secrets from you." Katie looked to

Mike for confirmation, Mike nodded his head yes. "Jenny is jealous of you. She thinks Ryan is in love with you, not her. We tried to explain to her that it is a part of our obligation to take care of you, but she is being unreasonable. Every time Ryan mentions your name or looks at you, Jenny gets all worked up."

"Jenny is jealous of me? That's completely ridiculous. Ryan is practically my brother." I didn't know why I felt the need to yell at Katie and Mike, as if they were the ones that didn't understand the situation, but I couldn't help it. I was annoyed with Jenny for this mess and I was taking it out on Mike and Katie. I took a deep breath and calmed down before I spoke. "I'm sorry guys, it's not your fault, its mine. I dragged all of you into this mess."

"No you didn't, silly." Mike rebutted me. "If I recall, you told us to stay home, but we didn't listen to you. Jenny included, so don't go blaming yourself. A little advice, though, I would avoid Ryan and Jenny for the time being."

"I know you are probably right, but now is not the time to procrastinate." I said over my shoulder as I was heading out of the wheel house. It wasn't just about the lack of time, or that there were more important matters to attend to, it was about not having to walk on egg shells around the people I care about. I didn't have a plan. I was just acting on instincts. I marched down to the sitting room where everyone else was gathered and walked right up to Ryan. He was facing away from me so I grabbed his long red pony tail and used it to turn him around and then I planted a kiss right on his lips.

He pushed me away immediately (I knew he would). "OW! What, in God's name, are you doing?" He yelled at me as he wiped my kiss off with his sleeve.

I saw Jenny hurdle a couch to get at me. She swung at me mid stride, it was a graceful move, but I was able to block her punch. She came at me again and this time I caught her fist inches from my face. "Do you see, Jenny? He doesn't love me like that, stop fighting with him!" I pushed her back enough to throw her off balance. She was in shock, and it looked like she was about to break down into tears.

I wanted to make a dramatic exit to drill my point home, but Kai blocked the doorway. He was smirking, on the verge of uncontrollable laughter. "What is so funny?" I snapped at him. I stepped around him and swept out of the room.

He let me by and then followed me out. "That was amazing! Although, I have to admit I felt a pang of jealousy when you kissed Ryan, but I figured out what you were trying to accomplish. You always did have a flare for the dramatic."

My annoyance subsided as soon as I was out of the room. "Did it work? Can you hear what they're saying?"

"I can hear them, but they aren't speaking to each other. I think you would call it a 'make up kiss.'"

"Good, mission accomplished. Is there anything else that needs to be fixed?" I asked sarcastically.

"Yes." He said seductively, "I need to be fixed as well." He took my hand and pulled me closer. He began kissing the inside of my forearm, running his nose softly across my sensitive skin. He worked his way up my arm to my neck. I shivered with pleasure. Wanting more, I took his chin in my hand and pulled him closer so I could kiss him on the lips. He kissed me hard and passionately for a brief moment before he pulled away. I tried to hold on to him tighter, but he was so strong that it was a simple matter for him to break my hold on him. "I'm sorry, that was not appropriate."

I'm sure I was pouting, "No, that was too appropriate. Why do you always pull away from me?"

Before he could answer, Katie and Mike came down the stairs from the wheel house. "I'm glad we're using the GPS, otherwise we would get lost in these freak fog banks." Katie said teasingly. As they walked past us heading to the sitting room, Mike patted Kai on the shoulder. "Just ask her, how hard can it be?"

I waited until Mike and Katie were inside before I questioned him. "Ask me what?"

He was silent for a long moment looking down to avoid making eye contact with me. I was about to repeat the question when he chuckled softly and shook his head. "I have been alive for one hundred four thousand years, but I never truly lived until you came into my life. I cannot be killed; therefore I fear nothing, except for loosing you. I have never experienced the feeling of nervousness until this very moment, the moment that means more to me than all of the thousands of years before." Kai took my hand and knelt before me. "Anyanka Paylea Cain, I would be the happiest being alive if you would join me."

I was confused at first with what he was saying, and then it dawned on me that this was a marriage proposal. I was stunned. I just stood there staring into his eyes without answering. Marriage was not one of those events on my priority list. I was only eighteen for goodness sakes. Besides, getting married now, I didn't see the point if the world was going to end in five months.

"Annie?" Kai was becoming concerned with my silence, but I still had no idea what to say to him. "Annie?" He repeated as he stood up and shook my shoulders gently.

I had no choice but to answer him. "Kai, I have loved you my whole life. You are the only man I could ever love." I paused trying to find the right words to say to him.

"But you are not ready to be joined with me." He stated for me, though he didn't understand the reasoning behind it.

"Kai, let's try to live through the next five months before we discuss that kind of union. When forever has meaning to me, then maybe I will be ready to commit to forever." I wasn't certain if I explained myself very well.

"I understand how you feel, but I want you to understand that I do not agree. If this world is going to end, then I want it to end with you as my wife. I do not want to spend another minute of this life without you."

Kai spoke with such passion. I could see the world through his eyes, his point, not to waste what precious little time we have, but I was not going to give in. At the moment, that was a concept I couldn't wrap my head around. It felt like if I gave in now, I had no hope of surviving into the new era. Hope was the only thing I had to hang on to, I wasn't willing to give that up, and so I wasn't willing to give in to Kai's proposal.

Kai cocked his head to the side looking at me inquisitively perhaps trying to see into my soul. I don't know what he saw, but he seemed deterred for the moment, "Fine!" He snapped at me, "But this conversation is far from over." He took my hand and led me back into the sitting room.

There was a map lying across the piano and everyone was gathered around it. Mike and Jesse were discussing the best place to go to shore and Katie was checking weather conditions, water currents and topographical maps to verify access to the island.

"Kai," Jesse responded to us entering into the room. "Do you know where Ariel built this effigy?" He tried to keep his voice normal but I detected a little bit of discord when he asked. Perhaps it was a twinge of jealousy for the man who had died centuries ago and had stolen the heart of the woman he loves.

"Yes, it is on the northeast side of the island on top of the cliffs. It will be easier for the rest of you if we anchor on the west side of the island and trek to the other side . There will be some rock climbing required. Is anyone opposed to that?" No one said a word. "Then it is settled."

"What is it that we are going to see? Why do we have to be on this island?" Jenny asked. Her mood had improved greatly. I was amazed my antics had worked so well.

Kai was reluctant to answer. "With any luck, all we will see is an eclipse."

Sami, who had been silently sitting in the corner with her nose stuck in a book, interrupted on Kai's behalf. "Kai, when did your transformation occur?" She seemed completely oblivious to the previous conversation.

He looked at her questioningly, "February nineteenth of the twenty-second year of mankind, why?"

Sami jotted a few notes on the edge of the connect-the-dots paper. "I'm just trying to piece things together. What about Ariel and Buddy? When did they transform?"

"Ariel transformed on May thirtieth, twenty-two-eighty-three B.C. And Buddy transformed on August twenty-seventh, three-hundred-nineteen B.C."

Sami was silent for a long moment writing more notes on her paper. Everyone was looking at her, waiting for her to say something. Even though we were all expecting it, we still jumped when Sami shouted, "A-ha! I figured it out!"

"You figured out the constellations?" Jenny asked as we all swarmed around her to look at the notes she had been writing.

"Yes. Look at this." Sami laid a spreadsheet on the floor for everyone to see.

	Spring–Buddy		Summer–Annie		Fall–Ariel		Winter–Kai
	Valhalla		Chichen Itza		Giza		Atlantis
BB	Mar21–Apr. 19	AnB	June 21–July 22	ArB	Sept. 23–Oct.22	KB	Dec. 22–Jan 19
	Aries–Fire		Cancer–Water		Libra–Air		Capricorn–Earth
KC	Apr. 20–May 20	ArC	July 23–Aug. 22	BC	Oct. 23–Nov. 21	AC	Jan. 20–Feb. 18
	Taurus–Earth		Leo–Fire		Scorpio–Water		Aquarius–Air
ArR	May 21–June20	BR	Aug. 23–Sept.22	AnR	Nov. 22–Dec. 21	KR	Feb.19–Mar. 20
	Gemini–Air		Virgo–Earth		Sagittarius–Fire		Pisces–Water
	B–Buddy		An–Annie		Ar–Ariel		K–Kai
	B–Birth		R–Rebirth		C–City		

She started talking very quickly from the excitement of her revelation. "All twelve of the Astrological constellations are on here in groups of three, located at the four corners of the room. We knew this was not a map of the skies because the constellations were not arranged in their appropriate places, so I went on the assumption that this was a code. What confused me is that each of your astrological signs, accept for

Ariel's, didn't make any sense. Take Kai for example, his birthday is the winter solstice. He has the gift of water but his astrological sign, Capricorn, is an Earth sign. Makes no sense, right? But, if you take into account his second birth, or the day of his transformation, February nineteenth, he is a Pisces, a water sign. Look here on the diagram. We have Capricorn, Pisces and Taurus, the third astrological sign. I think the third sign represents the city you need to be in at the time of the apocalypse. The Taurus falls in the spring time, Buddy's season. Also, if you look at each of the seasons, they consist of three of the four elements, spring is missing the water sign, and Kai will balance the season. Kai, I think you need to be in Valhalla for the apocalypse."

"This here is Ariel's corner." Sami pointed to another section of the diagram. "The fall equinox is the Libra, an air sign. And paired with it is Gemini, representing her transformation, also an air sign. And with it is Leo, which falls in the summer months and summer is missing the Air sign, which means Ariel will need to be in Chichen Itza. Are you guys following all of this?" She paused to take a breath. I think it was the first one since she started rambling on. No one answered, I couldn't speak for everyone, but I was beginning to think that Sami was either a genius or absolutely insane, and she was leaning way over the line on the insane side.

Kai stood up straight and headed towards the glass doors. He stood with arms crossed silently staring out at the open sea while Sami continued with her astrology lesson. "This corner represents Buddy. He is an Aries by birth and a Virgo by transformation. The Scorpio, here, is a fall sign, so Buddy will need to be in Giza. And this is Annie's corner. We have Cancer and Sagittarius paired together with Aquarius, so Annie gets Atlantis." The discussions ensued as soon as Sami had finished, I didn't hear any of it. I was more concerned with what was bothering Kai.

I walked over and stood behind him and wrapped my arms around his torso. I laid my head on his back and quietly stood with him. The minutes ticked by with the conversation behind us turning into nothing more than white noise. I was content to just hold him and wait patiently until he was ready to talk. Finally he turned to face me, I kept my arms around him, refusing to let go, he didn't seem to mind. "If Sami is correct, and I believe she is, then you should transform sometime between November twenty-second and December twenty-first, if you are meant to transform this year. You may not be ready yet."

"Kai, you have overlooked something. That timeline could have referred to the first Anyanka, not me."

"Do you still doubt who you are?"

"No, it's just that my circumstances have changed. Even Mama wasn't certain if I would ever transform."

He was silent again after that. I could tell he was lost in thought.

"Kai," I tried to break through to him. He looked back to me slowly, but his mind was still elsewhere. "What are you thinking about?"

"Nothing of consequence; we will be at the island by noon tomorrow. I suggest that all of you try to get some rest." It was already late evening and I knew he was right, but it felt more like a ploy to avoid telling me what was on his mind.

I looked into his deep blue eyes trying to read the turmoil that boiled beneath the surface, but Kai remained composed, he showed no outward emotions. I tried to distract him. "Will you stay with me until I fall asleep?"

"Yes," He smiled down at me. "Sleep Anyanka" He ran his fingers down my face, and that was the end of me until Kai woke me up when we reached the island the next day.

When he woke me up, I snapped at him immediately. "Why do you keep putting me to sleep?" but when I looked into his eyes, I sobered immediately. I had never seen such dead eyes before this and it terrified me. "What is it?" I whispered as I reached up to caress his face. He turned his head to kiss the palm of my hand, and when he looked back at me his eyes were back to normal. I must have imagined it, but the image was stuck in my head and haunted me.

He smiled down at me. "We have arrived at the island; it is time to get moving. We have to hike to the other side of the island before two o'clock this afternoon." My stomach growled, reminding Kai that I was still human. "Come, Mike has made breakfast for everyone."

"What about you, aren't you hungry?" I tried to remember the last time he had gone hunting; I couldn't remember him leaving my side when we were in Spain, or before the flight to Chile, or even before we left the docks.

"You can stop worrying about me Annie. I went hunting last night while you slept. I didn't want you to miss me while I was gone, that's why I put you to sleep."

"Oh, what was on the menu?" My morbid curiosity got the better of me, and I had to ask.

He raised an eyebrow at me, wondering if I really wanted to know or if I was just trying to make pleasant conversation. "Shark," He responded very nonchalantly. He dragged me out of bed and led me up the stairs back into the sitting room where there was a huge spread of food sitting on the bar.

Mike and Jesse were standing behind the bar making toast as requested. Jesse caught sight of me first. "Morning sunshine, nice 'do you're sporting there."

I caught a glimpse of my reflection in the polished brass trim on the bar. The view was distorted but I could tell it was bad. Jenny was my salvation, she handed me a hairbrush. "Got ya covered, girlfriend." she whispered and winked at me. I was grateful that our friendship was back on track, I was a little surprised that my antics had worked so well.

Kai leaned in and whispered in my ear. "You will always be beautiful in my eyes." I couldn't stop the blood from rushing to my cheeks for a full-fledged blush. I still couldn't comprehend how someone as beautiful and perfect as Kai could ever find me attractive.

We all ate like kings for breakfast. It had been so long since we had a decent meal that Mike overcompensated by making too much food. By the time we were done eating, Kai looked anxious to get moving. I was expecting to pile into a dingy with everyone and paddle our way to shore, but Kai had an easier way. With all seven of us in the dingy, Kai stepped off of the yacht *onto* the water, took the tow rope and began walking us to shore.

"I thought only Jesus Christ could do that?" Ryan shouted out jokingly to Kai.

Kai had his own snide comment for Ryan. "Who do you think taught him?"

Kai pulled us up onto a small sandy beach. The rest of the island looked to be rolling hills and grass lands, there were no trees on the island, and as I stepped onto the sandy beach, I knew why. The island was made up of volcanic rock. The sun was shining bright but the wind was bitter cold and whipped at our exposed skin. We all bundled up into our sweatshirts and began our trek across the island, most of which was uphill. Halfway up the first hill, no one was complaining about the cold anymore.

In the spirit of being on a long trip, Katie called out to Kai, "Are we there yet?"

Kai must not have understood the humor, because his answer was definitely not funny. "Two more miles uphill, and then we have a sixty foot rock wall to climb." By the time we made it to the rock wall, even Katie, the sports nut, was complaining about her legs burning, Kai had hiked us up three miles of hills in an hour and was actually surprised that we all insisted on taking a break before going rock climbing without safety ropes. We sat at the base of a huge cliff that slightly resembled a face, and behind it was another mound of rock that was unrecognizable.

"What is this?" Mike asked Kai as he waved his hand towards the cliff.

"This is a monument to the Mayan chief Itzamna, it used to resemble his face, but it is made up of volcanic rock and is crumbling away. Behind it is a crouching jaguar, a sign of royalty."

I looked up at the stone wall, trying to discern a face out of the crumbling rock and spotted a tree, the only tree on the island sitting on top of the effigy. I wondered if there was any significance to it.

"Let's go guys!" Kai the drill sergeant demanded after only a few minutes. I volunteered to go first because of my experience rock climbing with Mama, but Kai would not allow it. Mike and Katie went first instead, then Sami before I was allowed to go with Kai right below me as a safety net. Mike stood on the edge up above, giving directions for the best hand and foot holds. Several times I grabbed a rock and it crumbled in my hand making the climb even more treacherous. At the top, Mike grabbed my wrist and pulled me up the rest of the way. It was a miracle that we all made it to the top without incident.

Once on top of the cliff, I walked out to the edge overlooking the ocean. The view was breathtaking. I could see for miles, the beautiful blue of the ocean, and the contrasting dark gray of the rocks of several small islands nearby. I could hear the waves crash against the rock wall below and the cawing of the seagulls. There was a peace and serenity about the island that I had never felt before. And for all of the natural beauty I was surrounded by, the most fantastic thing here was the moon. It was a beautiful soft white contrast to the azure skies. It was so huge that I felt like I could reach out and touch it.

Kai came up behind me, and whispered in my ear. "For all the beauty God has created, there is nothing more beautiful than you." He had me blushing immediately. He wrapped his arms around my waist and held me tight. We stood in silence, watching as the moon made its way towards the sun. The rest of my friends came and stood beside us along the edge of the effigy. Waiting and watching in silence. It could have been hours or just minutes, time meant very little to me when Kai held me like this. As the moon finally reached the sun, I could feel Kai stiffen with anxiety. He still hadn't told us what we were looking for, so his reaction to the eclipse was disheartening.

As the moon crept slowly to the center of the sun, the anticipation was becoming unbearable. I turned to look into

Kai's eyes. I didn't like what I saw in them. Not only was he anxious, but he looked terrified as well. I turned back to watch the eclipse, but all I could envision was the look in his eyes. The moon finally made it to the center of the sun. It was bathed in a blood red glow. Everything around us was in total darkness, the only light I could see was the sun peeking out around the edges of the moon. It was then that I heard Kai sigh. He squeezed me even tighter and buried his head in my shoulder, like he was afraid to let go, afraid that I would be pulled out of his arms.

"What is it, Kai? What's going to happen?"

Kai pointed just below the sun and the moon. "Do you see those two spheres to the left of the sun?"

"Yes, I see them. What are they? What do they mean?"

"That is Mercury and Venus. We came here today for the eclipse so that I could see their positions on the horizon. We are heading for a full planetary alignment." The tone of his voice was ominous.

I didn't understand what that meant, or what he was implying, nor did anyone else. We all looked at him questioningly, but no one spoke. The sickening look in his eyes was still there, and made my stomach churn uneasily.

Kai finally started to explain, his voice was sullen. "Every twenty-six million years, there is a planetary alignment. All the planets in the solar system will line up." Kai stopped, and looked down, apparently, what he was about to tell us was not good news, he wouldn't make eye contact with anyone. "Six hours before the full alignment, and six hours after are the most critical." Kai stopped for a moment and squatted down to touch the ground. I felt a strange vibration beneath my feet, but no one else reacted to it, so I must have been imagining it. He stood back up before he spoke again. "Planets are nothing more than giant magnets. If they are far enough apart, they do not react with each other, but if they come too close to each other they will either attract or repel from each other throwing one or both planets out of orbit. In a full planetary alignment, all of the planets and their moons are reacting to each other." Kai paused, he looked sick, but he found the strength to continue. "The last planetary alignment caused the poles to reverse. The moon was thrown into an eccentric spin around the Earth so that it is gradually moving away from the planet. We can expect earthquakes, volcanic eruptions, tidal waves, violent storms, meteorites and mass extinction of life on this planet." I was beginning to understand why he looked sick.

I felt a darkness descend on me like no other moment in my short life. The darkness of the eclipse was nothing compared to the darkness that engulfed me. How could the four of us save this planet from an entire solar system? What was the point of allowing me to live again if there was nothing I could do to help? What purpose do I have? It felt like a dagger had been stabbed into my heart. I couldn't breathe. The hopelessness was crushing me, crushing my will to go on. I looked out across the island, a desolate place, the peace and serenity that I had felt earlier was replaced by despair. I caught sight of a glimmer out in the ocean, and though part of me was wallowing in self-pity, the other part of me was mildly curious as to what I saw. I realized it was just the yacht, Pandora's Box, lulling on the waves.

My mind wandered numbly through the story of Pandora's Box. Pandora was a gift to mankind from the goddess Aphrodite (Ariel was Aphrodite, I wondered if Pandora was her daughter). Pandora was given a box with instructions to never open it, but out of curiosity, she did open the box and out of it came disease, famine and war. Pandora slammed the lid down on the box before the remaining item escaped. Seeing what had been released upon the world, Pandora rationalized that there could be nothing worse than what had already been unleashed, so she opened the box again, and out of it came the true gift of the gods, hope.

Hope, what hope is there against a planetary alignment? What hope is there that I could live to see the next era? What hope is there that mankind could survive into the next era? What hope is there that mankind could find a balance with the Earth instead of destroying it? I looked into Kai's eyes, my stomach lurched. I knew what that look was, I knew what he was feeling. He had lost all hope. I couldn't stand it any longer, but what could I do? I had to find hope in this hopelessness.

God would not leave us to die without giving us a fighting chance, would he? Even Kai said we just had to figure this out and save ourselves. All the clues that we had been given, they have to mean something, there's hope in that. What about the pyramids created by the hand of God? There has to be hope in that too. My mother died because she had hope of us saving this Earth. That was all I needed to continue on, the faith, hope and love of my mother. I felt the darkness lift off of me, I was free from the overwhelming weight of it. I just had to help Kai find hope.

As I stood contemplating a plan to help Kai, Ariel showed up out of nowhere. She wasn't alone; with her was a man that was equally as beautiful as Kai with glowing brown eyes. It had to be Buddy, but he was nothing of what I expected. Maybe I was expecting him to wear a robe and sandals, or maybe try to blend in by wearing common clothes. Buddy was exactly opposite of blending in, he was dressed in full ceremony garbs of a Sioux Indian chief, complete with the long feathered head dress and war paint on his face and well defined arms. He even had a bow in one hand, a quiver of arrows on his back and a tomahawk at his waist.

"You called, brother?" Buddy asked. He must have been speaking a different language because he had that Japanese martial arts film effect going on. He made eye contact with me and smiled. "You're looking much better Annie. How ya feeling, kid?" He was speaking English this time with a hint of an Australian accent. He walked up to me and gave me a big hug like we were long lost friends. He was a comfortable person to be around despite the enormous personality he exuded.

Kai didn't give me a chance to answer him. "We are headed for a planetary alignment." He stated for Buddy and

Ariel. Both of them immediately understood the implications of that.

"How many planets will align?" Ariel asked with a hint of hope in her voice.

The look of dread was still apparent in Kai's eyes. "All of them."

I couldn't stand seeing Kai in so much pain and misery. I had to do something quickly and it had to be dramatic. In that moment, I knew exactly what I had to do. "Is that it, Kai? Is there nothing we can do? Are we just giving up now?" I was practically yelling at him.

The look of death still didn't lift from his eyes. He snapped back at me. "One planet, maybe two, we can handle that, but all eight planets pulling at us all at once, we are not capable of counteracting that."

"So that's it? There is no purpose of me being here? You were right Kai. I am not supposed to exist." I tried to keep the sarcasm out of my voice but I just couldn't help it. I took off at a dead run across the effigy, I had never run so fast in all my life, it felt like I had wings. I ran straight for the edge overlooking the ocean and with my last step I launched myself out into the open air.

Chapter 26

HOME

Call it a shock and awe campaign, call it a leap of faith. It wasn't about killing myself, it was about getting Kai to snap out the depression he was in. I knew I had to do something drastic. This is what I came up with, the only option I had available, cliff diving. Mama took me cliff diving lots of times, not from these heights, but I had the experience and I knew what I was doing. I enjoyed the free fall, the wind whistling in my ears, the thrill of the speed, I was truly happy in that moment. I knew who I was, I knew what purpose I had, and I knew with absolute confidence that Kai loved me and I loved him. I still didn't know what I would give to save the world, but I knew what I was willing to do to save Kai. Anything.

As the water came rushing up to greet me, I took a deep breath and put my hands straight out in front of me to minimize the impact. I slipped beneath the surface smoothly. The water was frigid cold and felt like thousands of tiny pins poking me simultaneously. I just had to hold on for a few seconds until Kai would come and rescue me. I knew with absolute certainty that he would save me. I dove deeper and deeper into the icy water until my momentum slowed, far below the turmoil of the crashing waves above. I stopped and hovered in the cold depths, waiting in the darkness.

I didn't have long to wait. I truly thought that Kai would jump in after me. What was I thinking? I was treading water for mere seconds when a surge of bubbles rose beneath me. I was being pushed to the surface very quickly. I broke the surface and took a huge breath, not certain if I was going back under or continuing to rise up. I did neither. Kai was standing on the surface and took my hand as soon as he saw me. He wasn't mad, and the look of death in his eyes was gone, he was laughing.

"You always had a flare for the dramatic, but that was the best one yet." He said to me as he helped me to my feet. "I got the message loud and clear though. As Sami put it, I need to pull my head out of my ass, suck it up and dig in. Not that I understood a word of what she was saying to me, but I think it meant, don't lose hope and don't give up. I should probably tell her that I don't own a donkey, though."

"You got it exactly right." I said through chattering teeth. I was soaked, the water was freezing and the wind was bitter.

Kai realized I was freezing and held his hands up in front of me. Within seconds, I was completely dry. I didn't bother to ask him how he did it. I found it was easier to just thank him. We walked around the island, staying on the water all the way back to the yacht. I was a little leery about walking on water so I clutched Kai's arm tight all the way back. All around us, the waves rolled and peeked, but directly in front of us was a smooth path leading to the yacht. "Where to next?" I asked casually as we were waiting for the rest of the crew to trek back across the island and paddle out to us.

"I thought you wanted to go home, back to New London." I was thrilled to hear him say those words. Home, I missed home.

"What about you? Where would you like to go?" I felt like all I ever worried about was what I wanted, and I never considered what Kai wanted.

"Home sounds good to me too." He looked down at me and smiled.

"Where is home for you, Atlantis?"

"For me, home is anywhere that you are, but if I were to choose a place to call home, it would be New London."

"Really? You never said one word about New London when we were there. I didn't think you noticed it."

He gave me a puzzled look, "You don't know, do you? New London is the location of the Garden of Eden. That's why I was able to find you so easily. That is why I knew the code to get into your home. The code spells EDEN on the keypad. I knew Lilith would never call any other place home. I knew that is where she would be hiding you."

"Wow!" There was nothing else to say to that. "O.K., let's go home."

Epilogue

"This is CNN World News tonight and I am your host Kim Lavengood. The top stories tonight, business tycoon Zachary DeSanto was found dead in his mountain top retreat in Spain. Foul play is suspected, the investigation continues. His son Cavin DeSanto is taking over the New York based business, DeSanto Industries."

"San Miguel, Mexico, a new cult is on the rise led by a Methodist Priest, claims that the fourth horsemen of the apocalypse has been sighted in the area. The priest has attracted a large following and police are at a loss to deal with the growing crowds."

"Geologists have detected micro earthquakes in the South Pacific Ocean and fear that a larger earthquake is eminent. Authorities are alerting coastal residents in Chile and Peru of potential tidal waves."

"A bombing in Cairo, Egypt has killed three people and uncovered an old fallout shelter. The shelter appears to have been constructed during World War I. It was empty but there was evidence of recent activity."

"Anthropologists have discovered a first century gravesite in Jerusalem where a large golden tablet has been found with writings of an unknown language. Theologians are protesting any research on the grave site believing it to be a possible last resting place of the body of Christ."

"This is CNN World News Tonight. I'm Kim Lavengood, on to David McCallaster with the weather forecast."

Ariel picked up the TV remote, threw it at the TV, and buried it halfway into the screen. The impact caused the TV to teeter and fall off of the stand.

Kai saved the day; with his lightning fast speed he was able to catch the urn with Mama's ashes before it hit the floor. Mama had spent several weeks on the front porch while we were gone. I could only imagine her looking down on me with a scowl on her face for making her wait outside.

"Well, I guess we didn't really need a weather report from ole Dave McCallaster with you two around, anyways." I replied sarcastically, dreading the cleanup of the mess on the floor.

Ariel barked at me. "Well that sucks."

"What's wrong with you Ariel?" She growled at me. I forgot that she wanted to be referred to by her given name. "Sorry, I meant Avinion."

"That's better. The problem is, they found one of my vaults."

"Who?"

"The Illuminati; now they are better funded."

Kai sat forward on the couch and moaned. "That isn't the biggest problem Ari . . . I mean Avinion. Buddy's tablet has been found, now we are going to have to deal with a bunch of crazy people looking for aliens at the pyramids again."

I couldn't help but laugh at him. "What's so funny?" He gave me a queer look.

"You; we have to deal with a planetary alignment and you're worried about crazy people looking for aliens."

"I suppose I am being ridiculous." He laughed at himself. "No more news for today, let's go for a walk." He took my hand and pulled me off the couch.

"Where to?" It really didn't matter to me where we were going as long as we were together.

"Buddy has been working on a project out in the woods. He said it was ready for you to see." Kai was being mysterious, he had my interest peeked. He led me out the back door and through the back yard towards one of my favorite hunting spots. The sun was dipping down on the horizon and the woods were already getting dark. Kai pulled me in closer so I wouldn't stumble on any unseen roots or get cut by any branches. We walked for several minutes until we stepped into a clearing that had been once full of briars and weeds. It was now the most beautiful place I had ever seen, a true piece of the Garden of Eden. There were strange luminescent plants all around the edges that bathed the entire area in soft lights. There were huge fragrant flowers hanging down from vines that crept up the surrounding tree trunks, as well as a hundred different types of flowers I had never seen before. And in the center of the clearing was an apple tree.

I heard someone singing softly. Buddy stood up from behind an evergreen bush, holding handfuls of weeds that he had pulled out of the ground. "Hey, Geronimo and Kai, you two made it. I hope you like the garden." With that, Buddy turned to leave us alone in the clearing.

"Oh, no you don't." Kai interjected. "You can't give someone else your name."

"Would Bonsai work?" Buddy asked innocently.

"No, that one's yours, too." Kai was laughing at him. "Let's stick with Annie for now."

"He's Geronimo?" I pointed at Buddy. "That would explain the feathered headdress." I concluded.

Buddy gave me a hug and ruffled my hair. "You and I are kindred spirits. We both like cliff diving." He nodded at Kai and turned to leave.

"Buddy, Where are you going?" I still hadn't gotten the chance to get to know Buddy. He always seemed so busy. I felt like he was avoiding me.

I heard his disembodied voice from the woods. "You and Kai need time alone. Besides, I have a date."

"Wow, really?" Kai seemed genuinely surprised by that bit of information. "Is the world about to end?"

"Maybe," Buddy answered back "Or maybe I finally found the right woman."

Kai called back to him, "Be careful, it's a full moon tonight, and she's still young." The whole exchange was a mystery to me. I had no idea what they were talking about.

Kai turned to face me. He didn't say a word. He just gently picked me up and held me in his arms. I reached my hands around his neck and kissed him with all the strength and passion that I had in me. He understood my mood and pulled back after a few seconds, his normal response before either one of us got carried away. I was not about to be denied so I kissed him again.

He simply held me out farther so I couldn't reach him. "Not until we are joined my love; until then, this is all the farther we go."

"Really? Then why did you bring me out here?" I was so frustrated I could scream. Every ounce of me was on fire. I ached to have him.

"I wanted to torment you until you agreed to join with me. Why else would I bring you here?"

"So that's it? This is going to be a battle of will power? You won't give in to me if I don't give into you."

He smirked at me, so confident that he would get his way. "Let the games begin."

"Alright, but keep in mind, I don't play fair." I hopped down out of his arms, gave him one last kiss, and strutted away through the fog.

CPSIA information can be obtained at www.ICGtesting.com
Printed in the USA
BVOW032041061111

275428BV00005B/2/P